spy school

Also by Stuart Gibbs

STUART GIBBS

spy school REVOLUTION

A spy school NOVEL

Simon & Schuster Books for Young Readers

New York London Toronto Sydney New Delhi

SIMON & SCHUSTER BOOKS FOR YOUNG READERS
An imprint of Simon & Schuster Children's Publishing Division
1230 Avenue of the Americas, New York, New York 10020
This book is a work of fiction. Any references to historical events, real people, or real places are used fictitiously. Other names, characters, places, and events are products of the author's imagination, and any resemblance to actual events or places or persons, living or dead, is entirely coincidental.
Text © 2020 by Stuart Gibbs
Cover design and principal illustration by Lucy Ruth Cummins © 2020 by Simon & Schuster, Inc.
American flag illustration by nazlisart/iStock
Declaration of Independence signatures by duncan1890/iStock
All rights reserved, including the right of reproduction in whole or in part in any form.
SIMON & SCHUSTER BOOKS FOR YOUNG READERS
and related marks are trademarks of Simon & Schuster, Inc.
For information about special discounts for bulk purchases, please contact Simon & Schuster Special Sales at 1-866-506-1949 or business@simonandschuster.com.
The Simon & Schuster Speakers Bureau can bring authors to your live event. For more information or to book an event, contact the Simon & Schuster Speakers Bureau at 1-866-248-3049 or visit our website at www.simonspeakers.com.
Also available in a Simon & Schuster Books for Young Readers hardcover edition
Interior design by Lucy Ruth Cummins
Map art by Ryan Thompson
The text for this book was set in Adobe Garamond Pro.
Manufactured in the United States of America 0721 OFF
First Simon & Schuster Books for Young Readers paperback edition August 2021
2 4 6 8 10 9 7 5 3 1
The Library of Congress has cataloged the hardcover edition as follows:
Names: Gibbs, Stuart, 1969– author.
Title: Spy school revolution / Stuart Gibbs.
Description: First edition. | New York : Simon & Schuster Books for Young Readers, [2020] | Sequel to: Spy school British invasion. | Audience: Ages 8 to 12. | Audience: Grades 4–6. | Summary: With SPYDER apparently defeated, thirteen-year-old Benjamin Ripley is hoping for some peace at spy school, but when the CIA conference room next to where Ben and Alexander are trying to explain everything to Ben's parents (no easy task) is blown up, suspicion falls on fellow trainee (and secret crush) Erica.
Identifiers: LCCN 2019045055 (print) | LCCN 2019045056 (ebook) | ISBN 9781534443785 (hardcover) | ISBN 9781534443792 (pbk) | ISBN 9781534443808 (ebook)
Subjects: LCSH: Central Intelligence Agency—Juvenile fiction. | Spies—Training of—Juvenile fiction. | Traitors—Juvenile fiction. | Conspiracies—Juvenile fiction. | Schools—Juvenile fiction. | Friendship—Juvenile fiction. | Spy stories. | Adventure stories. | CYAC: Central Intelligence Agency—Fiction. | Spies—Fiction. | Traitors—Fiction. | Conspiracies—Fiction. | Schools—Fiction. | Friendship—Fiction. | Adventure and adventurers—Fiction. | LCGFT: Action and adventure fiction. | Spy fiction.
Classification: LCC PZ7.G339236 Sq 2020 (print) | LCC PZ7.G339236 (ebook) | DDC 813.6 [Fic]—dc23
LC record available at https://lccn.loc.gov/2019045055
LC ebook record available at https://lccn.loc.gov/2019045056

For the Montessori crew: Andrea Berloff; Drew, Dashiell, and Sasha Filus; Mieke Holkeboer; Joel, Asher, and Vander Delman; Kira Meers; Chris, Aria, and Kai Kuklinski; and Carol, Bill, Milana, and the real Sasha Rotko. Thanks for being such great friends to my entire family.

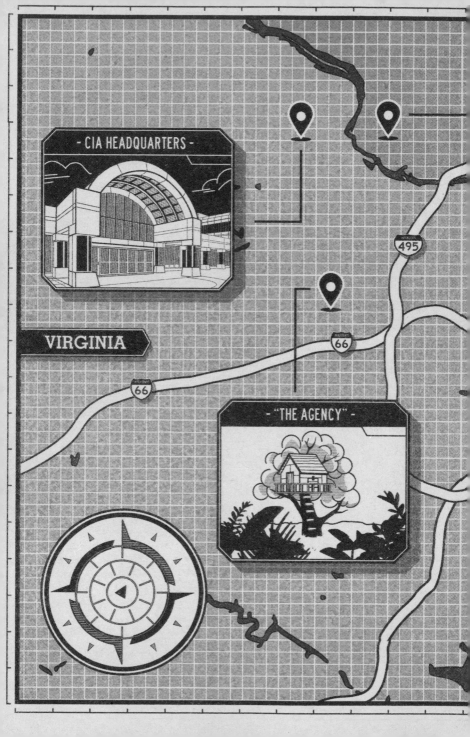

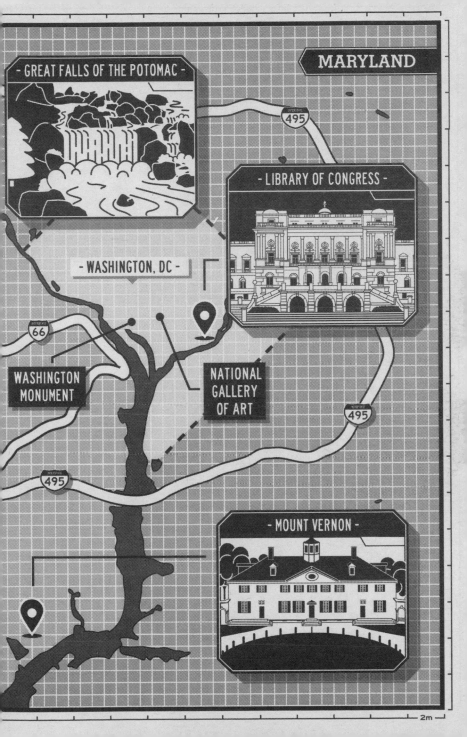

Contents

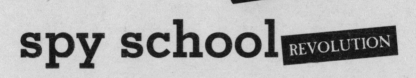

spy school REVOLUTION

April 15

To: ███████████████
Federal Witness Protection Program Liaison
Central Intelligence Agency Headquarters
███████████████

Langley, Virginia

From: ███████████████
CIA Agent Emeritus

Re: Federal Protection for ███████████████

As you are aware, while our junior operative ███████████████
was recently in Europe on Operation ███████████████, it became
evident that the identity of his family was known to ███████. Both
parents' lives were threatened and used as leverage, jeopardizing the
entire operation. If not for the actions of fellow junior agents ███████
███████ and ███████████████, Western civilization as we know
it might have been destroyed.

While the CIA believes that ███████ has been thwarted once and for
all, that has not been confirmed. Furthermore, ███████ had moles
throughout the Agency (for which reason it was necessary to conduct
███████████████ as a rogue operation in the first place) and thus,
it is possible that sensitive information about the family of ███████
███████ could have been leaked to other nefarious organizations.

Therefore, it seems prudent to provide for the safety of ███████
███████'s family. I authorize your office to begin domestic
reassignment procedures IMMEDIATELY. If action is not taken,
███████████████ could end up in very dire circumstances. Or
dead. I already have intel that another evil organization may be ramping
up their operations, now that ███████ is no longer around.

Sincerely,

Agent ███████████████

P.S. The last time the Federal Witness Protection Program came to the
CIA, one of them used my parking spot without permission. Please let
them know that this is not acceptable, and if it happens again, I will
blow up their car.

DECLASSIFICATION

CIA headquarters
Langley, Virginia
April 16
1000 hours

"I'm afraid we have lied to you," said Alexander Hale. "A lot."

My parents regarded him with surprise for what might have been the twentieth time that morning. They had already been surprised when Alexander and I had arrived at their house as they were leaving for work; they had been even more surprised to learn that their bosses had already given them the day off so that we could have an emergency meeting; and they had been *extremely* surprised when Alexander had driven us to CIA headquarters and been allowed through the imposing gates with nothing more than a grin and a cursory examination of his ID. Their eyes had been wide and their jaws agape almost nonstop.

"What exactly have you lied to us about?" my mother asked.

"Er . . . Just about everything," Alexander replied.

The four of us were sitting in a conference room on the top floor of the main building at headquarters. For security reasons, there were no windows, and the door had a coded keypad entry lock. There were no pictures on the walls, and every piece of furniture was a bland beige-like color. It was the most nondescript room ever built.

The building we were in didn't even have a name. Everyone simply called it "the main building." It sat in the center of the CIA campus, a sprawling tract of land in suburban Virginia, about thirty minutes from Washington, DC. There were a few smaller buildings arrayed around the main building, and all of that was ringed by acres of woods.

A box of doughnuts sat in the middle of the conference table: an assortment of glazed, chocolate, coconut, jelly, and ones with pink icing and sprinkles. My parents had each taken a doughnut but barely touched it. I had eaten two already; they were fantastic.

My parents were still dressed for their day jobs; Dad had

his butcher's clothes on for work at the grocery store, while Mom was dressed for a day of accounting. I was in my usual school uniform, shorts and a polo shirt. Meanwhile, Alexander wore a custom-made three-piece suit and shoes so polished they were almost blinding.

I said, "Remember, back in February, when I got that medal for saving the president's life?"

"How could we ever forget?" Dad asked. "That was one of the proudest days of our lives."

"Well, the day I saved the president, I wasn't at the White House to hang out with his son," I said. "I was there on a mission."

"A mission?" Dad repeated, confused. "What do you mean?"

"Perhaps we should start at the beginning," Alexander suggested. "As I'm sure you recall, around fifteen months ago, I came to your home and told you that Benjamin here had received an all-expenses-paid scholarship to St. Smithen's Science Academy for Boys and Girls."

"That wasn't true?" asked my mother.

"Not a single word," Alexander admitted. "In fact, there *is* no St. Smithen's Science Academy for Boys and Girls. And I am not a professor of astrophysics there. Instead, I am a spy for the Central Intelligence Agency—and Benjamin was recruited to our top secret Academy of Espionage, where he has been training to be a field agent."

My parents' eyes grew even wider. Their jaws dropped even farther. Finally, my father managed to formulate a response, although he was so stunned, it took him a while to get each word out. "That . . . is . . . amazing."

My mother turned to him. "You think it's amazing that this man lied to us and that our son has been training to be a spy?"

"Yes!" Dad exclaimed. "In fact, it might be the most amazing thing I've ever heard!" He turned to me, beaming. "We thought you were just going to some boring science school! But you're training to be a spy! My son, a spy!"

Alexander heaved a sigh of relief, pleased that things were going well with at least one of my parents.

On the other hand, Mom wasn't as easy a sell. She fixed Alexander with a stern look and said, "Benjamin is only thirteen! What gives you the authority to recruit him without our permission?"

"The government of the United States of America," Alexander replied. "Mrs. Ripley, I understand your concerns about this. But there is simply no way that we could have asked for your consent. The whole point of being a secret agent is that it's . . . well, a secret. No one at the Agency can tell their family what they do."

"Even you?" Dad asked.

"I'm sort of a special case," Alexander said. "My father is an agent. And so was his father. And his and his and his and so on, going all the way back to Nathan Hale."

"That's incredible," Dad said. "So it's like your family business?"

"Yes. My daughter is also training to be a spy—along with young Benjamin here. And my ex-wife is a spy as well, but being British, she works for MI6. Although, to be honest, Catherine even kept that a secret from *me*. I only found out the truth a few weeks ago."

"Wow," Dad said. "She sounds a lot more interesting than *my* wife." The moment the words were out of his mouth, he realized they had been a mistake, and he turned to Mom apologetically. "Which isn't to say that you aren't interesting, darling . . ."

"You should probably just stop talking," Mom told him. Then she shifted her attention to Alexander. "So what changed?"

Alexander looked at her blankly. "Excuse me?"

"For the past fifteen months you've been keeping all this a secret. And now it's not secret anymore. What changed? Does it have something to do with the events at the White House?"

"In part," Alexander said. "You see, Benjamin's experience at the academy hasn't exactly been . . . traditional.

Normally, our students study and train at the school for seven years before moving on to work at the CIA. But Benjamin has already been activated for several missions."

"*Several* missions?" Dad swiveled toward me in his chair, glowing with excitement. "You've done more than just save the president? What else? Have you faced any bad guys?"

"A few," I admitted.

"A few?!" Alexander crowed. "Mr. and Mrs. Ripley, your son is being humble. He has faced a great number of miscreants. In fact, he recently helped defeat SPYDER, the most nefarious organization of evildoers on earth!"

"Wow!" Dad exclaimed again. He was grinning from ear to ear.

Meanwhile, my mother wasn't happy to hear this at all. She glared bullets across the table at Alexander. "You let my son confront the *evilest* organization on earth before he even finished his training?"

Alexander shrank under her gaze. "It wasn't like this was standard CIA policy," he explained. "Benjamin kind of got roped up in all this by accident."

I winced, knowing this was only going to make things worse. Alexander wasn't a very good spy, and he was prone to making mistakes. But he *looked* like a good spy, and since he had been the one who had recruited me in the first place, the CIA had felt it made sense for him to deliver the bad news to my parents. Plus, no one else at the Agency wanted to do it.

Ordinarily, my mother wasn't so prone to anger. She was merely being protective, like a mother bear who had just learned that her cub had been recruited by a shadowy organization and sent out on covert missions against hunters. She was gripping the arms of her swivel chair so tightly that her knuckles were white. "Are you telling me that this agency is so incompetent that you *accidentally* allowed my son to confront evil enemy operatives?"

"Yes and no." Alexander took out a silk handkerchief and mopped his brow with it. "It's complicated. But I assure you, Mrs. Ripley, that young Benjamin here was rarely without adult supervision in the field . . ."

"Rarely?" Mom echoed crossly.

". . . and he has proven to be an extremely adept young agent!" Alexander said quickly. "In fact, if not for his keen intellect and quick thinking, we wouldn't have thwarted SPYDER's evil plans on multiple occasions."

Dad riveted his gaze on me. "Like what? Let's have some details!"

"Well," I said, "remember how, a few weeks ago, you thought I stayed at school over spring break to work on a science project? I was actually in Mexico, preventing SPYDER from melting Antarctica and flooding the earth. And then I went to England and France to help defeat SPYDER once and for all."

After all that, my friends and I had been forced to lie low in France for a while until the CIA said it was safe to come home. We had only returned to Washington a few days before. I had thought my life was going to return to normal—or at least, as normal as spy school got—until I had received a coded message from Alexander the previous afternoon, detailing how the time had come to reveal the truth to my parents.

"Benjamin also saved Camp David from being blown up in a missile attack," Alexander added proudly. "And prevented the nuclear annihilation of Colorado."

"Oh right," I said. "I forgot about that."

"You *forgot* about preventing Colorado from being nuked?" Dad asked, stunned.

"It's been a busy year," I said.

Finally being able to tell my parents the truth was a massive relief. Lying to them had been one of the worst things about being a spy. (It wasn't as bad as having people try to kill me on a regular basis, but still, I didn't enjoy it.) However, it was also gratifying to let them know about everything I had accomplished, and the pride in my father's eyes made me feel wonderful.

Conversely, my mother was giving me the same skeptical

look she'd given me when I was six and had claimed burglars had broken into the house and eaten all the chocolate cookies. She was obviously having a hard time believing the stories Alexander and I were telling. "*You* did all that?" she asked doubtfully. "No offense, Benjamin, but you're not the most coordinated person in the world. When you played Little League, you had a negative batting average."

"I wasn't the one who handled the physical stuff," I explained. "Alexander's daughter, Erica, did most of that. She's really good at beating people up and defusing bombs and that sort of thing. I do more of the figuring out what the bad guys are up to."

"He's extremely good at it," Alexander said. "Which is why the bad guys want all of you dead."

The suspicion instantly vanished from Mom's face and was replaced by fear. "What?!"

Alexander paled as he realized he had made yet another mistake. "Er . . . You asked what had forced us to admit the truth about Benjamin being a spy-in-training. Well, this is it. Regrettably, Benjamin's identity has been compromised. Which means that *your* identities have been compromised as well. And thus, any of Ben's enemies can potentially get to you."

To my relief, Alexander did not tell my parents that this had already happened. When I was in France, SPYDER had posted operatives outside our house, threatening to harm them unless we aborted the mission. Thankfully, my friends from spy school had captured the killers without my parents ever knowing they had been in danger.

However, my parents were still very shaken by the idea that this *could* happen.

"So . . . ," Dad said, getting his head around the idea. "We're potential targets for assassination?"

"Yes," Alexander replied.

"Can we tell our friends?" Dad asked.

"No!" Alexander exclaimed. "This is highly classified."

"I wouldn't tell *everyone*," Dad said. "Only a few people. Like the Petersons."

Mom looked at him, confused. "The *Petersons*? Why would you tell them?"

"They think they're *so* much better than us," Dad said. "Bob's always going on about his fancy golf club and how they went to Hawaii for vacation. I bet no one's ever targeted *him* for assassination."

"You can't tell anyone, Dad," I said.

"All right," Dad agreed, though he sounded almost as upset about this as he had about finding out his life was in danger.

"The bigger issue here is your safety," Alexander said. "I'm afraid the only way to protect you is to place you both in the Federal Witness Protection Program."

Mom, who had finally taken a bite of a doughnut, spit it right back out again in shock. "You mean, we would have to give up our lives here, move to a different place, and pretend to be entirely different people?"

"Yes," Alexander said gravely.

Mom considered that a moment, then shrugged and said, "I'm cool with that."

The fact that my parents would have to go into the Witness Protection Program had not been news to me. I had suggested it myself, after their lives had been threatened. But my mother's reaction threw me—and Dad, too.

"You are?" Dad asked her.

"Don't take this the wrong way," Mom told him, "but our lives could use a little shaking up." She turned to Alexander. "Is there any chance we could be relocated to Florida?"

"That's definitely a possibility," Alexander replied. "From what I understand, there are entire communities down there that are nothing but relocated federal witnesses."

"I've always wanted to live in Florida," Mom said dreamily.

Dad looked at her curiously. "You do realize that we'd have to give up our jobs?"

"We don't like our jobs," Mom told him.

"And you would never speak to your family again?"

"That just might be the best part of all this," Mom said.

I had always known that my mother didn't get along

with her parents or like her job, but even so, her response to all this surprised me. Just as my father's response to learning that I was a spy-in-training had surprised me. I wondered if my parents were thinking clearly. It was possible they were in shock. I tried to imagine how I would have reacted if I had suddenly discovered that *they* were covert operatives; I probably would have been dumbfounded.

Two CIA agents suddenly entered the room. They were women I had never met before. Both wore suits and clutched coffee cups from the CIA Starbucks. One was stick-thin with severe features, while the other was heavyset and round. Next to each other, they sort of looked like the human version of the number 10.

"Good morning!" the rounder one said cheerfully. "I'm Heather Durkee, the CIA liaison to the Witness Protection Program."

"We were just discussing that," Alexander said. "Mrs. Ripley here is very open to relocating to Florida."

"Also," Mom said, "I'd like to work with animals, if possible. Maybe at a veterinarian's office?"

"Ooh!" Agent Durkee exclaimed. "That sounds fun!" She turned to my father. "And what would you like to do?"

"I still can't believe we have to move," Dad said. "Is it really necessary?"

"I'm afraid so," said the extremely thin woman. She

spoke in a tone as sharp as her features, like she was perpetually annoyed. "My name is Agent Nora Taco. I'm in charge of—"

"Did you say 'Nora Taco'?" Dad interrupted.

Agent Taco gave him a severe look. "Yes."

"That's a pretty unusual name," Dad observed.

"So I've been told." Agent Taco spoke as though she had gone through this every day of her life and was sick of it.

My father didn't pick up on this. "Is it weird, being named after a food?"

"My family is not named after a food," Agent Taco said curtly. "The food is named after my family. My ancestors invented it."

"Your family invented the taco?" Mom asked, astonished. "I had always thought . . ."

"Tacos always existed?" Agent Taco said. "They didn't. The same way that sandwiches didn't exist until the Earl of Sandwich invented them. There were no tacos until Don Diego Taco came along."

"Wow," Dad said, impressed. "You learn something new every day."

"As I was trying to say," Agent Taco went on, "I'm in charge of internal investigations concerning double agents here." She grabbed one of the neon pink doughnuts with sprinkles and then shoved the box toward Agent Durkee.

"None for me, thanks," Agent Durkee said. "I don't eat gluten. Or refined sugars. Or anything that's a color that doesn't exist in nature."

"More for me, then," Agent Taco said, grabbing a second pink doughnut.

"Unfortunately, we've had a bit of a mole problem here at the CIA," Alexander explained to my parents. "SPYDER, the evil organization that Benjamin was instrumental in bringing down, had corrupted a great number of our agents. That's how Benjamin's identity—and yours—were leaked. Thankfully, Benjamin managed to not only thwart SPYDER but also recover a list of the moles . . ."

"Which I'm currently using to root out corruption throughout the Agency," Agent Taco concluded. There was now a tiny fringe of frosting on her upper lip that made it look like she had a thin pink mustache.

"How could the CIA have let so many agents get corrupted?" Mom asked accusingly.

"Obviously, mistakes were made," said Agent Taco, then added, "By other people. Not me. That's why *I* have been tasked with cleaning up this mess. And, to ensure that nothing like this ever happens again, I am creating a new division at the CIA with the sole purpose of policing the Agency. I'm calling it the Double Agent Detection Division."

"DADD?" I said.

"Yes?" my father asked.

"Sorry," I said. "I wasn't talking to you. I was referring to the acronym of the division: DADD."

"Yes?" my father asked again.

Agent Taco sighed. "I might have to rethink the division name."

"Ooh!" Agent Durkee said excitedly. "You could call it the Mole Patrol!"

"I will do no such thing," Agent Taco said flatly. "Anyhow, I'm assembling an elite team to track down and neutralize any agents who have been corrupted."

"But the damage has already been done where you're concerned," Agent Durkee told my parents. "The best we can do now is to relocate you. I apologize for the inconvenience."

"Inconvenience?" Dad echoed. "It's a bit more than that. You're asking us to give up everything!"

"I know," Agent Durkee said. "But I promise we are going to do everything possible to protect you from now on. That's why we decided to have this meeting here, at CIA headquarters, rather than at your home. This building is the most secure facility in America. You're as safe as—"

The air was suddenly split by the scream of something moving very fast, after which came the sound of an explosion extremely close by. The entire room shook. A lighting fixture fell out of the ceiling and landed on the doughnuts with such force that all the jelly-filled ones exploded.

"Take cover!" Alexander Hale shouted. "We're under attack!"

Apparently, we weren't nearly as safe as the CIA had hoped.

EVACUATION

CIA headquarters
April 16
1030 hours

"We need to clear this room and get to safety!"
Agent Durkee announced. Even though it was an order given
in the face of danger, her naturally cheerful voice still made
it sound like she was suggesting we all go do something fun,
like getting ice cream or going roller skating.

My parents were petrified, literally so frightened that
they weren't moving. I had to remind myself that they had
never experienced a direct threat to their lives before. "Come
on!" I told them, grabbing their arms and tugging them
toward the door.

Alexander came to my aid, guiding my mother while I took care of my father. My parents snapped out of their dazes and allowed themselves to be led from the office.

Agent Taco grabbed the last of the pink-frosted doughnuts and followed us.

We stepped into a hallway full of chaos.

In part, this was because the CIA was designed to be confusing on purpose. While hallways in normal buildings went in nice, straight lines, the CIA's zigged and zagged to discombobulate any bad guys who might have happened to infiltrate the building. Unfortunately, they also were discombobulating to any good people who happened to be there as well. And having a full-on crisis didn't help things. Directly next to where we had been meeting, the door had been blown off another conference room and thick smoke was pouring out, creeping along the ceiling like an incoming tide. Through the charred doorway, I caught a glimpse of flames and a gaping hole in the outer wall, revealing blue sky and green trees.

Agency employees were running every which way. There were agents and analysts and support staff and cleaning crews. Some were fleeing from the site of the explosion, seeking safety, while others were running toward it, intending to fight the flames or rescue people or do something equally heroic.

Luckily, it appeared no one had been hurt. The conference

room where the explosion had occurred had been empty.

However, Agent Durkee still went pale at the sight of it, as though something was seriously wrong. She quickly led us away from the disaster, joining the flow of people heading for safety. We were all moving toward a stairwell; the elevators had shut down due to the emergency.

The sprinkler system came on, jetting water from the ceiling and dousing us all.

"Does this sort of thing happen often in this business?" Dad asked me.

"Not really," I assured him, even though I had experienced plenty of danger. To my surprise, I wasn't shaken at all by the current crisis. Once you've dangled from a helicopter over a chasm to defuse a nuclear bomb, a midsize explosion in an office building isn't really that big a deal. I was far more concerned for my parents than for my own safety.

"To be honest," Alexander added, "I don't think we've ever had an attack on this building in the history of the Agency."

"There's a good chance it wasn't an attack at all," Agent Taco said, obviously displeased that Alexander had told my parents the truth. "It might have been a gas line rupture."

"Right," Alexander said, doing his best to sell this. "A gas line rupture. That's probably what it was."

We funneled into the stairwell. Hundreds of people were

heading down while a few emergency responders were trying to come up, so we couldn't descend very fast.

In the crush of people, Alexander and I let go of my parents, allowing them to file down ahead of us. Now that they were no longer close enough to hear her, Agent Durkee whispered to Alexander and me, "The room where the explosion occurred . . . That was supposed to be *our* conference room."

Now I felt frightened. I stumbled slightly on the stairs. "What do you mean?"

"I had originally booked that room for our debriefing this morning," Agent Durkee explained. "But I changed it half an hour ahead of time. I found out that the room had been used for a retirement party yesterday, and apparently it got a bit crazy. There was quite a mess left behind. So I moved our meeting to the other room instead."

"But the bomber didn't get the message," Alexander concluded. "And so they attacked the wrong room in their attempt to kill us."

"Not *us*," Agent Durkee corrected, then looked to me. "*You*. And maybe your parents, too."

This news rattled me even more. My legs got wobbly as I descended the stairs. "How many other people knew where we were supposed to be having that meeting?"

"None," Agent Durkee said. "The location was classified."

"Apparently, it wasn't classified enough," Alexander mused. "Someone obviously found out about it."

"Could it have been SPYDER?" I asked.

"We *defeated* SPYDER," Alexander reminded me.

"There could still be some double agents who weren't on the list we recovered," I suggested. "And they might want revenge."

"Or it could be an entirely new evil organization that wants to get rid of you," Agent Taco suggested ominously.

I considered that as I continued down the crowded staircase. The possibility of another evil organization had been raised before. In fact, it was rumored that one might have covertly helped us undermine SPYDER to get them out of the way. But I had considered those ideas to be slightly paranoid until now.

My stomach began to tie itself in knots. After defeating SPYDER, I had really been hoping to not have any attempts on my life for . . . well, the rest of my life. Which I had additionally hoped would be quite long. And now I had barely returned to spy school before someone was trying to kill me again. At CIA headquarters, no less. If they could target me at an extremely secure location like that, where would I be safe?

We reached the ground floor. All the other CIA employees were leaving the stairwell, most likely headed for the closest exit from the building. My parents started to follow them, but Agent Taco held them back.

"Not that way," she said. "*This* way." She continued down the stairwell, heading into the basement levels of the building.

The rest of us followed her, although not without concern. "But everyone else is leaving the building," Mom protested. "Shouldn't we be doing that?"

"Just because everyone else is doing something, that doesn't make it the smart thing to do," Agent Taco said bluntly.

"I agree with that in theory," Mom said, sounding slightly offended. "But in this case, the building we're in happens to be *on fire*. Not to mention under attack by bad guys . . ."

"It might have just been a gas line rupture . . . ," Agent Durkee suggested.

"Oh please," Mom said. "We're not morons. We can handle the truth."

"We'll be safe down here," Agent Taco said. "The lower levels of this building have been built to withstand a nuclear attack."

"That's good," Dad said, then thought to ask, "Um . . . There's no chance of a nuclear attack, is there?"

"Probably not." Agent Taco led us through a door at the lowest level of the stairwell, two floors below ground level.

She needed a keycard to pass through it, and there was a sign on the door that said AUTHORIZED CIA PERSONNEL ONLY. VIOLATORS WILL BE PROSECUTED.

We found ourselves in another maze of twisting hallways, although this one appeared to be empty except for us. Every door had a coded keypad entry, but no signage or even office numbers. There was no way to tell what any of them led to.

And yet, Agent Taco seemed to know exactly where she was going. She led us through the maze without pausing for even a second to figure out where we were. "Benjamin, might I have a word?" she asked.

"Sure." I hurried to catch up with her as we zigzagged through the halls.

Agent Taco said, "I didn't get the chance to mention it before we were interrupted, but I'm looking for a junior member for DADD. Would you be interested?"

"Me?" I asked, surprised.

"You have proven yourself quite adept at uncovering double agents so far. You found one within only a few weeks of starting at the academy, and we wouldn't have the list of SPYDER operatives if it wasn't for you, either. In fact, it might be safe to say that you have uncovered more moles than most people who specialize in it."

I should have been flattered by Agent Taco's words, but they were delivered in the flat tone of someone who was bored to death. "So . . . I'd be working with you here?"

"Part-time. You would remain a student, as there is still plenty for you to learn. For example, I understand that you're at the bottom of your class in advanced weaponry."

"Yes."

"In fact, your instructor reports that you're so bad, 'bottom of the class' doesn't do it justice. They really need to come up with a new term to describe just how bad you are. Like 'basement of the class.' Or 'sub-basement.'"

"I'm more of an idea person."

"Anyhow, this would be a very good opportunity for a young agent-in-training. You'd start immediately, helping me and my team track down moles at the Agency, and then after graduation, you'd have a plum job waiting for you."

"Ooh," said Agent Durkee, who'd overheard all this. "That's a nice offer, Ben. The Mole Patrol is going to be a very high-profile division."

"It is not called the Mole Patrol," Agent Taco said through gritted teeth. "It's called DADD!"

"Yes?" my father asked.

Agent Taco rolled her eyes, then looked to me. "So? Are you interested?"

"Can I have some time to think about it?" I asked, trying to be diplomatic. I was flattered by the offer, but I didn't like the idea of committing to a specific division of the CIA when

I was only in my second year of school. Especially one that solely policed the CIA itself. Obviously, uncovering double agents was important, but I feared it might lack excitement. While my previous missions had been terrifying at times, they had ultimately been quite thrilling. Saving the world was a rush; I wasn't ready to give it up. Plus, I was pretty sure no one in law enforcement ever liked the people assigned to investigate *them*. At least, that was always the case in the movies.

Agent Taco didn't seem pleased with my answer. "I can give you some time, but not much. Staffing this division is a high priority." She arrived at a door that looked exactly like every other door we had passed and entered a code on the keypad. The door clicked open. Agent Taco led us through it.

We found ourselves in a security-monitoring station. Dozens of agents were at work before a bank of monitors that displayed video feeds from cameras around the CIA campus. Spy school had a similar station, but this one was far more up-to-date and much better staffed.

An agent stationed by the door went on the alert as we entered, her hand dropping to the weapon holstered on her belt.

"At ease," Agent Taco said. "They're with me. We've just come from the site of the explosion. Any intel on that yet?"

The agent overseeing the operation was an older man with a graying mustache. He gave my family a wary glance, then said, "We believe it might have been a gas leak . . ."

"Oh, don't start this again," Mom said.

"There's no need for a cover-up here," Agent Taco said. "We need the facts."

The agent with the mustache considered us carefully, but then told the truth. "The explosion appears to have been caused by a short-range rocket-propelled grenade launcher."

"Short-range?" Agent Durkee echoed. "Meaning someone fired it from within this property?"

"Yes," Agent Mustache said. He pointed to a monitor that displayed security footage of the attack.

The footage showed the RPG being fired from a clump of trees not far from the headquarters building. There was a puff of smoke as it launched, and then there was a stream of fire and exhaust, followed by it striking the building. It was chilling to think that, had the shot been only a few feet to the right, it would have struck the conference room where my parents and I had just been.

"However," Agent Mustache went on, "we may have a lead. The attacker was recorded by one of our cameras. The image is blurry, but we're enhancing it."

He pointed to another monitor, where an agent was examining a portion of the footage from before the blast. She had zoomed in on a shadowy blob back in the trees. The magnification had pixelated the image, but the computer was working hard to refine it. Before our eyes, the blob started to look more human.

"I assume a manhunt is underway?" Alexander asked Agent Mustache.

"Every available agent is sweeping the property from here to the Potomac," Mustache reported. "Although as far as I know, they haven't found anything yet."

My parents were watching everything, rapt with attention. Until that morning, their lives had been normal. The most exciting thing that had happened to them in the past few years was when our neighbor, Mrs. Fielding, had lost control of her car while swerving to avoid a squirrel and ended up parked in the middle of our begonias. Now, within the space of an hour, they had learned that I was actually a spy-in-training, been told their lives were in enough danger that they had to join the Federal Witness Protection Program, experienced an actual enemy attack, and become privy to a high-tech digital identification session.

"This is fantastic," Dad gasped. "I'll bet Bob Peterson's never seen anything like this."

"*Most* people haven't seen anything like this," Mom corrected, just as amazed.

Dad noticed me watching them and asked, "Is it fun, training to be a spy?"

I had never thought about that before. At times, spying

had been terrifying, tense, exhausting, unnerving, and exhilarating, but fun? I considered that a moment, then answered, "I've made some really good friends doing it. So that's been fun."

"Good," Dad said. "That's important." He turned to Agent Durkee and said, "When we go to Florida, I think I'd like to have an ice cream shop. Is that possible?"

Agent Durkee seemed slightly puzzled, as though no one in the history of the Federal Witness Protection Program had ever requested this before. "Maybe."

"I think that'd be nice," said my father. "People are always happy when they're getting ice cream."

"Oh dear," Alexander Hale said suddenly. The color had drained from his face.

He was staring at the monitor with the image of our attacker. The resolution was getting better and better as the computers enhanced it. Even as I watched, the features grew clearer, so I could make out the attacker's face.

I immediately understood why Alexander was so upset.

The attacker who had launched the grenade at us was his daughter. And my friend.

Erica Hale.

DISAGREEMENT

Armistead Dormitory

The Academy of Espionage

Washington, DC

April 16

1400 hours

"I can't believe your girlfriend tried to kill you," Chip Schacter said. "That sucks."

"First of all," I told him, "Erica isn't my girlfriend . . ."

This provoked a variety of responses around my dorm room, where my closest friends were gathered with me. We were supposed to be in class, but I had called an emergency meeting. I knew I wouldn't be able to concentrate on my Introduction to Deception and Subterfuge lecture after that morning's events, and my friends had readily agreed to skip their classes as well. (Often, our classes were far less exciting than they sounded, and some, like Self-Preservation 102, could be quite painful.)

My room was small, barely able to hold all five of us. By the time I had arrived back at school, my friends had already learned about Erica attacking the CIA, even though the information was classified. It was impossible to keep secrets at spy school—and a juicy bit of gossip like this had spread like wildfire.

My relationship with Erica was extremely complicated. So complicated, *I* wasn't even sure where things stood. I'd had a crush on Erica from the moment I met her, when she had tackled me during a fake enemy attack designed to test my combat skills upon my arrival at spy school. At the time, Erica had seemed way out of my league, being somewhat older and far more talented at spying than me—or anyone else at school. (Her grandfather, Cyrus Hale, had been training her in spycraft since she was old enough to walk.) However, fate had put us together on several missions, during which I had occasionally risen to the challenge and proved my worth to her. In a few rare instances, Erica had dropped her guard around me. She had even kissed me once, in the few seconds before we thought we were going to be annihilated by a nuclear weapon in Colorado—although she had later claimed that she was trying to calm *me* down and then threatened to kill me if I ever told anyone what had happened. (I presumed she was joking, but wasn't 100 percent sure.) Later, while under the influence of truth serum, Erica had told me that she thought having a relationship in the spy business was a liability and discouraged me from pining away for her. So I had turned my attention elsewhere—notably, toward my friend Zoe Zibbell, a fellow spy-in-training, who I had discovered had a crush on me. But even though I liked Zoe, I was still carrying a torch for Erica. Zoe knew this and had told me she wasn't going to wait much longer for me to sort things out.

It wasn't exactly your standard middle school romance.

To complicate matters further, Erica wasn't around to explain herself. She had vanished after her attack. The CIA had swept its own property to no avail, finding no sign of her save for the used grenade launcher, which had been wiped clean of fingerprints. Erica had not returned to campus, although that was understandable; the perimeter was surrounded by CIA agents who had orders to arrest her on sight.

As it happened, Zoe was one of the friends gathered in my room. She wasn't pleased that Chip had referred to Erica as my girlfriend, though she tried to hide it, because the last thing she wanted to do was let Chip think she was jealous.

Chip smirked at her reaction; half the reason he had called Erica my girlfriend was certainly to get under Zoe's skin. Chip enjoyed causing trouble, with friends almost as much as enemies. He wasn't the smartest student at spy school by a long shot, but he was one of the toughest, and the spy business always needed thugs who didn't question orders. It was good to have him on my side. He was one of the people who had saved my parents' lives when SPYDER had threatened them . . .

. . . along with Jawa O'Shea, who was also there with us. If it hadn't been for Erica Hale, Jawa would have been the star student at spy school; he was smart, athletic, clever, and capable. Jawa and Chip were unlikely friends, but they made a good team. Jawa seemed to find Chip's needling of Zoe and me funny as well.

The fifth person in the room was Mike Brezinski, who was the most recent recruit to spy school. Mike had been my best friend while we were growing up. About a year after I had left to start my top secret spy training, Mike had figured out what was going on, after which the Agency had no choice but to recruit him as well. Mike was an outside-the-box thinker who everyone found charming—especially girls. Most recently, he had been dating the president's daughter (although she was upset at him for ditching their spring break plans to go on an unauthorized covert mission and now wasn't returning his calls). Mike was also the most loyal friend anyone could ever hope for. He always had my back—and the backs of the people I cared about. "Erica didn't try to kill Ben," he told Chip before I could do it. "That's ridiculous."

"It's not ridiculous if there's *proof*," Jawa argued. "I heard there's CIA security footage showing Erica firing that grenade."

"There's a perfectly good explanation for that," I said.

"Which is . . . ?" Jawa challenged.

"I don't know yet," I admitted. "But there's no way Erica would have ever done something like this."

"Maybe she doesn't like you as much as you thought she did," Chip said, only partially teasing. "Or maybe she got jealous of you and Zoe here making goo-goo eyes at each other."

Zoe turned red and glared at Chip. "Ben and I have not been making goo-goo eyes."

"Yes you have," Chip said. "Ever since you came back from your last mission. Like this." Chip did an overblown, purposefully insensitive imitation of Zoe, fluttering his eyelashes and gazing at me dreamily.

"That's not funny!" Zoe shouted. Though she was much smaller than Chip, she was an exceptionally good fighter. She might have lunged across the room and pummeled him if Mike hadn't restrained her.

I tried to get us back on topic before things got out of hand. "If Erica really *did* want to kill me, there are a thousand better ways she could have done it. Far less complicated ways. She could have poisoned me, gassed me, stabbed me . . ."

". . . or shot you," Mike said supportively. "She's the best sniper at school by far."

"Exactly," I agreed. "Plus, Erica cares more about her reputation than anyone else here. She's determined to be the top of her class, if not the best spy in the history of the CIA. So why would she do something as reckless as infiltrating the CIA's headquarters and firing a rocket-propelled grenade at me from within sight of the security cameras?"

"Heat of passion?" Jawa suggested.

"I might buy that for anyone else," I said, "but not Erica."

"Ben has a point," Zoe agreed. "This is the Ice Queen we're talking about. I've seen rocks with more passion than her."

"Fine," Chip conceded. "Erica didn't try to blow the CIA up because she was angry at Ben. She did it because she's a double agent."

"She is not!" I said. "If Erica really did want to attack CIA headquarters, she would have figured out where every security camera was on the property and then mapped out the exact route to avoid them. She would have probably done it with something far less obvious than an RPG—and if she really wanted me, or anyone else in that room, dead, then we'd be dead. Because Erica doesn't fail at *anything*."

"But she *did* attack CIA headquarters," Jawa protested. "It's on camera. How do you explain that?"

"Maybe it wasn't her," Mike suggested. "It was only someone pretending to be her. Like wearing one of those incredibly lifelike masks that they have in the *Mission: Impossible* movies."

"We don't have masks like that in real life," Jawa told him.

"Really?" Mike asked, sounding disappointed. "Why not?"

"Because they're impossible to make," Zoe said. "The CIA's been trying for years, and the closest they've gotten still makes you look like someone whose face is melting off their head. Which is great if you need to blend in with a bunch of zombies, but not very useful otherwise."

Chip looked to Mike. "No one here has ever told you those *Mission: Impossible* masks don't really exist?"

"Oh, plenty of people have," Mike said. "But I thought maybe everyone was just keeping them a secret."

No one argued against that, because it was a perfectly reasonable line of thought at spy school.

Instead, I said, "An impostor wouldn't have needed a

perfect mask to fake being Erica. All the footage was taken from cameras that were a long distance away, and then they used computers to enhance the images. So maybe someone could have fooled them with a mask that was only halfway decent. Or even a life-size photo of Erica's face over their own."

Everyone shifted their attention to Jawa, because he was the one who would best know if this theory was any good.

"I suppose there's a chance that might work," he said, "but I'd doubt it. Ben, you said it really looked like Erica in the footage?"

"Yes."

"Then I'd bet it really *was* her. The CIA's image-enhancement systems are top-of-the-line."

"So I guess she's guilty," Chip declared. "Man, of everyone here, I can't believe *she* would go to the dark side."

"Because she *wouldn't*," I argued. "Erica has done more to defeat evil than most adults at the Agency have. You've been with her on missions!"

"We were also with Warren Reeves on a mission," Chip countered. "And he went dark."

"Erica was a much better student than Warren," I said, trying to keep the anger out of my voice.

"Doesn't matter," Jawa said. "Joshua Hallal was the best spy-in-training here before Erica, and *he* went to work for SPYDER."

That was true. In fact, despite his young age, Joshua had been one of the leaders of SPYDER and had run some of their major operations. He was no longer an issue, though, because he was dead. Or suspected to be dead. The last time I had seen him, he had plummeted off a viewing deck at the Eiffel Tower—although Joshua had been presumed dead before, only to turn out to be alive and well, if in need of a few bionic limbs.

"Erica is different," I told the others. "She *despised* Joshua for joining SPYDER. And Warren."

"Maybe it was all an act," Chip suggested. "She pretended to be the person you never suspected would switch sides so that no one would ever suspect her of switching sides."

"Agents flip all the time," Jawa added. "Ben, you found a whole list of moles that SPYDER had corrupted. I'm sure every one of them had friends who thought they would never turn bad either."

Chip continued, "The Agency suspects that some other evil organization was looking to get rid of SPYDER so that they could steal their business. Well, maybe Erica is part of that. So she acted like a good soldier here all along, helping to destroy SPYDER, and now that they're gone, she's free to move on to their other operations."

I was feeling awfully hot under the collar, and it had nothing to do with the fact that the air-conditioning in the dormitory was barely functioning; I hated that two of my friends were questioning the loyalty of another. I was on the edge of losing my temper when Zoe waded into the argument.

"Look," she said, "I've never been Erica's biggest fan. She's been cold and arrogant to me for years. But even *I* can't imagine her working for an enemy organization. Erica might be a jerk sometimes, but she's not evil."

"It's not always a question of evil," Jawa said. "She might simply be greedy. Like Murray Hill."

Murray was another spy school student who had gone to work for SPYDER, but he had made no secret of the fact that he was only in it for the money. In fact, Murray had gone back and forth between SPYDER and the CIA, playing everyone off each other to further his own interests, becoming a double, triple, and possibly even quadruple agent. He'd flipped more times than a pancake.

"Erica's not greedy and you know it," Zoe said sternly. "I've never met anyone with less interest in money than her."

Chip flopped back on my bed, exasperated. "Well, if she's not working for the bad guys and it's not someone in a mask, then what's she doing on camera firing an RPG at the CIA?"

I turned to him, struck by an idea. "Maybe she *wanted* everyone to see her. So someone would *think* she really was trying to kill me."

"She *was* trying to kill you!" Jawa exclaimed. "She fired a rocket-propelled grenade at you!"

"No," I corrected. "She fired a rocket-propelled grenade *near* me. Think about it. We all agree that if Erica had really wanted to kill me, she could have done it easily, right?"

Everyone looked to one another, then nodded agreement—although Chip and Jawa did it begrudgingly.

"So," I went on, "the only reason Erica would do a bad job of something is if she was *trying* to do a bad job. Maybe someone was forcing her to attack me. Maybe they were blackmailing her into it somehow."

"How?" Chip asked dismissively.

"Maybe they were threatening to kill her parents," I said pointedly. "The same way SPYDER threatened to kill mine. If you guys hadn't saved them, I would have done whatever SPYDER asked."

Chip and Jawa both had to concede that was a valid point.

"You're welcome for that, by the way," Chip said.

"Ben's thanked you like a thousand times," Zoe reminded him. "He even bought you a cake."

"The bad guys couldn't have been threatening Alexander," Jawa said. "Because he was with you, Ben."

"True, but Erica has other family members," I said. "So imagine these bad guys used them as leverage to blackmail

Erica into killing me. Now she's in a bad spot. She has to attack me to satisfy them, but she doesn't really want to hurt me—or anyone else—so she does a job that *looks* decent, but really isn't. She lets herself get seen on camera—because she needs to prove it was her—and she hits the one room she *knows* is empty."

"How would she know that?" Chip asked. "I heard the meeting was moved from that room only shortly before Erica attacked."

"Her father was notified about the change of location," I said. "And if anyone knows how to access her father's email, it's Erica. Since the location was changed so shortly ahead of time, Erica knew the original room probably wouldn't be occupied. I mean, there must be a few hundred rooms in that building. What are the chances that an attack like this hits the *one* room no one was in?"

My friends took a moment to ponder this.

"Makes sense to me," Mike said.

"Does it?" Chip sat back up on my bed. "Because it seems awfully complicated to me."

"Tying your shoes is complicated to you," Zoe said.

"Chip has a point," Jawa said. "In our Analysis and Deduction class, Professor Gomez always says that the simplest explanation is usually the right one."

"Usually," I repeated. "But not this time. Erica's innocent."

"Professor Gomez also says that emotions can often cloud judgment," Jawa added. "And you definitely have emotions in play here, Ben." He glanced at Zoe to make sure she was okay with him saying this.

"I'm not being emotional," I said.

"This, coming from a guy who still sleeps with a teddy bear," Chip said. He got up off my bed, holding the stuffed animal that had been hidden under my pillow. "I gotta go. I'm supposed to meet Hauser in the gym. See you guys later." He turned to me. "Unless Erica takes care of you for good before then."

"That's not funny," Zoe said.

"I'm just saying, if I were Ben, I'd sleep with both eyes open. Erica's not going to miss a second time." Chip tossed the bear to me, then headed out the door.

Jawa got up to follow him, but paused to look at me. "I hate to say this, but Chip's right. Even if you truly believe Erica isn't after you, there's still a chance she *might* be. So be careful." He stepped into the hall and shut the door behind him.

Despite the gravity of Jawa's words, I barely paid any attention to them. Because something had changed in the last few seconds that made me even more convinced I was right about Erica.

"Are you okay?" Mike asked.

I turned to him. "I think so."

"Because you're looking really rattled all of a sudden," Zoe said.

"Not rattled," I said. "Surprised. I *don't* sleep with a teddy bear."

I held up the stuffed animal. It certainly *looked* like someone had slept with it for thirteen years. It was missing large patches of fur and one eye, and surgery had been performed on it multiple times to keep the limbs attached. I had never seen it before in my life.

"Who would break into your room to stick a decrepit teddy bear in your bed?" Mike asked.

"Isn't it obvious?" I replied. "Erica Hale."

DECEPTION

Armistead Dormitory

The Academy of Espionage

April 16

1430 hours

Before I had a chance to explain anything, Cyrus Hale burst into my room.

Cyrus was Erica's grandfather—and Alexander's father. He was a highly respected agent, although he was also crusty and difficult to please. He had come out of retirement to battle SPY-DER, and now that SPYDER had been vanquished, the plan had been for him to retire once again. He had missed a good portion of our last mission after suffering a bad whack on the head that had left him thinking he was a spy in the American

Revolution. He had recovered, but was still under orders to take it easy. Apparently, the events of the day had changed his plans.

Mike, Zoe, and I all started to ask what he was doing there, but he put a finger to his lips and gave us a harsh stare that indicated he would gag any of us if we made so much as a peep. He grabbed a pen, noticed my Reverse Psychology homework on my desk, and scrawled right over it: *We need to leave. NOW!!!!*

We didn't question his orders. Cyrus generally knew what he was talking about. So we all started for the door.

Cyrus let Mike and Zoe pass into the hall, then stopped me and wrote another message on my homework: *Get an extra set of clothes.*

Once again, I followed his instructions. I grabbed extra shorts, a T-shirt, and a baseball cap and crammed them in a backpack, along with the teddy bear, as it was the only clue I had to where Erica might be. Then Cyrus and I joined the others in the hallway.

The dormitory was almost empty, as most of our fellow students were at class. As we raced through the narrow halls, we only passed one other student. Cyrus fixed her with a cold glare and said, "You never saw us, got it? If I find out you squealed, I will hunt you down and ruin your life."

The student nodded meekly and scurried back to her room.

I figured it was now safe to speak. "What's going on?"

"You nimrods blabbed that Erica had made contact with you," he snapped.

Normally, I might have taken offense at this, but "nimrods" was practically a term of affection compared to the other things Cyrus had called people. Instead, I tried to grasp the logic of what had caused our sudden exodus. "Does the CIA have my room bugged?"

"Of course they do!" Cyrus exclaimed. "My granddaughter's the prime suspect in an attack on Agency headquarters, and you're her best friend."

"Erica said I was her best friend?" I asked before I could stop myself. The moment I said it, I knew it was a mistake, but I was too excited.

Zoe glowered. "That shouldn't surprise you. You're her *only* friend."

Cyrus wasn't pleased by my response either. It probably seemed very childish to him. Although, in my defense, I *was* a child. "The Agency has agents posted all over campus, and now they're certainly on their way to get FooFoo BinkyBum."

For a moment, I thought that Cyrus had suddenly gone senile, but then grasped what he meant. I held up the teddy bear. "You mean this?"

"Yes. That's Erica's, from when she was little."

"Erica Hale had a teddy bear?" Zoe asked with the same

amount of amazement she might have shown if she had learned Erica had a third arm growing out of her forehead.

"Her grandmother gave it to her," Cyrus groused, as though he still disapproved. "It's not like she slept with it or anything. She only pretended to send it on covert missions to overthrow dictators."

I heard footsteps pounding up the staircases at both ends of the hall: the CIA coming for us, boxing us in.

Cyrus led us into a room with a trash chute.

This was where we dumped our garbage. The ancient chute dropped several stories through the walls to the trash room of the dormitory. I had never given much thought to the trash room before, but now I did. Because I realized what Cyrus's plan was.

So did Mike. "Oh no!" he exclaimed. "We're going down there?"

"It's that or get arrested by the CIA for collusion." Cyrus opened the chute door.

The rancid fumes of the garbage of two hundred teenagers wafted out.

"I'd rather get arrested," Mike said, although he didn't really mean it.

There was no point in arguing. I squeezed through the door and dropped feet-first into the chute.

It wasn't as bad as I had expected—but that was only

because I had been expecting it to be one of the worst experiences of my life.

It barely made the top fifty.

For starters, the chute probably hadn't been cleaned in at least a generation. The metal sides were coated with various oozes and slimes, the origins of which I didn't want to think about.

Second, I was falling, which was never a good feeling. Somehow, the scum-slicked sides of the chute made me fall even faster than usual, like I was firing down the world's worst waterslide.

Then I landed in a pile of filth. Luckily, there was enough to cushion my fall—but that also meant it had been sitting around for a while, so the stench was toxic.

I tumbled into a pile of pizza crusts so old that they had petrified. Then I scrambled out of the way before the next person down landed on me.

The room was a dull concrete square. An incinerator was built into the wall for the trash to be shoveled into, although given how much trash was there, it seemed that happened only on rare occasions. Foul-smelling fluids trickled out of the pile and into a drain in the floor.

Mike was the next one down. He landed in the garbage, clambered out, and joined me at the side of the pile. "Why do our escapes always have to be so disgusting?" he griped, flicking a wad of ancient chewing gum off his sleeve. "Sewer lines! Trash chutes! Tunnels full of skeletons! Why can't we ever escape through something pleasant, like a room full of puppies?"

"Where are we going to find a room full of puppies?" I asked as Zoe dropped down into the trash pile.

"An evil dog-breeding operation, maybe? I don't know. The point is, it'd be nice to have an escape route that wasn't putrid for once."

Zoe clambered out of the way and Cyrus crashed down a second later, having barely given her any time to avoid him. He landed on his butt but snapped right to his feet and strode out of the garbage, casually brushing a fetid banana peel off his shoulder. "This way," he said, then ran out the door.

The trash room was in one of the many subterranean levels of campus. I had been down in them many times, although I had always found negotiating them nearly impossible. A labyrinth of hallways stretched on for miles beneath the school grounds, and each doorway looked exactly like all the others.

Cyrus knew his way around, though, just like Erica did. Which made sense, as Cyrus had taught Erica almost everything he knew. He moved through the maze at the speed of a much younger man, expecting us to keep up with him. "Let's see that bear," he ordered.

I fished FooFoo BinkyBum out of my backpack and handed him over.

Cyrus promptly twisted the bear's head off.

Zoe gasped, horrified by Cyrus's treatment of what was obviously a cherished toy.

Cyrus gave her an annoyed glance. "Don't lose your lunch, kid. The head's designed to come off. Erica altered him back when she was a kindergartner so she could use him to send me secret messages. See?" He held out the disembodied head of FooFoo BinkyBum.

The bear hadn't been torn at all. Instead, young Erica had sewn a screw top into the neck, so that the stuffed bear worked somewhat like a shaggy thermos bottle, only instead of storing liquids inside, you stored information.

Most children used their teddy bears as toys; Erica had turned hers into a covert messaging system.

Cyrus jammed his fingers into what would have been the esophagus of a real bear and removed a piece of paper that Erica had concealed there. He glanced over it as we rushed through the halls, then handed it to me. "What do you make of this?"

I took the paper from him. *LOC 198* was scribbled in what I recognized as Erica's handwriting.

I held it out so that Zoe and Mike could see it too.

"Location One Hundred Ninety-Eight?" Zoe guessed, which was what I had come up with as well.

"Where's that?" I asked Cyrus.

"Beats me," Cyrus replied. "That's why I showed it to *you*. I thought you might know. You're her friend."

"And you're her grandfather," I pointed out. "I thought she told you everything."

"Apparently not. The two of you never established a burrow?"

"No." A burrow was an espionage term for a secret meeting place. If something went wrong on a mission and everyone had to split up, you would meet up at the burrow. It was recommended that all students establish them with their friends, in case of emergency. "I suggested it, but Erica wouldn't agree to one. You know how secretive she is."

"I do." Cyrus suddenly froze in his tracks, like a rabbit that had just sensed a wolf.

The rest of us took his cue, falling silent and still as well.

In the distance, I heard footsteps running through the halls, along with a murmur of adult voices. Fortunately, I'd had a test on footstep recognition in Advanced Evasive Action only the week before. Given the loud clack of the steps, I could tell they were from hard-soled shoes, which were favored by CIA agents—as well as most other security agencies. However, I couldn't pinpoint what direction the noise was coming from, as the halls were bare and sound echoed through them wildly.

The agents were definitely somewhere on our basement level, though. Which meant they were coming for us.

Cyrus turned to Mike and me. "Take off your clothes," he ordered.

"What?" Mike demanded. "How does being naked help this situation at all?"

"You're not getting naked, you dingus," Cyrus snapped. "You're changing. You're putting on Ben's clothes. While Ben is putting on *these*." He pulled the spare set of clothes he'd asked me to bring out of my backpack.

"Oh!" Zoe exclaimed. "It's a decoy situation!"

"Exactly," Cyrus said. "Those agents are looking for Ben and me, so Mike and I are going to lead them on a goose chase." He looked to Zoe and me expectantly. "That ought to give the two of you time to track Erica down."

"But we don't know where she is!" I protested, pulling off my shirt.

"Well, you better figure it out fast," Cyrus told me.

I wasn't crazy about stripping in front of Zoe, but I did it anyhow, as both she and Cyrus would have chastised me for letting my personal issues interfere with a mission. I slipped out of my pants and held my dirty clothes out to Mike, who shrank away from them as though they were crawling with rats. He hadn't bothered to take off his own clothes yet. "No," he said firmly. "It's bad enough that I have to wear *my* garbage-coated clothes. I'm not putting on yours! Why don't *I* get to wear the clean clothes while *you* wear my laundry?"

"Because you're the decoy," I informed him.

"I didn't agree to that!" Mike argued. "Why can't you and Cyrus be the decoys while Zoe and I track down Erica?"

"Because Erica won't trust you and me," Zoe explained. "The only people she trusts are Ben and Cyrus. And her mom, but she's not here right now."

"So take off your dang clothes," Cyrus growled to Mike. "Or I'll take them off for you and then make you eat them."

"Fine," Mike said, in a way that indicated he didn't think this was remotely fine at all. He sullenly began to remove his clothes, grumbling the whole time.

Meanwhile, I was pulling on my clean clothes, which smelled much better than the clothes I had just taken off. Plus, they didn't have bits of garbage sticking to them.

Still, this did little to lighten my mood. I was worried about Erica. She was obviously wrapped up in something dangerous—and now I had been dragged into it as well. I wanted to help her—after all, Erica had come to my aid plenty of times—but I wasn't sure I was up to the challenge. Not only would I have to elude the CIA; I also had to figure out where Erica was in the first place. I looked back at the clue she had left for me: *LOC 198*. Erica had obviously expected it would make sense to me, or that I would be able to figure it out, but my brain was stubbornly refusing to do that. I had no idea what she meant.

Cyrus took the garbage-smeared clothes that Mike had shed and tossed them and my backpack into a random room to hide them from the CIA. "Here's the plan," he told us while impatiently waiting for Mike to put my clothes on. "Mike and I will head to street level via the secret stairwell that leads to the ATM vestibule across from the main entrance of the school. The CIA knows about that access point and is probably monitoring it." He looked to Zoe and me. "Meanwhile, the two of you will go up the other secret route that leads off campus."

"Other secret route?" I repeated. "Erica told me the ATM vestibule was the only way off campus."

"I've been around longer than Erica," Cyrus told me. "It's possible I might know a bit more than she does." He held out a small radio transmitter that was designed to fit in my ear. I had used one several times before. "I'll keep you posted over this." At that point, many leaders would have said something encouraging, like "Let's do this" or "Good luck." Instead, Cyrus warned me, "Don't screw this up."

"I won't," I replied, hoping I sounded confident enough.

Cyrus pointed down a hall to our left. "The secret route is that way. Make the first right, then take the fourth door on the left." Without another word, he turned and ran in the opposite direction.

"I know you'll find her," Mike said, showing that at least *he* had decent leadership skills, even though he was still visibly peeved about wearing my clothes. Not only were they smelly and grubby, but they were small on Mike. He was done complaining, though, and ran down the hall after Cyrus.

The footsteps of the CIA were much closer now, although I still couldn't tell exactly where the agents were.

Cyrus took care to make his own footsteps as loud as possible to draw the attention of the other agents.

Zoe and I raced the way Cyrus had shown us. We took the first right, into a hall that looked like it had almost been forgotten. It certainly hadn't been maintained as well as the rest of the subterranean maze. There were cracks in the concrete ceiling through which tree roots poked, and the lights flickered ominously. As we ran down the hall, we startled a family of bats that was roosting in a gap in the ceiling, and they took to the air, swarming around us. Just in case our day hadn't been unsettling enough already.

"You really don't know where Location One Hundred Ninety-Eight is?" Zoe asked me.

"No." I found the fourth door on the left. It wasn't locked, but it hadn't been used in so long, the hinges had almost rusted shut. I had to throw my shoulder into it to get it to open.

It led us into a dank, dripping shaft with a ladder of metal rungs bolted to the side. It was very similar to the manhole shaft that we had encountered in the sewers of Paris while on our last mission. It was completely dark inside, so there was no way to tell how high the shaft was. But the only way out was up, so I started climbing the damp rungs of the ladder.

"Do you think Erica actually numbered every location in the city somehow?" Zoe asked, following below me.

"If she did, there'd be a lot more than one hundred ninety-eight locations," I observed.

"Obviously. But maybe she put her favorites at the top of the list."

"And she's only at her one hundred ninety-eighth favorite?"

"She might have thought that the other one hundred ninety-seven were compromised."

I sighed, frustrated once again by my inability to understand what Erica meant. If Erica had wanted to lie low in Washington, there were thousands of places to do it—including a few that almost no one else was aware existed. For example, Erica and Cyrus had the keys to the secret entrance to the Washington Monument, and seemed to be the only people who knew that it had originally been built as a sentry post on the eve of the Civil War; the whole tourism thing was a cover story cooked up by the predecessor of the CIA. I would have bet that Erica knew plenty of other secret hideaways like that. But if she had wanted to direct me to them, then writing

LOC 198 seemed like an unnecessarily cryptic way to do it. And Erica definitely wanted me to find her; otherwise, she wouldn't have left FooFoo BinkyBum in my bed.

My thoughts were suddenly interrupted by me smashing my head into the roof of the shaft. It was so dark inside, I hadn't even seen it coming.

Whatever was capping the shaft was made of metal, so it rang dully as my skull banged into it. "Ow," I groaned, then warned Zoe, "Hold up. We're at the top." I clung to the top rung with one hand while feeling the metal above me with the other.

There was a crank built into it. It was creaky with age, but still functional. I twisted it clockwise, which released a latch. The metal cap above me popped open slightly, letting in a sliver of daylight that was blinding after having been in so much dark.

Once my eyes adjusted, I could see that the cap had the latch on one side and a hinge on the other. I cranked it up enough to widen the gap even farther, then pulled myself up and peered through it.

I found myself looking at more garbage.

A small pile of it was on the ground in front of me, lying in a puddle of something that I really hoped wasn't urine.

"Where are we?" Zoe whispered from below.

"In a back alley," I replied. From my vantage point, I

had a rat's-eye view of it. The alley ran behind several businesses, each of which had a foul-smelling dumpster. It was paved with old asphalt that was cracked and pitted; clumps of weeds grew along the sides of buildings.

It was the perfect location for a secret exit. No one spent any time in dirty, trash-strewn alleys if they could avoid it. So there was no one around to witness Zoe and me as we pushed the metal cap open farther and scrambled out into the alley. Then we shut the cap again. There was a soft click as it locked back into place.

Once the cap was closed, I could see that the top of it had also been covered with asphalt, so it blended into the alley. In fact, it blended so well that I almost couldn't tell where the cap was, even though I had just closed it.

At the end of the alley, across the next street, was a dull gray wall that I recognized as the perimeter of spy school. One of the buildings at the end of the alley was a bank: the same institution whose ATM vestibule had the other secret access to the spy school tunnels.

Zoe and I ducked between two noxious dumpsters before anyone could see us.

"Mike has a point," Zoe said, pinching her nose. "We do end up escaping through an awful lot of places that stink."

Cyrus's voice suddenly rang in my ear. "Benjamin, are you back on the surface yet?"

"Yes," I replied.

"Find someplace to hide. There are some agents by the school entrance, keeping a lookout for us. We're going to decoy them. The next thing I say isn't going to be meant for you."

"Roger," I said, then fell silent and waited.

After a few seconds, Cyrus yelled, "Run, Benjamin!"

It was so convincing, I almost snapped to my feet and bolted from my hiding place. But the "Benjamin" Cyrus was yelling to wasn't me; it was Mike, and it had obviously been done for the sake of confusing the CIA agents.

A moment later, Cyrus and Mike ran past the far end of the alley. Although, since Mike was wearing my clothes and had a baseball cap yanked down over his eyes, it really did look like *I* was running past. If I hadn't been me, I would have been fooled.

A screeching of brakes and a concert of angry car horns followed. I figured that was due to the CIA racing across the street in pursuit, forcing traffic to skid to a stop, and sure enough, a few seconds later, three agents ran past the end of the alley.

One of them was Agent Nora Taco.

"All right, Benjamin," Cyrus said, breathing heavily as he ran, speaking to me now instead of Mike. "Coast is clear for you to move."

Zoe and I bolted for the opposite end of the alley, hooked a right, and kept on running down the street.

"Where are we going?" Zoe asked.

"I don't know," I answered. "I'm just running away from campus."

"Wouldn't it be better if we were running *toward* something, rather than away from something? What if Location One Hundred Ninety-Eight is back on campus? Then we'd be going in the wrong direction."

I realized this was a good point and stopped running. Since I didn't want to be out on the street where the CIA could spot me, I ducked into the closest store, which turned out to be a coffee shop. This wasn't really surprising, as it seemed that every single block in Washington had a coffee shop, if not two or three.

"This is good," Zoe said. "Now let's figure out where we're heading."

"That could take hours," I said, exasperated.

"What else would you have us do, run around in circles and hope we magically stumble upon Erica?"

"That might be faster than figuring out what Erica means." I held up the piece of paper she had hidden inside FooFoo BinkyBum and groaned. "Why does she always have to be so cryptic? If she really wanted me to find her, you'd think she would just write it down in a simple, easy-to-understand way . . ." I trailed off suddenly.

"What's wrong?" Zoe asked.

"I'm an idiot," I said.

"You're not an idiot," Zoe told me. "You're very smart."

"Well, maybe that's the problem, then. I've been over-thinking this." I held out the paper to Zoe. "Erica *did* use a simple, easy-to-understand way to write this. I think I know where she is."

TRACKING

The National Mall
Washington, DC
April 16
1530 hours

An hour later, Zoe and I were standing in front of
the Library of Congress.

The *LOC* in Erica's note hadn't stood for "location." It
had simply been the initials of the name of the building.

Normally, it wouldn't have taken an hour to get there,
but we had been cautious to avoid detection and cover our
tracks, using all the tricks we had learned in Advanced Not
Being Noticed. First, we had opted to avoid the subway,
because there were only a few Metro stations near campus

and thus, the CIA could easily monitor all of them. Plus, the Metro was loaded with security cameras.

So we decided to hitch a ride instead. Only, we couldn't hail anything on our phones, because that was traceable. (Our phones weren't even turned on so that the Agency couldn't track us with them.) That meant finding a cab the old-fashioned way: hoping one would pass by. To be safe, we headed a good distance from campus before flagging one down, because nothing made you more obvious than stepping into the street and waving your arm wildly.

Then we had to get through Washington traffic, which was moving at a speed that made glaciers look fast. The trip was much more expensive than the Metro would have been for both of us, but we had also learned to always have cash stashed on us in case of emergencies. I kept mine in my sneaker. Since I was only a kid, my emergency cash reserve was only twenty dollars, but Zoe had the same amount, which was good enough to get us to downtown DC.

We didn't get out right at the Library of Congress, because if anything went wrong later and the cabbie got grilled by the CIA, we didn't want him telling them he had dropped us off there. So we got out by the Smithsonian National Museum of Natural History instead. That was a much more likely place for two kids to be heading than the Library of Congress and, therefore, less suspicious. The museum was close to the LOC, but not *that* close. Again, if the CIA questioned the cabbie, we wanted there to be many potential places we could have gone.

To avoid being noticed, we didn't make a beeline for the LOC. Instead, we wandered slowly, like tourists—and, since this was spring in Washington, there were thousands of tourists to blend in with. This worked to our advantage. There were many places where two kids on their own might have stuck out, but the National Mall in April wasn't one of them. It seemed as though half the middle schools in the country were on spring break; everywhere we looked, there were enormous herds of children our age.

We blended in with a school group that was leaving the Museum of Natural History and followed it into the National Gallery of Art across the street. The National Gallery was actually two buildings that were radically different in style. The classical arts building looked like it could have been built in ancient Rome, an enormous symmetrical structure full of traditional paintings and sculptures, while the modern arts building was itself a work of modern art, all crazy angles and misshapen rooms arranged around a central atrium, which was dominated by a massive Calder mobile that dangled from the ceiling. The buildings were connected by an underground tunnel, which Zoe and I used to pass from one to the other; we entered the classical building and emerged from the modern one.

From there, we joined another middle school group and

circled the US Capitol, which had just been refurbished. The last of the scaffolding was still being removed, and the dome, which had spent the last few years being scrubbed, buffed, and polished, shone brightly in the afternoon light. There was going to be a big rededication ceremony in a few days, so bleachers were being erected on the western balcony, the same way as for a presidential inauguration. Between the workers, the school groups, and all the tourists and lobbyists funneling into and out of the Capitol, there were people everywhere. Zoe and I were able to slip amongst them in a way that would have shaken anyone who had managed to follow us that far. Or so I hoped.

The Library of Congress sat across the street from the Capitol.

The LOC was the largest library in the world, housing more than 150 million items, ranging from books to photographs to motion pictures to audio recordings. (I remembered all that from a field trip I had taken there back when I was in elementary school.) On the outside, it looked more like a British mansion than a library, with two great wings flanking a large central building. Because the library had been built in the 1800s, the main entrance was designed to accommodate horse-drawn carriages, although very few people arrived that way nowadays, so it had been modified into a drop-off area for cars.

And since it was a federal building, it was open to anyone who wanted to visit.

A small security staff presided over some metal detectors. Zoe and I blended in with yet another tour group and passed through without any trouble at all. From there, we followed the tour to the main reading room, which might have been one of the most beautiful places that humans had ever built. It was octagonal in shape and three stories high with a soaring ceiling. There were marble columns and intricate mosaics and bronze statues of great artists and thinkers. Our tour group fell silent in reverence.

Dozens of arched doorways led away from the reading room, and through each, I could see books. Hundreds of thousands of books, arrayed on miles of shelves—and those were merely the ones within sight.

"Wow," Zoe gasped in awe. "I need to come back here sometime when I'm not being hunted by the CIA."

"C'mon," I whispered. "Let's find room one-nine-eight. I'm betting that, if Erica's hiding there, it's not on the regular tour."

Unfortunately, much of the library was off-limits to us. Except for the small viewing area where we were standing, we weren't allowed into the reading room without an appointment. In this way, the LOC wasn't much like a normal library. Normal libraries were often full of kids, who could read whatever they wanted and hang out almost anywhere, while the Library of Congress seemed to be exclusively for adults who were doing research. There wasn't a single child in the reading room, besides those of us in the viewing area. It wasn't the type of place we could move around without attracting attention.

Our tour group left the viewing area and headed toward some galleries where notable items from the collection were displayed for tourists. Zoe and I fell in behind them once again, though we allowed them to get some distance ahead of us. We passed along a marble hall that was so well polished that it gleamed.

In the middle of the hall was a nondescript door marked LIBRARY STAFF ONLY. There was an electronic card-reader on it for security purposes.

Zoe tried the door anyhow. It was locked.

Neither of us had received instruction in lock picking yet—we weren't scheduled for Advanced Breaking and Entering until the next year—so we went to the closest display case, which was across the hall. It was full of first editions of notable nineteenth-century American classics like *The Last of the Mohicans* and *The Adventures of Tom Sawyer*. While the old books were impressive, what Zoe and I really cared about was the reflective glass of the display case. By focusing on that, we could watch the staff door behind us.

It was only two minutes and thirty-eight seconds before someone walked out of it.

Now Zoe and I employed a technique we had learned in Basics of Infiltration—the very first technique we had learned, in fact: "Fake It with Confidence." Often, you could get away with something that you weren't supposed to be doing (like sneaking into a restricted area of a federal library) by simply acting like you *were* supposed to be doing it.

Zoe and I waited for the staff member to start down the hall; then we turned and confidently strode toward the door, catching it right before it closed and locked. Then we slipped through into the staff area. If any tourists noticed us doing this, they didn't seem concerned by it.

While the main reading room had been an example of how beautiful a building could be, the staff area was an example of the opposite: It was as dull and industrial as the tunnels under spy school. The halls were floored with aging linoleum and painted a bilious green, with doors every few yards. The first one we came to was marked "2101."

A handy map of the building was posted on the wall nearby, which made sense, as there turned out to be hundreds of rooms in the LOC; it was hard to imagine that any visitors there—or even some employees—could have found their way around without a map. Room 198 was down on the basement level.

"Looks like we're going back underground," Zoe said with a sigh.

We found a staircase and hurried down it to the basement level, which was as sprawling and mazelike as the subterranean levels of spy school, although thankfully, there were more maps posted on the library walls. In addition to all the storage rooms and offices, there were also two cafés and several tunnels that led to other buildings. It occurred to me that a startling amount of Washington, DC, lay underground. It was almost as though the city had been partly designed by mole people.

Zoe and I were able to pinpoint room 198, although it took us a while to get to it. We had to work our way through a good quarter mile of basement hallways, and do so without being spotted by any staff members. Luckily, the underground librarians weren't nearly as obsessed with silence as the aboveground ones. Many of them were talking to each other, or to other people on their phones, or listening to music as they wandered about, so we could always hear them coming and hide before they saw us.

Eventually, we reached room 198. I felt a pang of worry as we approached, fearing that I had made a mistake interpreting Erica's note and that all the work Zoe and I had done to get there was for nothing. Then I cased the hallways to make sure we were the only ones within earshot and knocked on the door. "Erica," I said. "It's Ben. Are you there?"

There was no answer.

I decided to try the knob to see if the door was unlocked.

The moment I touched it, the door flew open. Before I knew what was happening, someone grabbed my wrist and yanked me into the room with such force that I was flung across it. I tumbled to the floor next to a metal shelf lined with books. A second later, Zoe landed next to me, having been flung there as well.

This wasn't a particularly unusual way to be greeted by Erica Hale.

She was standing by the door, dressed in her usual outfit, a sheath of black that allowed her to leap into action at any second, accented by a white utility belt that held everything from explosives to antidotes for poison. Erica was extremely beautiful and extremely dangerous. She scanned the hall to confirm no one had seen us, then closed the door and locked it. If she was pleased that we had figured out her clue and tracked her down, she didn't show it. Instead, she was all business. "Did anyone follow you here?"

"No," I reported. "Your grandfather and Mike diverted the CIA before we left campus. And we took precautions coming here."

Erica's gaze shifted to Zoe and seemed to narrow slightly.

Then she looked back to me. "I thought you'd be coming alone."

"Why? You didn't tell me to."

"I left the message for *you*. In your room. If I had wanted this to be a party, I would have sent out invitations."

"It's nice to see you, too," Zoe said sarcastically, getting to her feet.

I stood as well, taking in the room. It was obviously meant for storage, although it appeared to have been forgotten. The books on the shelves smelled musty and were covered with years' worth of dust. The closest ones to me were a full set of *Bunsen's Encyclopedia of Funguses and Molds*. Most of the other books in the room were about similar subjects, and quite a few appeared to have actual funguses and molds growing on them. I noticed a date stamped on the spine of one: 1952. I wondered if anyone had even touched it since then.

In one corner of the room was a small desk where Erica had obviously been working. A dozen books were stacked on it, along with a laptop computer. The books looked quite old, with cracked brown spines and yellowed pages. The laptop was open, revealing that Erica had been taking notes on her reading, although there was also a browser window displaying security camera feeds from the library's main entrance and the hall outside the door. Erica had apparently hacked into the building's security system.

Beside the desk was a case of energy bars. It was almost empty, and the nearby trash can was full of crumpled energy-bar wrappers.

"How long have you been using this place?" I asked Erica.

"A few years, on and off."

"I meant recently."

"Most of the past week. Except for this morning, when I had to run an errand."

"You mean attacking CIA headquarters with a grenade launcher?" Zoe asked. "You call that an *errand*?"

Erica grabbed a dictionary off her desk and flipped through the pages until she found the entry she was looking for. "Errand. Noun. A short trip taken to convey a message or perform a specified task." She slapped the book shut again. "That's what I did."

"Why?" I exclaimed, unable to control myself.

Erica didn't answer. Instead, she suddenly focused on her laptop, and her eyes filled with concern. "I thought you said no one followed you here."

I followed her gaze. She was staring at the security camera feed from the main entrance of the library.

The CIA had arrived. Five agents, led by Nora Taco. They stormed through the front doors, flashing their badges at security.

Erica grabbed a satchel from the floor and swept the books off the desk into it.

"They couldn't have followed us," I said. "We did everything possible to shake them. And if they *had* followed us . . . then why were they so far behind us right now?"

On the screen, the agents passed through security and made a beeline for the basement door.

That struck me as odd. Normally, the CIA would have fanned out to search the building. They wouldn't have headed straight for the basement unless . . .

"They know where we are," Erica said, echoing my thoughts, and then whirled toward Zoe. "You told them!" she shouted accusingly.

I started to tell Erica that she was being paranoid, and that accusing her friends of betrayal wasn't going to help the situation.

But then I noticed that Zoe had a gun aimed at us.

"Erica Hale," she said, "you're under arrest."

BETRAYAL

The Library of Congress
Basement level
April 16
1615 hours

I wasn't sure exactly when Zoe had alerted the CIA, but there had been plenty of opportunities on our long trek to the Library of Congress. I had been so busy keeping an eye out for people tracking us, it had never occurred to me that I needed to watch my own friend. She could have easily sent a text to the CIA, letting them know where we were going. As far as I was aware, Zoe didn't know Agent Taco personally—but if any alerts had come in about the whereabouts of a double agent, Agent Taco and the rest of

DADD would have been assigned to bring them in.

I didn't put all this together in the moment; I was too stunned by the fact that Zoe was aiming a gun at Erica.

The gun wasn't normal. It was made of plastic, which explained how Zoe had passed through the metal detectors with it.

"Zoe!" I exclaimed. "*You* told the CIA where we were?"

"Of course," she replied. "It was my sworn duty as a spy-in-training. Erica needs to be brought to justice."

"Why?"

"*Why?* For starters, she tried to kill you today!"

"I'm sure that's just a misunderstanding," I said.

Zoe gave me a look that said I was the world's biggest idiot. "Wow, Ben. You're even more in love with her than I thought. This girl fired a rocket-propelled grenade at you and you *still* think she might like you?"

"I'm not in love with Erica," I said, a little faster than I had intended. "But she's my friend. I thought you considered her a friend too."

A frown flickered on Zoe's face, indicating I was wrong about this last part, though she didn't say anything.

"We should at least hear her side of the story," I said.

"There's no point in reasoning with her," Erica told me, sounding surprisingly calm given everything that was going on. She was standing beside me, her hands in the air.

"If the situation was reversed, and Zoe was the one who'd been accused of attacking the CIA, I'd be arresting *her*."

"I would never attack the CIA," Zoe said coldly. "Because I care about the Agency. I would never betray it."

"Neither would I," Erica said. "I haven't betrayed anyone."

Despite the disturbing confrontation happening right before my eyes, I couldn't help thinking about Nora Taco and the other agents heading our way. My mind was racing, working out how long it would be until they arrived. (I might have lacked many of the skills that Erica had, but I was gifted in math and had an uncanny sense of time.) It had already been a minute since the agents had run for the basement door. At best, we only had another minute and a half . . .

"You were recorded in the act!" Zoe accused Erica, although she seemed to be saying it for my benefit as well. "Everyone knows you blew up the CIA!"

"But they don't know *why*," Erica said. "I'd explain it to you, but you'd just sleep right through it."

Zoe looked at her curiously. "Sleep through it? I'm not tired at alllllmnthpthh . . ." The strength seemed to suddenly drain out of her body. Her eyes rolled up in her head, and she sagged like a marionette whose strings had been cut.

Erica caught her. The gun dropped from Zoe's hand and clattered on the floor.

"Here," Erica said, shoving Zoe's limp body into my arms. "Find someplace to put her. Quickly." She picked up the plastic gun and slipped it into her satchel.

I cautiously laid Zoe on the floor, noticing, to my relief, that she was snoring softly, which meant she wasn't dead. Only sleeping. "You drugged her?"

"Of course." Erica grabbed her computer. "I'm not about to let her arrest me."

"*How* did you drug her?"

Erica was already running out the door. She had certainly been keeping track of how much time we had left and also knew we only had seconds to spare. "I darted her."

"But how?" I repeated, racing after her.

There were no CIA agents visible in the hallway outside the room . . . yet. But we could hear them coming.

Erica ran the opposite direction down the hallway, then hooked a left at the first opportunity. I stayed right on her heels.

A half second before I would have disappeared from sight, the CIA entered the far end of the hall behind us. "There he is!" I heard Agent Taco shout. This was followed by the sound of footsteps racing after us.

Erica gave a little groan of annoyance and picked up the pace. Then she continued our conversation, as though nothing unusual had happened. "I darted Zoe with this," she explained, pulling up her sleeve as she ran. A small launching mechanism was mounted on her left wrist.

"Where'd you get that?" I asked, impressed.

"Mom gave it to me for my birthday."

For my last birthday, my parents had given me socks. "Are there enough darts left in there to take out all the CIA agents following us?"

"Unfortunately, no. And the darts are so small, they don't hold enough sedative to knock someone out quickly. On the plus side, the person you shoot usually doesn't even notice they've been hit. You just have to keep them talking for ninety seconds until they pass out."

"Ninety seconds?" I repeated. "Zoe wasn't talking to us for that long after we realized she'd betrayed us."

"She wasn't talking to us for that long after *you* realized she'd betrayed us," Erica corrected. "I put it together when I first noticed the CIA arriving."

I grimaced, feeling dumb, which was a common occurrence when I was around Erica. "The whole thing with you pointing them out to us was a diversion?"

"Yes. So I could dart Zoe without her noticing. Although I'd suspected Zoe didn't have my best interests at heart from the moment she arrived." Erica was turning left and right through the underground tunnels with the confidence of someone who had planned out this escape route and run through it many times. This wasn't surprising; Erica was always prepared for the worst-case scenario. Which was wise, as worst-case scenarios occurred around us disturbingly often.

"Why is that?" I asked, gasping for breath due to our breakneck pace.

"Zoe and I don't know each other the way you and I do. If I'd seen *her* attacking the CIA this morning, I would have assumed she was a double agent. So it made sense she'd do the same to me."

I realized that made sense. No one at school really knew Erica as well as I did. Until recently, Erica had never been interested in making friends; instead, she had considered them liabilities.

However, I was still upset by how things had played out. Zoe was *my* friend—my closest friend at spy school—and she had used me. She had taken advantage of me, pretending to believe Erica was innocent in order to trick me into bringing her along.

Erica didn't appear to be nearly as bothered by this as I was. In fact, she seemed like she might have been somewhat impressed by Zoe's tactics. "Zoe *is* smart," she went on. "And she wants to prove herself as a spy. What better way is there to impress the CIA than arresting someone who attacked CIA headquarters?"

"You never explained why you did that," I said.

"I will," Erica replied. "But we have to get out of this building first." We reached a door marked CAPITOL DISTRIBUTION ACCESS: KEEP OUT. It was locked, but had an old-fashioned key entry that Erica quickly jimmied.

We stepped into the room, locked the door behind us, and found ourselves facing a bizarre mechanical contraption. A large conveyor belt passed into a three-foot square hole in the wall and continued on down a tunnel so long, I couldn't see the other end. What made it strange was that the machinery for controlling the conveyor appeared to be well over a hundred years old. It was a big, complex device, full of pistons, pumps, springs, and flywheels. Instead of a simple on/off switch, there was a four-foot-tall lever. Even the lighting in the room was extremely old: Large glass light bulbs with glowing filaments were screwed into pipes along the ceiling.

Several wooden pallets were stacked nearby. Erica set one on the conveyor and ordered, "Get on."

"What is this thing?" I asked, trying to keep the fear out of my voice.

"The original system for sending books to the Capitol. This is the Library of *Congress*, after all. Initially, this whole collection was started just for their use."

I warily climbed onto the wooden pallet. "It doesn't look like this machine has been used in a few decades."

"I don't think people in Congress read very much anymore," Erica said. "Or if they do, it's all electronic. Now lie down flat so you don't get decapitated."

Since I preferred having my head attached to my body, I did what she said. "What does this thing even run on? Steam?"

"It's electric. But just barely. The library was the first building in Washington to be wired for electricity. Grandpa says Thomas Edison built this conveyor himself. Unfortunately, it's not quiet. Our friends at the CIA are probably going to hear it. So I'll need to run it at top speed to make sure we get all the way to the Capitol before they can shut it down."

"How fast is top speed?" I asked worriedly.

"We're about to find out." Erica yanked on the large lever.

The conveyor gradually came to life with a great deal of groaning, as though it was waking up after a few decades of dormancy. Erica was right: It wasn't quiet at all. The room soon filled with a cacophony of clanking and hissing that certainly carried out into the rest of the basement and possibly reverberated through the entire library. I could imagine the librarians in the main reading room, aghast that their precious silence had been ruined.

The rollers beneath the belt started turning, slowly at

first, gently sliding me into the dark tunnel. But I soon began to pick up speed. I looked back over my shoulder to check on Erica and saw her grab another pallet and leap onto the conveyor with it in one fluid motion, like a surfer diving into the ocean. A second later, the machinery kicked into high gear and we began rocketing through the tunnel. It felt as though we were going at least thirty miles an hour.

It was only now that a very important question occurred to me.

"Erica!" I yelled. "How do we stop this thing when we reach the other end?"

"There's an automatic shut-off," she replied. "It's probably still working."

"Probably?" I repeated. This time, I made no attempt to hide the fear in my voice. I had a horrible vision of myself firing out of the far end of the tunnel and splattering on the wall like a ripe tomato.

"It's an old machine," Erica said matter-of-factly. "Old things break."

"You didn't think that was worth mentioning *before* we got on this conveyor?"

"If I had mentioned it, you might not have gotten on. And this is the only way out of the library."

"That's not true! There were plenty of other ways out of the library!"

"The CIA would have caught us using them, and I couldn't let that happen. Too much is at stake."

I wanted to ask what she meant, but several other things occurred at once.

The sound in the tunnel began to change, which I realized meant we were getting close to the end. I couldn't see anything ahead, though: Wherever we were heading, it was dark.

Meanwhile, at the end of the tunnel where we had started, people were shouting. It sounded like the CIA had found our escape route.

Then there was a disturbing clatter from much closer by, the distinct sound of something going wrong with the machinery. I had no idea if this was a result of the CIA futzing with the controls at the far end or simply the conveyor breaking down as a result of running at high speed after decades of neglect. Either way, it probably wasn't good.

"We should assume the crash position," Erica suggested.

I quickly balled myself up and wrapped my arms around my head.

A wooden flapper thwacked me on the shoulder. I figured it was the switch for shutting down the machine. In the past, the books on the conveyor would have hit the flapper, which would have set a series of other cogs and gears into motion, eventually causing the belt to stop. But that wasn't what happened now. Since the machinery was already falling apart, the flapper didn't trigger the brakes; it triggered the breakdown of the entire system.

Somewhere very close to me, a spring snapped with a cartoonish *boing*, followed by a hiss of air. Rather than working together to slow the conveyor down, the cogs and gears began to break loose and ricochet around the tunnel.

The result was that the conveyor belt did slow, but it didn't stop. I still came flying off the end of the conveyor into the darkness. Thankfully, I wasn't going fast enough to splatter on the wall, but then, the conclusion of my ride wasn't nearly as gentle as I would have liked. My wooden pallet splintered on the floor and I tumbled off it. Thanks to my crash position, I rolled like a human bowling ball, banging my arms and legs a bit until I bumped into the far wall.

All in all, I had gotten out of it with surprisingly little pain.

And then Erica slammed into me.

She had been tossed to the floor just as I had, but there hadn't been time for me to get out of her way. My body cushioned hers against the full impact of the wall, and we ended up in a tangle of arms and legs in the darkness.

I felt Erica's breath against my cheek. Our faces were now only inches apart.

I was glad it was dark, so that Erica couldn't see me turn red with embarrassment.

She quickly disentangled herself from me, rolled away, and snapped on the lights.

We found ourselves in a room that was a mirror image of the one at the other end of the tunnel, from which books would presumably have been sent back to the Library of Congress from the Capitol. The machinery that controlled the conveyor looked exactly the same, only it was oriented in the opposite direction—and it was quickly falling apart.

The entire contraption rattled as though it was experiencing a private earthquake. Metal shrieked and fountains of oil spurted from the joints. Increasingly larger pieces were flying off and caroming around the room. Inside the tunnel, so many bits of machinery were ricocheting about, it looked like the inside of a popcorn popper.

"Should we shut it down?" I asked.

"No," Erica said. "Let it self-destruct. The CIA will never be able to follow us through the tunnel while that's happening." She turned for the door, then noticed her satchel had burst open when she'd been thrown off the conveyor. She looked inside and frowned. "I'm missing a book!"

I glanced around the room and spotted the book in a corner. "There!" I ran to get it, dodging a few flying bits of metal on the way.

The book was small but thick, and so old it was falling apart. The leather cover was cracked and mottled with age. Many of the pages had come loose and stuck out at haphazard angles. There was handwriting on all of them, indicating that the book was a journal or diary.

Being thrown from the satchel had been the last straw for the aged binding. As I picked up the book, the front cover broke off, revealing the first page.

In faded handwriting were the words: *If found, please return to T. Jefferson, Monticello, Albemarle County, VA.*

I was so stunned, I forgot about everything else that was happening around me and stood there gaping at the book—until a piston ejected off the conveyor and whizzed past my ear, snapping me back to reality.

Erica was waiting impatiently at the door to the conveyor room. "Ben, let's go!" she yelled.

I ran after her, into the basement level of the US Capitol. It was far more populated than the basement of the Library of Congress. Dozens of low-level congressional staff members had their offices down there, and many of them now stood in their doorways, looking curiously toward the conveyor room and wondering what all the noise was about.

"The gas main's about to explode!" Erica warned them. "We need to evacuate the building, now!"

Even though this order was only coming from a teenage

girl, Erica delivered it with great authority. The congressional staffers joined us in the hallway, hurrying toward the exits.

As we passed a fire alarm, Erica pulled it. Urgent clanging rang throughout the building.

This brought more people racing from their offices, and when they saw the exodus underway, they joined it. Soon, we were amid a crowd of people.

I still had the book clutched tightly in my hand. While there were lots of people around, they were all too focused on evacuating to be paying us any attention, so I figured it was safe to speak. "This is Thomas Jefferson's private journal?" I whispered to Erica.

"My decision to lie low at the Library of Congress wasn't random," she told me. "The entire collection there was started with Jefferson's books. I figured that, if I needed to read them, it was easier to move the books around *inside* the library than to steal them."

"Why are you reading Jefferson's journal at all?"

"Because he was one of the only people on earth who knew anything about the Croatoan."

Although this was the first time Erica had mentioned the organization's name, I felt like I had heard it before.

At the far end of the hallway behind us came the sound of a large explosion. Erica and I knew it was the conveyor belt finally collapsing once and for all, but everyone else mistook it for a gas main eruption. They gibbered in fear and stampeded for the stairs, sweeping us along with them.

Through it all, I kept my gaze riveted on Erica, trying to make sense of anything she was saying. "What's the Croatoan?" I asked.

"The organization that forced me to attack the CIA this morning. It's probably time I told you about them."

NEMESIS

The US Capitol
Basement level
April 16
1645 hours

We did not head back to street level. Not right away.

Instead, there were more subterranean hallways. These connected the US Capitol to several congressional office buildings. Even though the Capitol was enormous, it was still much too small to house the offices of all 535 members of Congress and their staffs, so over time, additional buildings had been constructed around Capitol Hill for this purpose. Unlike the underground levels at spy school, the ones at the Capitol were not a secret; thousands of people commuted back and forth through them every day. (There was even a small Metro line in one of them, though it only ran a block and was more like a children's theme park ride than a subway.) At the moment, most of the staffers and congressional aides around us were using the tunnels to flee the Capitol, rather than heading up to the surface, so Erica and I stayed with them.

"There were only five CIA agents in the Library of Congress just now," Erica explained. "They've probably called for backup, but even so, there are twenty emergency exits for the Capitol on the surface alone. The CIA couldn't possibly muster the manpower to monitor them all on such short notice—especially when the entire Capitol is evacuating—let alone monitor all the buildings where these tunnels go."

I hoped she was right. Erica was clever, but Nora Taco had already proven a formidable adversary.

Still, I chose to trust Erica's instincts. Hers generally tended to be better than mine. So I stayed by her side and pressed her to continue explaining the Croatoan to me.

"Remember how secretive SPYDER was?" Erica asked as we moved with the crowd through the tunnel. "Until they surfaced right after you arrived at spy school, their existence had never been confirmed by the CIA—even though they had managed to corrupt dozens of agents and amass millions of dollars."

"Of course."

"Well, the Croatoan is even more secretive. Its existence has been only a rumor for over four hundred years."

"So how do *you* know about it?"

"My family is the one that's been spreading the rumor. I learned about the Croatoan from Grandpa, who heard about it from *his* father, and so on."

Our tunnel ended in the basement of the Rayburn Congressional Office Building. The evacuating crowd was surging up the stairs. We stayed with it.

"And what did Cyrus tell you?" I asked.

"The Croatoan was originally started by the Spanish in the 1500s as a covert organization to fight British influence in the New World. The Spanish had already conquered Florida, but the British had recently established a colony in the Carolinas, and the Spanish regarded it as a threat to their empire . . ."

"Roanoke," I said, suddenly remembering where I had heard the word "Croatoan" before.

"Right," Erica said. "The Lost Colony."

I had learned about Roanoke in elementary school. It was the first British attempt to colonize the New World, sponsored by Sir Walter Raleigh. It was also the location of one of the greatest mysteries in American history. "Roanoke's governor returned to England to request assistance from the king," I recalled. "And when he returned years later, the entire colony had vanished without a trace. There was only one clue left behind . . ."

"The word 'Croatoan,' carved into a tree," Erica said.

We arrived at the main lobby for the Rayburn Building, which wasn't big enough to hold all the evacuees from the Capitol, so everyone was heading outside. Once again, Erica and I went with the flow. We emerged into daylight a few blocks from the Library of Congress, although with our detour to the Capitol, I figured we had traveled more than half a mile underground.

The Capitol was across the street, though separated from us by a great swath of lawn. Hundreds of people were streaming out of the building and gathering on the grass to wait for further instructions.

The air was alive with sirens; since the Capitol was the seat of the legislative wing of the US government, any alarm there inevitably provoked a massive emergency response. Two dozen police cars and an equal number of fire engines were already parked around the building, and more were arriving. With so many people exiting the building and plenty of emergency responders trying to get in, the scene was beyond chaotic. Meanwhile, all the construction crews dismantling scaffolding and erecting bleachers for the upcoming ceremony made things even worse. I couldn't tell how many CIA agents were there, but they would all certainly have had their hands full.

The sidewalk in front of our building was thick with people watching the Capitol, as if waiting to see if it would go up in flames. Erica and I used them as cover, slipping through the crowd and heading west, toward the National Mall.

I said, "So, according to your family, the Croatoan at Roanoke was part of this Spanish organization?"

"It makes sense," Erica replied. "The Spanish and the English were already at war. That was why the English were having trouble funding the colony in the first place. The Spanish certainly wouldn't have liked the idea of an English settlement in territory they wanted for themselves. So they got rid of it."

"How?"

"No one knows for sure, but whatever they did was effective. No trace of anyone from Roanoke was ever found again."

Another memory from elementary school history struck me. "Why are they called 'the Croatoan?' Wasn't that the name of a local Native American tribe near Roanoke?"

"Yes. According to Grandpa, the Spaniards carved the name into the tree to point the blame for Roanoke at the natives. But it ended up sticking. Plus, the original name of the organization, the 'Sociedad para la Erradicación de los Infieles de los Territorios Españoles en el Nuevo Mundo,' took forever to say. Apparently, the Spanish hadn't invented acronyms yet."

While Erica spoke to me, she was constantly scanning our surroundings for any sign of Agent Taco and the other DADD agents. I was trying to do this as well, although I knew from experience that Erica would probably spot trouble well before I did.

"At the same time," Erica continued, "the Croatoan realized that pinning the blame on other people for their crimes had worked out pretty well. The British kept picking fights with the Native Americans, and the Spanish got off free and easy. So they decided to keep a low profile from then on. Over the next few hundred years, they did everything they could to undermine the British in the Americas. They attacked other settlements. They convinced the French and Indians to start the French and Indian War. They secretly backed the colonists in the American Revolution . . ."

"Wait," I said. "They *supported* the colonists?"

"As far as the Croatoan was concerned, the British were the real threat. The Spanish assumed that a war between the colonists and the British would weaken both sides, and then Spain could sweep in afterward and conquer everyone. Only, things didn't work out the way the Croatoan had hoped.

"First of all, Spain's presence in North America was growing weaker. The Spanish government had given up Florida in return for Cuba in the 1760s, and Spain itself was no longer the great power it had once been. Second, the colonists actually won the Revolution—and created a much stronger country than the Croatoan had expected.

"But the Croatoan didn't give up. Instead, the organization took on a life of its own. It dissolved its official ties to Spain, although its members remained convinced the Spanish were the rightful rulers of this land. And so, they grew to hate this country and everything it stands for. Over the past four centuries, the Croatoan has become more and more fanatical, with one singular mission: to destroy the United States of America once and for all. Are you hungry? I could really go for some ice cream."

Everything Erica had told me was so startling, it took me a moment to realize what she was talking about. There was an ice cream truck parked on the corner of the street, the kind that catered to tourists. Almost every item it sold came in the shape of a comic book character.

"You want to eat *here*?" I asked. "You never eat junk food."

"It's been a rough day. I deserve a treat." Erica plucked some cash out of her utility belt, approached the truck, and ordered a Spider-Man Strawberry Blast.

"Make it two," I said.

We were now a good distance from the Capitol and had returned to the realm of middle school field trips. There were plenty of other kids around us, many hungrily devouring their own ice cream, so we blended right in. However, I remained vigilant, on the lookout for an ambush by Nora Taco or her fellow DADD agents.

Erica said, "The Croatoan has been behind most of the great blows to the United States throughout its history. They provoked the War of 1812, then burned this city and framed the British for it. They inflamed the tensions that led to the Civil War and triggered the stock market crash of 1929. The Cold War, the Kennedy assassination, Vietnam . . . The Croatoan has been involved behind the scenes in all of it."

If anyone else had told me this, I would have thought they were paranoid and delusional, but in the time I had known Erica, she had told me many things that sounded paranoid and delusional—and all of them had turned out to be true.

I realized I was still holding Thomas Jefferson's journal, which I now tucked under my arm to avoid dripping strawberry ice cream on it. "So how does Jefferson tie into all of this?"

Erica started away from the Capitol again, eating her ice cream as she walked. "Like I said, since Roanoke, the Croatoan has done an amazing job keeping a low profile.

They have covered their tracks masterfully, never showing themselves, never leaving a clue behind. The CIA doesn't even have a file on them; the entire organization is dismissed as a fairy tale. But there's another tale from American history as well: about a spymaster who not only believed in the Croatoan but also investigated it."

"Who?"

"The very first spymaster of the United States."

I stopped in my tracks. I knew exactly who that was. It was the first thing I had learned in History of American Spying. "George Washington?!"

"Obviously." Erica didn't even break stride, forcing me to race after her again. "Washington established an extremely advanced spy network during the Revolution, and then kept it running throughout the early years of the country and his presidency. Our professors claim this was to monitor threats from the British and Native Americans, but Washington also knew the Croatoan was a serious threat. After all, they tried to assassinate him."

I almost stopped in my tracks again. "When?"

"Plenty of times. The Croatoan believed that the future of the United States depended on Washington. And they might have had a point. Washington was the perfect leader. He was smart, diplomatic, beloved, and completely incorruptible. His assassination would have thrown the country into crisis. So the Croatoan tried to kill him. Repeatedly. Luckily, Washington's spy network was extremely competent, and they thwarted the Croatoan each time."

"How come I never heard about any of this?"

"Because Washington quashed the story. He didn't want the public to know how close the country had come to disaster."

"How close *did* we come?"

"At one point, the Croatoan nearly poisoned Washington with a turtle soup laced with cyanide. An agent stopped him from eating it at the last second—although a little bit still splashed in Washington's mouth. That's why he had to get false teeth."

We arrived at the United States Botanic Garden. The centerpiece was the conservatory, a glass building within sight of the Capitol that looked like a greenhouse on steroids. It had fourteen rooms filled with plants from around the world. Erica led me inside it. Like almost everything else in DC, it was free to the public, so we walked right in.

I asked, "If Washington was the one who kept a file on the Croatoan, then shouldn't you have been reading *his* journals?"

"Yes," Erica admitted. "Only, I don't know where his journals are. No one does . . . except Thomas Jefferson."

The center of the conservatory was a soaring three-story glass structure with a tropical rain forest inside it. Massive trees grew inside the building, stretching right up to the roof, their branches bedecked with orchids and bromeliads. The ground floor was a riot of greenery with a man-made stream flowing through it. The glass walls and ceiling were supported by an intricate network of metal framing, beams, and girders. Erica headed up a spiral staircase to a catwalk that led through the forest canopy.

As was often the case, the moment I realized what Erica was up to, I was struck by how cleverly she had thought things through. The catwalk offered us a fantastic view of Capitol Hill through the glass walls of the conservatory. It was the perfect place to keep tabs on any CIA agents who might be searching the crowd—but at the same time, we would be almost invisible. The glass walls were reflecting the afternoon sun, which would have been blinding to anyone outside trying to look in, and there were plenty of plants inside for us to hide amongst—assuming any CIA agent would ever think to look for us there in the first place, which was highly unlikely. For all they knew, we were still inside the Capitol.

Erica fished a compact pair of binoculars from her utility belt and focused them in the direction of Capitol Hill. No one else noticed, not that there were many people in the room to begin with. The botanic garden wasn't as famous as the other museums on the Mall, and therefore didn't attract nearly as many tourists. It was surprisingly peaceful and quiet, save for the soft burbling of the stream.

Therefore, I had to whisper to avoid being overheard. "Why would Jefferson have known where Washington's journals were kept?"

"Because he helped Washington figure out where to hide them. Remember, when Washington was president, this city didn't even exist yet. It was still only in the planning stages. There was no permanent place to house anything. So the story goes that Washington decided to store his most sensitive documents at the one place he felt they would be safe."

"Where's that?"

"Mount Vernon."

I almost smacked my forehead, annoyed I hadn't thought of that. Of course Washington would pick his own house. It was his favorite place; he had been very open about how badly he missed it when he was president, and after retiring from public life, he rarely left it again. "Jefferson was an architect," I said, still trying to show Erica that I knew *something*. "Among many other things. So Washington asked him to design a place to hide his files on the Croatoan?"

"So I've heard. And they hid the files so well, no one has ever been able to find them again." Erica handed her binoculars to me. "Our friend is still sniffing around the Capitol."

I accepted the binoculars and held them to my eyes.

"South wing, by the temporary bleachers," Erica instructed.

A large crowd was gathered there: construction workers, congressional aides, firefighters, senators, perhaps a visiting dignitary and a few lobbyists as well. It took me a while to find Nora Taco. She was searching the crowd with a younger agent in tow, frustration etched on her face. It seemed that she knew her chances of finding us were fading fast.

While watching her, I asked, "Do you really think that Washington's files will be of any help? They'll be over two centuries out of date."

"They'll still be something, which is more than we have now. Beyond those, I don't even know where to begin looking for the Croatoan."

"You realize there's a good chance that, even if you figure out where Washington hid the files, they might not be there? Someone else might have stumbled across them over the years. Or maybe they got damaged. Or eaten by rats."

"Jefferson was one of the smartest men this country ever produced. If he wanted to build something capable of protecting a trove of secret documents for posterity, he'd do it right. So now all you have to do is break into Mount Vernon and find them for me."

My surprise ratcheted up several notches. "Me? Why can't *you* do it?"

"Because the Croatoan is watching me. If I head down to

Mount Vernon, they'll know exactly what I'm doing—and they won't be happy."

"So? Plenty of dangerous people have been unhappy with you. That's never stopped you before. I'm sure you can handle these guys."

"Not this time. The Croatoan has found my weakness."

"Weakness?" I repeated, surprised. "You don't have any weaknesses."

"I do have *one*," Erica said. "My sister. And they're using that against me."

LEVERAGE

The Conservatory

United States Botanic Garden

April 16

1730 hours

It was an extremely common experience to be astonished by something Erica Hale said. In fact, it could happen a dozen times in a single conversation. And yet, I had never been so completely gobsmacked as I was right then.

"You have a sister?!" I exclaimed.

"Why are you so surprised?" Erica asked. "Lots of people have sisters."

"Yes, and they generally tell their friends that they exist."

"I'm telling you now."

"I know, but . . . Usually, it would have come up before this. I've known you for well over a year and you've never mentioned her once."

Erica nodded thoughtfully, as though this made a slight bit of sense to her. "As you know, my family isn't normal. It has always been prudent to keep Trixie's existence a secret so as to avoid exactly what is happening with the Croatoan right now."

There were a lot of questions in my mind at that moment, all vying to be asked, but the one that came out first was: "Your sister's name is Trixie?"

"Yes."

"Is she older or younger?"

"Two years younger. So a little bit younger than you."

"Does she live in town?"

"No. She's at boarding school. A *real* boarding school. In Connecticut. Where they teach you how to be unusual things like doctors or engineers."

"Um . . . Being a doctor or an engineer isn't that unusual."

"It is in *my* family."

I hesitated before asking the next question, because I knew Erica would think it wasn't professional. But then I asked it anyhow, because my curiosity was overwhelming me. "Do you have a photo of her?"

Erica frowned at the request, but then took out her

phone and began searching through her pictures. While most people's collections were full of snapshots of friends and relatives, Erica's was mostly surveillance photos. Finally, she found one of her sister.

Once again, I was gobsmacked.

Trixie was just as beautiful as Erica—although she was beautiful in a different way. It was obvious that they were sisters, and yet, the way Trixie presented herself to the camera was the polar opposite of Erica. While Erica had a cold but strangely alluring presence, Trixie appeared open and friendly. She was wearing a dress and actually smiling at the camera, which was something I was quite sure that Erica had never done in her life. I could imagine Trixie as the kind of girl who would want to go for a picnic or a walk in the park, rather than a covert assault on an enemy compound.

Erica bristled slightly at my reaction. "I know. She's ridiculously pretty."

"Er . . . ," I said, unsure whether the right thing to do was agree or disagree, so I changed the subject. "Does she know what everyone else in your family does for a living?"

"No. Grandpa considered training her to be a spy too, but she didn't show much aptitude for it. When she was three, she couldn't even throw a knife or defuse a bomb."

"Um . . . *Most* people can't do that stuff when they're three."

"Really? Well, since Trixie couldn't do it, everyone decided to try to give her a normal life and keep her in the dark about the family business."

"So she thinks you're really at a science academy?"

"Studying to be a biochemist."

"And she thinks your mother is really a museum curator?"

"Yes."

"And your father . . . ?"

". . . is a diplomat."

"And your grandfather . . . ?"

". . . is a retired sporting goods salesman." Erica swiped away the photo of Trixie—somewhat reluctantly, it seemed to me—and tucked her phone back in her pocket.

"Do you have any other siblings?" I asked.

"No."

"You're not just saying that because you want to keep their identities secret?"

"Well, if I *was* just saying that to keep their identities secret, then I couldn't really admit to it right now, could I?"

"I suppose not." I frowned, now unsure whether or not Erica really had siblings other than Trixie, and aware that

I probably would never know. "So . . . If you're this secretive about Trixie's existence, how did the Croatoan find out about her?"

"I don't know."

"What did they do?"

"A few days ago, I received an envelope in my dorm room. It had just been slipped under the door. No one saw who delivered it. There were no fingerprints or any DNA material on it. It had been sanitized before delivery." Erica lifted the binoculars to her eyes again and resumed watching Agent Taco. "After I did a routine check for explosives or anthrax, I opened it . . . and found several photos of Trixie inside. Long-range photos, taken of her at her boarding school. Enough to make it clear that someone knew who she was and could get to her if they wanted to."

"That was it?"

"There was also a note ordering me to kill you on your visit to the CIA today."

I suddenly went weak in the knees. "Me?!"

"Who else in that room would our enemies want dead?"

"Er . . . Your father. Or one of the other agents who were there."

"None of them figured out how to thwart an evil organization's plans on multiple occasions. You did."

"Oh." I had suspected that I was the real target all along, but had been avoiding the truth. It was frightening to realize I was number one on someone's hit list. "Was the note signed by the Croatoan?"

"Sure. On personalized evil stationery. And they also left a nice little map with directions to their secret headquarters so I could find them and arrest them." Erica gave me a disappointed look. "Of course it wasn't signed."

"Then how do you know it was the Croatoan?"

"Because I've been hearing about the Croatoan since I was in kindergarten, and this is exactly how they operate: They're smart, secretive, and extremely devious. They found out about Trixie. They figured out how to get those photos to me without anyone seeing them. And they came up with the perfect way to neutralize both of us in one shot: Have me take you out. Then you're dead and I'm wanted for it."

"But you found a way to thwart their plans."

"Kind of. I sent my father and the other CIA agents an email telling them that the room they had selected for their conference was a mess. Once they switched locations, I attacked the room where you were all *supposed* to be, in the most obvious way possible . . ."

". . . to prove to the Croatoan that you were really trying to kill me. So that they wouldn't do anything to Trixie."

"Exactly. But even though you're not dead, we're still effectively neutralized. I'm wanted for the attack, and now the CIA is looking for you, too."

"But why would the Croatoan want us out of the way now?"

"Because it's good business. In theory, they're plotting something big and don't want us causing any trouble. But now they also have the CIA looking for *us* and not them. The only way out of all this is for us to find evidence that the Croatoan exists and that they're behind everything. Only, I can't do it, because they can still use Trixie as leverage over me." Erica suddenly grew concerned. "Nuts. We have to go."

"Why?"

"Take a look." Erica handed the binoculars to me.

I scanned the area outside the Capitol where I had last seen Agent Taco and located her quickly. Because she was talking to Zoe.

Zoe had awakened from her nap and was now engaged in a discussion with Agent Taco. She kept pointing toward the conservatory. Through the binoculars, it seemed that she was pointing directly at me.

"Zoe's figured out where we are!" I exclaimed.

"It's probably just an educated guess." Erica took the binoculars back, tucked them into her utility belt, and hurried for the spiral staircase. "She's always been a smart student. And Agent Taco's smart too, so she'll probably listen."

I followed right behind Erica. "I can't believe Zoe's ratting us out. She's our friend."

"I've told you before, friendships can be a liability in this business." Erica led the way down the stairs and back through the indoor forest.

I followed her sullenly. I knew that Zoe honestly believed she was right and I was wrong, but I still considered her behavior a betrayal.

Despite my concerns about all this, I remained worried about the Croatoan as well. "Can't your family arrange protection for Trixie somehow?" I asked Erica. "Maybe they could take her away someplace safe until all this blows over?"

"If the Croatoan is really keeping a close eye on Trixie, then they'll be prepared for something like that. And it might be a long time until all this blows over. I don't want my sister locked up in a safe house for months. Or finding out the truth about our family."

We used a crowd of tourists as cover as we exited the conservatory and paused for a glance back toward the Capitol. Even from a distance, I could see Agent Taco and Zoe running our way. It looked like a few other DADD agents had joined them.

"Nuts," Erica said again, then ducked around the side

of the conservatory, putting the building between DADD and us.

There was no longer any point in trying to keep a low profile in front of all the tourists. We ran.

To the west of the conservatory lay some outdoor exhibits that were also part of the botanic garden. We dashed across the formal terrace lawn and through the First Ladies Water Garden, which featured an ornately tiled pool and fountains. An unsuspecting group of Korean sightseers blundered into our path and we bowled them into the water, resulting in a lot of what I assumed were Korean curses shouted after us.

"We have to split up!" Erica ordered. "I'll divert them while you escape." She shoved her satchel into my hands and started to veer off through the rose garden.

I grabbed her arm before she could run away. "No."

"Don't be stupid," Erica told me. "If we both get caught, then neither one of us can go after the Croatoan. . . ."

"We're not going to get caught," I said with as much confidence as I could muster. "I have a plan." I pointed toward the nearest street.

Twenty tour buses were lined up there. It was the end of the day at all the museums on the Mall, and hundreds of middle school students were filing on board while their chaperones desperately tried to keep track of them.

Erica immediately grasped my plan and stopped trying

to run. Instead, we quickly melted into the horde of students.

"They won't notice two extra students on a bus?" Erica asked.

"You've obviously never been on a school field trip," I replied. "All the chaperones are doing is making sure they don't leave anyone behind. They'll notice if they're two kids short—but not if they have two kids too many."

We fell in with a group of disgruntled middle schoolers who were all griping about how boring the National Gallery of Art had been and climbed up the steps into their bus. The chaperones dutifully counted us, but didn't seem to have any idea that we didn't go to their school.

The bus was a hired coach with some amenities, like air-conditioning and tinted windows. Inside, it had the dense funk of sweaty teens who hadn't learned to use deodorant yet. The students were all chatting with their seatmates; apparently, the chaperones had confiscated all phones for the day. Erica and I took a seat at the very back. (In my How Not to Be Seen seminar, we had learned to always sit in the back of any mode of transportation, as everyone else would be facing away from you. Plus, there was almost always an emergency exit in the rear.)

Through the bus's tinted window, I observed Zoe, Agent Taco, and the DADD agents. They were all focused on the conservatory, apparently thinking we might still be inside.

The agents fanned out around the building, setting up a perimeter to catch us if we ran, unaware that we had already escaped.

The chaperones, pleased that they hadn't lost any students, gave the bus driver the okay to get moving and then got on the intercom to remind everyone of the official rules for proper bus etiquette.

"It's going to be an hour's drive back to our hotel," the lead chaperone announced. "During that time there will be no shouting, no food, no public displays of affection, and no unsavory language. Also, we will not be returning your phones until the end of the ride."

This provoked a lot of unsavory language.

Our bus pulled away from the curb. Erica and I kept an eye on the botanic garden through the tinted windows.

Zoe Zibbell was not part of the perimeter around the conservatory, probably because she was still only a student. Instead, she was left standing in front while the rest of DADD secured the building.

As our bus slipped into traffic, Zoe's gaze fell on the mass of middle school students still gathered on the sidewalk. Her eyes went wide as she appeared to realize it was the perfect place for Erica and me to blend in. She grew more concerned as she took in all the buses, then yelled after Agent Taco, but it was to no avail. DADD was too focused on the conservatory.

"I still can't believe Zoe turned us in," I said.

Erica kept her eyes locked on Zoe until she was sure we had escaped. Then she returned her attention to me. Although she seemed pleased by my idea to take the bus, she didn't say it. "Just because someone says they're your friend doesn't mean they always will be."

"But that's what a friend *is*," I argued. "Or what a friend is supposed to be."

"Not everyone thinks that way. You can't only look at what's on the surface. You have to read between the lines."

I frowned, unsettled by the thought of this. "You're my friend. I'd never betray you. No matter what."

"And that's highly unusual. Though I appreciate it. Which is why you're the only person I'm not related to who I trust. I'm still not going to be able to go with you to Mount Vernon, though. I have something else I need to take care of tonight."

"What is it?"

"Something I need to keep secret for now. Do you think you can find the Croatoan files?"

My immediate thought was that the mission was impossible. The files had been hidden for over two centuries, and I would have to avoid both DADD and the Croatoan. Plus, the idea of going on a covert mission without Erica was daunting. "Can I at least bring Mike?" I asked. "So I have someone to help me?"

"Sure, you can bring him," Erica said. "But I'm also sending along someone else."

"Who?" I asked.

"Who else? The best secret agent I know."

MARITIME APPROACH

The Potomac River
South of Alexandria, Virginia
April 17
0200 hours

"My goodness," Catherine Hale said. "It's a lovely night for a covert operation."

We were in a rowboat, drifting down the Potomac River, and it was well past my usual bedtime.

Catherine was Erica's mother, and as Erica had indicated, she was an incredible secret agent. For example, she had managed to hide the fact that she even *was* a secret agent from all the other secret agents in Erica's family until a few weeks before, and the only reason they knew was because she had decided to tell them. Officially, she worked for MI6, the British intelligence agency, though she freelanced when Erica needed her to. Like now.

Catherine was also irrepressibly cheerful, even in troubling times, such as when the fate of humanity hung in the balance. Or when you were in a leaky boat on a murky river at a time when all sensible people were in bed.

"What's so lovely about it?" Mike grumbled. He had originally been excited about helping out on the mission, but once again was feeling that this wasn't living up to his expectations. Mike had seen far too many spy movies. He had been very disappointed to find out that we were only using a dinghy to make our approach, rather than a speedboat. Also, Catherine wouldn't let him have any weapons save for a slingshot.

"For starters, the weather is quite pleasant," Catherine observed. "Nice and warm. Sure beats a covert op in the dead of winter in Siberia. Plus, the honeysuckle is in bloom!" She inhaled deeply and then gave a blissful sigh. "Ah! It smells heavenly, doesn't it?"

I had to admit, it did. Although I was worried about the task at hand, it was nice to be with someone who took the time to stop and smell the honeysuckle, rather than Cyrus, who was always crotchety and smelled like liniment.

Erica and I had ridden the field trip bus out of Washington, DC, without incident. Since the middle schoolers were traveling on the cheap, they were staying at a hotel way outside the city, near Dulles Airport in Virginia. And since the bus was full of middle school kids, it was only halfway to its destination before everyone on board had to go to the bathroom. (Erica sparked this by loudly declaring that she had to go, and was immediately seconded by a chorus of other tweens who'd had way too much soda before boarding the bus.) So the bus had made a pit stop at a mall in the Virginia suburbs, where Erica and I had gotten off and never got back on again.

Instead, we walked to a nearby hotel. Erica had used the computer in the business center to send an encrypted message to Catherine while I used the gym showers to finally clean myself off. (I still had a bit of residue on me from my trip down the garbage chute that morning.) Catherine had handled things from there, making plans for our infiltration of Mount Vernon, arranging a covert pickup of Mike from school, and packing us an astoundingly delicious dinner (meat-loaf sandwiches and homemade brownies).

As for Mike, Nora Taco hadn't been pleased to discover that he and Cyrus had led her on a wild goose chase, but technically, hanging out with Cyrus wasn't evidence of any collusion with Erica. So Agent Taco had let him return to school but left a team to keep an eye on him, suspecting he was up to no good. Unfortunately for her, Mike had always been a master at sneaking out of the house without his parents noticing he was gone, and that skill set worked just as well at spy school. He had slipped out of the dorm, evaded the DADD agents, slunk through the forty acres of woods on campus, and vaulted over the perimeter wall to meet up with Catherine.

While all that had been going on, I was in the hotel business center, following up on email. Erica had taught me how to log into the school system with a dummy account so that the school computers thought I was in Kuala Lumpur, rather than only a few miles away. (The school computer system's security was archaic, which was usually a bad thing, but at times like this, that could be useful.)

I had received over 150 emails. Most were from friends at spy school, wanting to know if the rumors about Erica attacking the CIA were true; since I was Erica's closest friend on campus, I was the go-to person for any information about her. There were also a few emails from my professors, chiding me for missing class that day, along with my homework assignments. And there was a threatening message from the school principal informing me that it was school policy not to consort with suspected terrorists; the punishment was expulsion.

I wasn't surprised to receive this. The principal was an ineffectual blowhard who didn't like me much because (1) I'd had more successful missions than him, and (2) a few months earlier, I had accidentally blown up his office. (He was still working out of a storage closet while waiting for renovations.) But even if that hadn't been the case, I had known that allying myself with Erica would be trouble at school. I simply didn't care. Erica had saved my bacon many times; I owed it to her to return the favor. Once we proved that Erica was right about the Croatoan, the administration would allow us back in with open arms and would probably even pretend like they had never threatened us at all.

The emails I was most interested in were from Agent Heather Durkee. Given the events of that morning, the process of putting my parents into the Federal Witness Protection Program had proceeded even faster than originally planned, but everything was going well. Mom and Dad had been temporarily relocated to a safe house, and plans were underway for finding them a nice condo near the beach in Florida. My mother's pet chinchilla, Roscoe, had also been collected from the house and was doing fine. Meanwhile, Witness Protection was disseminating a cover story to their employers and neighbors: Our family had suddenly come into a large inheritance from a distant relative and had left town to deal with the estate.

I had been so concerned with Erica since the attack on the CIA that I hadn't stopped to really think about my parents. I felt bad that my life was affecting theirs in this way. It had been *my* choice to go to spy school, not theirs; they hadn't even known about it until that morning. And now they were giving up their lives, their community, and their home.

I found myself dwelling on this as I floated down the Potomac. My parents lived only about twenty miles from where I was at the moment. Our neighborhood was much less affluent than the ones we were drifting by, but it had still been a nice place to live. Mom and Dad had spent most of their lives there, and Florida would be different in almost every way: the weather, the terrain, the heat, the wildlife. Even though my mother was surprisingly excited to relocate to Florida, I knew the transition wouldn't be easy. I wondered how well they would adapt, if they would make new friends, and how often I would get to see them.

My parents had also emailed that day, assuring me that everything was fine and that they were enthusiastic about their new jobs and lives, but I wasn't sure how much of that was true. I knew they wouldn't want me to worry about them. They had always looked after me, but now, thanks to the spy business, they needed someone to look after *them*.

"I can't believe Zoe betrayed you and Erica," Mike said suddenly, snapping me out of my thoughts.

I had explained everything that had happened before we had gotten into the boat. Mike had been extremely upset, and now I could see that he had been stewing over it the whole time we'd been on the river. It seemed to be what he was really irritated about, rather than the low-rent nature of our mission. Mike valued loyalty more than anything else—and thus, he was probably the most loyal friend I'd ever had.

"She thought she was doing the right thing," I said.

Mike frowned at me. "Why are you defending her? Friends don't accuse friends of high treason. Or use them to further their missions. Zoe was supposed to be your friend. Maybe even more than that."

This last bit caught me off guard. "What do you mean, 'more than that'?"

"I saw the way you two were always looking at each other while we were in Europe. I kind of thought you might be a thing."

"We weren't."

"Really? Because I know she liked you. Like *serious* liked you. You knew that, right?"

"Yes."

"And you liked her too, right?"

"I guess."

"And nothing ever happened between you two?"

"No."

"Why not?"

I was growing extremely uncomfortable with this conversation. The issue of Zoe and me would have been prickly enough, but the biggest reason nothing had happened between us was that Zoe knew I still had a crush on Erica, which I couldn't really talk about, since Erica's mother was only two feet away. There was no such thing as privacy in a rowboat. I glanced toward Catherine uneasily, certain she had heard everything, but she was staring downriver, at least pretending like she wasn't listening.

I found myself wondering exactly how much Catherine knew about Erica and me, which made me even more uncomfortable.

"It's complicated," I said.

"Life is *always* complicated," Mike replied. "You shouldn't let that get in the way of making you happy. That only complicates things even more. I mean, what if Zoe's all upset at you because she thinks you're giving her the cold shoulder? Maybe *that's* why she betrayed you."

Or maybe she did it because she thinks of Erica as a rival, I thought. Although I didn't say it in front of Catherine.

Instead I said, "It's not like *you* have been so great at handling your relationships. You messed things up with the president's daughter so badly that it screwed up our mission in Mexico."

"That wasn't my fault," Mike argued. "I was totally honest with Jemma . . ."

"You left the country without telling her!"

"What was I supposed to tell her? That I couldn't go to Hawaii with her because I had to go on a top-secret spy mission?"

"You weren't supposed to be on the mission. And you were never honest with her about not wanting to go to Hawaii in the first place."

"Why are we talking about how my relationship got messed up?" Mike asked defensively. "We're supposed to be talking about how you messed up *your* relationship."

"I'm only pointing out that relationships aren't always that easy."

"Especially in this business," Catherine said suddenly. She was still looking down the river, her head turned away from us. There was a melancholy tone to her voice that I had never heard before. "More so than any other, perhaps. This won't be the last time you find yourselves with your job and your heart at odds. I was asked to lie to Alexander for our entire relationship. Obviously, I did it, but it never felt right. And that was one of the less complicated decisions I had to make. If you remain covert agents, your lives will be full of them."

"Like what?" Mike asked.

"I'm afraid that's a conversation for another time,"

Catherine said. "We're here." She pointed to a house that loomed high on a hill above the river.

Mount Vernon. I had visited it once on a school field trip as well. George Washington's home had a commanding view of the Potomac, one of the finest panoramas I had ever seen. It was so beautiful that the states of Virginia, which surrounded the property, and Maryland, which sat across the river, had taken steps to preserve it forever, declaring the land on both sides of the Potomac as parkland. Thus, even though we were only a few miles downstream from the modern-day city that had been named after Washington, it felt as though we had gone back in time to colonial days.

Mount Vernon was the only building visible along that stretch of river. There were no roads or streetlights. No other boats were out. A herd of deer grazed along the riverbank, unconcerned by our presence.

"Maybe we should take a look at what Mr. Jefferson has for us," Catherine suggested, fishing the journal out of Erica's satchel.

Erica had given me the satchel at the hotel that evening, then claimed she was going to the bathroom and had never come back. There had been a note in the satchel telling me not to worry; she hadn't been abducted. Instead, she had obviously left on the secret mission she had mentioned earlier. I figured that maybe she was drawing the attention of the Croatoan, clearing the way for the rest of us to infiltrate Mount Vernon, but I wasn't sure. I had no idea when I would see or hear from her again.

Erica and I had spent much of our time on the bus discussing the journal, and after she had vanished, I had spent the rest of the evening reverently leafing through it. In addition to being president, Jefferson had extremely wide-ranging interests, and his journal had reflected that: There were architectural diagrams, observations on astronomy and horticulture, mathematical calculations, planting schedules for his estate—and what might have been the first scientific analysis of the prairie dog. (Lewis and Clark had sent him one from their expedition. Jefferson had named it Fluffy.)

Catherine ignored all that and flipped to a page that Erica had flagged for us. It was unusual in that it featured a poem, the only one in the entire set of journals Erica had examined. It was titled, "In Honor of George Washington, Upon His Retirement from Public Life." Although, in the weird fashion of the time, Jefferson had used lowercase *s*'s that looked like *f*'s, so that it appeared to read, "In Honor of George Wafhington."

Catherine read the poem out loud, her melodious voice carrying through the quiet night.

All hail our leader, Washington,
Who hast served every last man and son
Of this great land at our behest
But seeks only at his home to rest.
Thus we wish you many a peaceful day
With your grave concerns all locked away.
You shall no longer have to roam.
All you require lies within your home.
Yet should you feel the need for taking stock,
Just keep in touch with your faithful flock.

She closed the journal again and asked, "Now, what can we deduce from this?"

"Jefferson was a lousy poet," Mike said. "He sounds like a cheesy greeting card."

"He wasn't going for poetic greatness," I observed. "Erica thinks it's a clue to where he hid Washington's files on the Croatoan. That's what the 'grave concerns' Jefferson mentions are. If the Croatoan had been successful, Washington would have been in a grave."

"That certainly makes sense," Catherine agreed. "And the line 'All you require lies within your home' indicates the files are hidden somewhere inside Mount Vernon. But as to where in the house, Jefferson is being quite coy."

"Of course he is," Mike muttered. "Because no one can ever make anything easy on us. Why simply say where the files are when you can write a stupid riddle?"

"You're talking about one of the founding fathers of your country, Michael," Catherine said sharply. "Be respectful. Nothing Thomas Jefferson ever did was stupid. If he had openly stated his secret hiding place for the files, it wouldn't be much of a secret hiding place anymore, would it?"

"I guess not," Mike said with a sigh.

We had drifted past the hill that Mount Vernon sat atop. Now the land sloped gradually down toward a small wharf that had been in use since Washington's time. However, mooring the dinghy there would have sent an obvious signal that we were trespassing on the property. So instead, we paddled to the shore before the wharf and hid our small boat amongst a copse of trees along the water's edge.

Catherine tied the dinghy to a sapling and hopped to land. "I suspect the answer to where the files are hidden lies within the final couplet of Jefferson's poem: 'Yet should you feel the need for taking stock / Just keep in touch with your faithful flock.'"

"What do you think that means?" I asked.

"I haven't the foggiest idea," Catherine admitted. "Hopefully, we'll be able to make far more sense of it once we're inside. Come along, gentlemen." She scrambled up the hillside through the trees.

And so, we set off to break into the home of the father of our country.

DISCOVERY

Mount Vernon

April 17

0230 hours

One thing quickly became evident as we worked our way across the estate: George Washington was stinking rich.

The property was enormous, an entire community unto itself. Hundreds of people had been required to keep it all running—including, it should be noted, over 300 slaves. A foundation now oversaw the estate and had restored it to look much as it had when Washington lived there, right down to the livestock. As we slunk through the night, we passed fields, cattle pens, stables, servants' homes, storehouses, smokehouses, and even an eighteenth-century version of a garage, where Washington's horse-drawn carriage was still kept.

We knew the foundation also provided security to patrol the property, but there was a lot of ground to cover and the guards seemed to be few and far between. Even so, we stuck to the shadows and kept our voices as low as possible. When we reached the great lawn that rolled from the back porch of the house down to the river, we lay prone to scope out the scene.

Catherine gave the orders. "Benjamin, you and I will infiltrate the main building. Michael, you stand guard . . ."

"Stand guard?" Mike groaned. "That's so boring. Why can't we all infiltrate the building?"

"Because we don't want any guards or Croatoan members to catch us with our knickers down," Catherine informed him. "A boring mission is a successful mission. So stay on alert." With that, she scurried across the lawn.

Although Mount Vernon was an impressive building, the design was very simple: It was a perfectly symmetrical two-story building. We approached it from the rear, where a long porch lined with rocking chairs looked out over the grand view of the river. The back door was true to Washington's time, so it had a simple key-operated lock—although we also noted the electrical wire of a modern-day alarm system running up the jamb. Catherine quickly spliced in a second sensor, designed to send a permanent signal that the door was closed. Then she disconnected the original sensor and deftly picked the lock. The door swung open soundlessly.

We stepped inside Washington's home, entering the central passage, which led from the front door to the back. The walls were paneled with wood, and a staircase curved up to the bedrooms. The ancient floors creaked under our feet.

Erica and I had spent some time that afternoon studying maps of Mount Vernon that we had found online. "Washington's office ought to be to our left," I whispered. "Erica thinks the files would probably be hidden there."

Catherine nodded agreement and led the way to the office. We skulked through the dining room, where the table was laid out with a sumptuous feast of plastic food, designed to show tourists what dinner was like at the Washington household. Apparently, George and Martha ate quite well; there was enough meat, fish, fruits, vegetables, and bread to feed a small platoon.

Washington's office occupied a large, rectangular room at the southern end of the house, with windows on three walls and a grand marble fireplace on the fourth. The great man's desk sat in the dead center of the room, facing the fireplace. There were no shades on the windows, so enough moonlight spilled in from outside to let us see. A cordon ran across the room to prevent people from touching the desk; we stepped right over it.

I took a moment to reflect that I was standing before the very desk that George Washington himself had used. And then I started rummaging through the drawers.

They were empty, save for a dozen stray paper clips, a pencil, and an outdated phone charger, which indicated that someone had used that desk a lot more recently than Washington. It didn't surprise me that the desk was empty; anything Washington had touched would have been invaluable, and thus spirited off to some archive or another over the years. I was more interested in the desk itself; it seemed a decent location for a secret hiding place, so I yanked out the drawers and searched the whole piece of furniture for any concealed files.

I didn't find any.

Meanwhile, Catherine was slinking about the room, tapping on the walls and thumping on the floor, looking for telltale hidden spaces.

"Find any possible locations?" I whispered.

"I've found plenty," she responded, "which is a bloody nightmare. There are two dozen air pockets behind these walls, and this entire floor is hollow underneath. It'd take weeks to rip this place apart and search everywhere. And that's assuming the hiding place is even in this room, which, let's face it, is mere speculation."

"Then what do we do?"

"Figure out *this*." Catherine set Jefferson's poem on the desk in front of me.

I read it over again, focusing on the final couplet once more: "'Yet should you feel the need for taking stock / Just keep in touch with your faithful flock.'"

Something about the words struck me. I looked up from the poem and took in the room.

Catherine and I had been so focused on the desk, walls, and floor that we hadn't taken the time to observe the room's decorations. There was a distinct agricultural theme. Every painting was a pastoral landscape, full of farmers and shepherds and cows and sheep.

"Stock," I said. "Like livestock."

Catherine looked to me with excitement. "And 'flock' could refer to birds or sheep as well as one's followers. So then, when Jefferson advises Washington to 'keep in touch with your faithful flock' . . ."

"He could mean it literally," I concluded.

"I think you're onto something, Benjamin." Catherine quickly scanned the room, taking everything in.

So did I. Almost immediately, my eyes fell on the fireplace directly in front of me.

Even in the faint light, the white marble of the mantel seemed to shine. It was decorated with agricultural motifs as well. Directly in the center, right where Washington would have been looking every time he was seated at his desk, was a bas-relief of a shepherd, his wife, and their son.

I approached it for a closer look. For some reason, the family seemed to be from ancient Greece and were wearing togas. (Or *partially* wearing togas. Neither parent had their entire chest covered.) They were overseeing a cow, a dog . . . and a flock of sheep. The sheep were front and center in the sculpture, their woolly bodies bulging out from the mantel.

"Keep in touch with your faithful flock," I repeated, then ran my hands over the sheep.

The marble was cool to the touch. The most prominent sheep was a ram, his head turned back toward his flank. It shifted ever so slightly beneath my fingers. "Here!" I exclaimed.

I tried to twist the ram's head, and then its whole body, but nothing happened. I could still feel it shifting, though. So I leaned on it and shoved with all my might.

There was a click from inside the fireplace, followed by the groan of old cogs turning. The entire central section of the mantel retracted into the wall, revealing a hidden space on the left side.

"Benjamin!" Catherine cried in awe. "You've done it!"

The central section stopped retracting once it was a foot back into the wall. I began to reach into the hidden space, but Catherine caught my arm.

"Not so fast," she whispered. "Jefferson might have built in a little extra protection, just in case his enemies found this." She took the pencil I had found in the desk and cautiously extended it into the gap in the mantel.

A set of metal teeth hidden within the fireplace snapped shut, cleaving the pencil in half. It was like a small bear trap, designed to bite off the hands of thieves.

I heaved a sigh of relief. If it hadn't been for Catherine, my new nickname might have been "Lefty."

Catherine tore out the trap, then reached into the space behind it. She gave a cry of triumph, then removed a single envelope.

It was musty and yellowed with age. It had once been sealed with a wax stamp, but this had dried out over the years and most of it had crumbled away. On the front, in faded handwriting, were the words: *To the attention of Spymafter Wafhington.*

"Oh my goodness," Catherine gasped. "This is it!"

Before we could see what was inside the envelope, Mike's voice rang out through the night. "Ben! Look out!"

Catherine reacted with incredible instincts, tackling me

to the floor. A moment later, one of the glass windows shattered. Something whistled over our heads and thudded into the opposite wall with a puff of plaster.

Sadly, I had been in a situation like this enough times to immediately grasp what was happening:

Someone was shooting at us.

11

EQUESTRIAN SKILLS

Mount Vernon

April 17

0300 hours

Our attacker fired into the room several more times. Most of the other shots hit the wall, but one knocked a painting of a waterfall to the floor while another shattered a vase on the mantel.

"Stop shooting, you heathen!" Catherine yelled angrily. "You're destroying priceless artifacts!"

Being a museum curator wasn't merely Catherine's cover. She had an advanced degree in art history. She now seemed far more upset about the damage to the artwork than she did about someone trying to kill us.

"Give up the files!" a man's voice yelled. "Or we'll put some holes in you, too!"

The voice was notably high-pitched for a man's, but I didn't recognize it.

However, I could tell that the shooter was yelling from rather far away, possibly a good distance across the lawn. Which meant it would take him a while to get to the house. We had time to move.

Catherine intuited the exact same thing. Both of us scuttled across the floor, staying as low as we could to avoid getting shot. The bullets had come from the rear of the house, so we moved toward the front door.

A few more shots were fired. A second vase shattered, which provoked a grimace from Catherine.

We made it back through the kitchen and central hallway, then raced out the front door. This took us out to the grand front lawn, which had been designed back in Washington's time to impress approaching visitors. To me, it looked like a death trap. It was wide and open without any cover to shield us from our attacker.

The quiet night was suddenly filled with the clopping of hoofbeats. Two horses came racing toward the house, hauling Washington's antique carriage behind them. The carriage was wooden and ornately painted, without a roof. It was merely a chassis and two seats mounted on enormous wheels, although the rear seat was cushier, designed for the passengers. Mike sat in the driver's seat, snapping the reins.

"Have no fear!" he shouted. "The cavalry is here!"

"Don't stop!" Catherine yelled to him. "There's no time for that!"

"Good!" Mike yelled back. "Because I don't know how to stop this thing!"

The carriage rumbled across the lawn toward us. I had never realized quite how big and powerful horses could be until two of them were bearing down on me.

Catherine stood by my side. "We need to time this just right," she warned, stuffing Washington's file into her satchel. "Get ready . . . and go!"

As the horses charged past us, we leapt for the open carriage. Both of us caught the wooden siding. Catherine sprang into the driver's seat with the practiced ease of someone who had done this before, while I failed with the ineptitude of someone who knew diddly-squat about horses. I ended up hanging on for dear life, my feet dragging across the ground, as the carriage rolled onward. The great wooden wheels churned along, mere inches from me. If my hands slipped, I would fall and be run over.

I heard the whinny of more horses behind us.

Someone else was riding after us with a second horse in tow. Meanwhile, the man who had shot at us emerged from the house, having followed us through it, clutching a rifle. It was too dark to make out the features of either one of them. The one with the horses slowed, but just barely, while the rifleman deftly vaulted into the saddle of the second.

The CIA didn't shoot without warning. So I assumed they were the Croatoan.

Hands clutched my arms. Mike was leaning over the edge of the carriage to help me aboard. Catherine had taken the reins.

"Let go!" Mike yelled. "I've got you!"

I was running out of people I could trust, but Mike was still one of them. I let go, and he held tight enough so that I wasn't crushed beneath the wheels. Then he leaned back, using his own weight to pull me up and into the carriage. We tumbled onto the floor between the seats.

A gunshot rang out. The wood paneling at the back of the carriage splintered as the bullet struck it. Given that our attacker had fired from atop a galloping horse at a moving target in the dead of night, the shot was disturbingly accurate.

Our own horses whinnied in fear. Catherine snapped the reins and spurred them on.

We hurtled off the lawn and onto a dirt road that was the main route across Washington's estate. Since we were in a horse-drawn carriage, being pursued by enemies on horseback, racing through well-preserved colonial farmland, it was easy to imagine that we had somehow time-traveled back a couple of centuries. I found myself wondering if any of Washington's own spies had ever ended up in a situation like this.

"Benjamin!" Catherine yelled. "Could you take a look at that message we found and see what it says?"

"Now?!" I exclaimed.

"We might not have the chance to examine it later," Catherine explained. "And you're not doing anything at the moment."

She had a point. Technically, I was doing *something*: cowering in fear. But that really wasn't contributing much to our mission.

So I reached into the satchel and removed the aged envelope we had found in Washington's office.

Mike gaped at it. "Whoa! You stole Washington's mail?"

"You stole his carriage!" I pointed out.

"It was an emergency," Mike said defensively.

The dirt road led through the part of the estate where animals were still kept. We raced past meadows surrounded by wooden fences and heard the distant bleating of sheep and grunting of pigs. Two chickens that had made the mistake of going for a late-night walk scurried frantically out of our path, squawking and desperately flapping their wings, as if hoping that the ability to fly would suddenly kick in.

Our pursuers fired upon us again, their gun barrels

flaring in the night, but this time, their shots went wide.

I opened the envelope and removed the letter inside. It was so old and brittle with age that it crackled as I unfolded it.

My heart sank when I saw what was written on the page:

Mike looked at it over my shoulder and groaned. "It's in code? They couldn't have just written in English? Would it be too much to ask for someone to make life easy on us for once?"

Although I didn't say so, I was frustrated as well. We had gone through so much trouble to get this message that we couldn't even read. I stared at the letter, trying to make sense of it, which would have been hard enough to do in my nice, cozy, well-lit bedroom. Jouncing around in the back of a carriage in the middle of the night, I could barely even see the page, let alone decipher it.

Suddenly, the world grew even darker. I looked up from the letter to find that we had left Washington's farm behind and entered a forest. A canopy of trees arched over us, blotting out what little light there had been. Our pursuers were hidden by the gloom, although I could still hear the pounding of their horses' hooves on the ground.

The dirt road made a sharp turn around a stand of majestic oaks, and as we took it, the carriage shimmied wildly.

"Michael," Catherine said, sounding as though she was worried but trying to hide it, "do you know the proper way to hitch a carriage to a team of horses?"

"No," Mike answered honestly. "Since I don't live in colonial times, it's never come up. So I kind of winged it and tied everything together."

"Ah," Catherine said.

"Is that a problem?" Mike asked.

"It might be one quite soon. Our carriage is threatening to come loose from the horses that are pulling it."

"And just when everything was going so well," I said with a sigh.

"How are your equestrian skills?" Catherine asked us.

"I don't really have any," I replied.

"Me neither," said Mike.

Catherine frowned, as though this was a failing of our schooling somehow. "Have either of you ever ridden a horse at all?"

"Does a carousel count?" Mike asked.

"Seeing as those horses aren't alive, no."

"Then I haven't."

"I rode one at a petting zoo once," I said. "Although it might have been a donkey."

"None of that is very encouraging," Catherine replied. "Michael, please come up here, posthaste."

"Right." Mike clambered up to the front seat. "What do you need me to do?"

"Do you see how those knots you've tied in the harnesses are starting to come undone?"

"Yes."

"Make sure that doesn't happen."

"Okay." Mike edged down between the horses and the

carriage so that he could try to fix the harnesses. This was quite dangerous and involved having his face disturbingly close to the rear ends of the horses, but he didn't waver for a second. He *did* complain, though. "Oh man. These horses' butts reek!"

"And Benjamin," Catherine went on. "The faster you could decipher that letter, the better. Our enemies are gaining on us."

I looked behind us and discovered this was true. Our pursuers were now close enough that I could make out their silhouettes in the forest, right down to the rifles in their hands.

"Here," Catherine said, handing something back to me. "This might help."

I was hoping it would be a guide to deciphering Colonial Era codes, but it was only a small flashlight. Still, I needed it. It was extremely hard to crack a code that I couldn't see.

I crouched in the well between the seats, where I was less likely to be shot, and examined the letter again. It wasn't easy, as there was so much else going on, but I willed myself to focus on it.

As I inspected the letter, I noticed that the symbols were in clumps with spaces between them every now and then, the same way that letters would be clumped in words. Which gave me an idea.

I started searching for patterns and quickly noticed a trio of symbols that repeated a few times:

$$\oplus \vdash *$$

The word "the" came up with about the same frequency in English.

"It can't be that easy," I said.

"What can't?" Catherine asked.

"This looks like it's just a substitution cipher. Where one symbol stands for *A* and another stands for *B* and so on. It's like the simplest code imaginable."

"So what's the problem?"

"You really think George Washington's spies would use something this easy? This is the kind of thing you find on restaurant kiddie menus!"

"There weren't a lot of restaurant kiddie menus in Washington's day," Catherine reminded me. "It was a simpler time. Codes and ciphers were all rather new. What looks simplistic to us now might have been quite advanced back then. So try it out and see if it works . . ."

"Catherine!" Mike yelled, drawing both her attention and mine. "We've got a problem!"

Ahead of us, a security gate blocked the dirt road. Unlike everything else we had encountered at Mount Vernon, this one wasn't designed to look as though it was left over from the

1790s. Instead, it was part of a modern chain-link fence with a padlock on the hasp and barbed wire curled along the top.

The horses were barreling straight for it, either unable to see it in the dark or unaware that horses can't run through metal.

"I've got it," Catherine said calmly, then withdrew a gun from her belt and fired at the gate. She nailed the padlock with her first shot. It dropped to the ground and the gate swung open.

This triggered an alarm, but at the moment, alerting the police was the least of our problems.

"You've had that gun all along?" Mike asked Catherine, incredulous. "Why haven't you been using it on the bad guys?"

"I don't like shooting people," Catherine replied. "Violence never solved anything."

"I've noticed the bad guys never have that philosophy," Mike said.

Our horses galloped through the open gate and we suddenly found ourselves in the suburbs. An upscale community began directly outside the Mount Vernon property: luxury homes on large lots with perfectly manicured lawns. The residents didn't seem very concerned about crime; scooters lay in front yards and bicycles were propped on porches, rather than being locked up inside.

We raced down a wide, tree-lined street with our enemies

right behind us, the horses' hooves clattering on the asphalt.

Through all of this, I was doing my best to translate the coded document. If I assumed the three symbols I had found to be a *T*, an *H*, and an *E*, then the second line read:

$$\overset{E}{\daleth}\!*\!\cap e \quad \square\square\overset{}{\xi}\triangleright\cap\square\overset{TE}{\oplus}*e \quad \overset{}{\Lambda'}\cap\square\overset{H}{\vdash}\triangle\triangle\overset{T}{\underline{\mathbb{E}}}\oplus\acute{\delta}\triangle$$

The pattern of the last word struck me as interesting. I figured there was a relatively good chance it was the name of the person the letter was delivered to: Washington.

A loud snap from the front of the carriage diverted my attention. It sounded disturbingly like an important part of the harness coming apart.

Even more disturbing was Mike's response. "Crap!" he shouted. "This is bad!"

The carriage began to judder wildly, as though something had gone very wrong.

"Benjamin," Catherine said, in a voice that she was struggling to make calm. "Could you join me here, please?"

I climbed into the front seat with her. From this vantage point, I could see that Mike was still down between the horses, trying to fix the connection to the carriage, which didn't look good. Part of the harness system had come free and dropped to the ground, where it was now scraping along the street.

Behind us, our pursuers were gaining.

"I'm sorry, Benjamin, but I have to take some drastic measures here," Catherine said. "Please don't be upset with me."

"What do you need to do?" I asked worriedly.

"This," Catherine said, and shoved me out of the carriage.

At the time, we were turning a corner, passing a yard that had an abundance of landscaping. Still clutching Washington's message, I toppled into a bush and plunged through the foliage. A hundred twigs scraped me at once, but the plant cushioned my fall so that I landed on the ground with only moderate discomfort as opposed to extreme pain.

Catherine had timed her actions perfectly so that, due to our turn, the carriage was blocking me from the view of our pursuers as I fell. And the bush was thick enough to hide me from sight as they galloped past. They continued down the street in pursuit of the carriage.

Ahead of them, Catherine leapt gracefully from the carriage onto the back of one of the horses. Mike was struggling to get onto the other.

The carriage was weaving wildly behind them.

I fought my way out of the bush and ran back the way we had come.

I understood what was going on: The carriage wasn't going to stay connected to the horses for long, and two horses could only support two riders, not three. (Perhaps one could support two competent riders, but Mike and I didn't qualify.) So Catherine had dumped me before things went wrong and was distracting our enemies so that I could escape.

It was working so far.

In the distance, I heard what I suspected was the sound of a vintage Colonial Era carriage breaking loose from two horses and then crashing into a tree.

Close to me was a backyard with a relatively low wooden fence, which I vaulted over.

It would probably take the bad guys another thirty seconds to examine the wreckage of the carriage and confirm that I wasn't in it. Then, they'd have a choice to make: Split up or stay together. That might take another few seconds. Most likely, they'd hedge their bets and split up. One would go after Catherine and Mike, while the other would come looking for me.

Chances were, they wouldn't catch Catherine and Mike, whose horses were no longer burdened by the carriage. Assuming Mike didn't fall off his horse. Mike didn't know horses, but he was a natural athlete, so hopefully, he would be all right.

However, even if both bad guys came looking for me, I had the advantage. I had a two-minute head start on them, and there were thousands of places to hide. If the bad guys really were Croatoan, they wouldn't want to attract attention, which meant they'd have to be cautious about their search so as to not wake the whole neighborhood.

As it was, some of the homeowners were already up. I could hear them emerging onto their front porches, roused by the sounds of Mount Vernon's fence alarm and the chase and the crash, groggily asking one another if anyone knew what was going on.

Police sirens wailed in the distance, coming our way.

There was a good chance that the bad guys, seated atop stolen horses, would simply flee the scene.

All of which took care of the issue of my getting captured, but still left me with one equally big problem:

I was on my own.

DECRYPTION

Somewhere near Mount Vernon, Virginia

April 17

0330 hours

The backyard I had jumped into was shielded from the street by the fence. No lights in the house had come on, indicating that the owners of this one either hadn't been wakened by the ruckus or were on vacation.

It was a nice, large backyard with a pool, a hot tub, a patio, and a barbecue station. There was plenty of landscaping, which featured a disturbing number of garden gnomes, as well as a large storage shed. The shed looked like a great place to hide.

So I didn't hide there.

One of the first things I had learned in my Evading the Enemy class was Titley's Maxim of Not Getting Caught: The best hiding place is always the first place they look for you.

What you really wanted to do was find the tenth-best hiding place, if not the hundredth. The place that no one would think to look for you at all.

The shed wasn't merely obvious; it was also a dead end. If I had hidden there and been found, I'd be trapped inside.

The area with all the garden gnomes was much more promising. It was right out in the open, which in theory was a terrible place to hide. But it was dark, which meant someone probably wouldn't notice me there right away, and it was exposed, so there were plenty of ways to run if they *did* notice me.

There was a great variety of gnomes. They ranged in size from six inches to two feet, and they were all engaged in odd activities: riding rabbits and turtles, proudly displaying fish they had caught, reading newspapers while seated on little ceramic toilets. I sat down among them. I was bigger than they were, but ideally, the whole cavalcade of gnomes would look like a bunch of shadowy human forms and I would blend in.

Then I got to work decoding Washington's letter.

Shortly afterward, the police arrived. I heard them out in the streets, interviewing neighbors who had been roused by the noise and assuring them that there was no danger. The police seemed to be working under the theory that some teenagers had stolen the horses and carriage from Mount Vernon and gone on a colonial-style joyride. I heard one officer express disdain for "young hooligans with no respect for this country's history."

For the record, I felt terrible about destroying Washington's carriage. Although, as far as I was concerned, the Croatoan were really to blame. If they hadn't been trying to kill us, we never would have stolen anything.

Except the document in my hands, of course.

As I had suspected, it was a simple, restaurant-kiddie-menu-style substitution code. Now that I had figured out a few words, it wasn't very difficult to translate the rest. The only real problem was that I didn't have a pencil, so I had to memorize everything I deciphered. But even with that, I quickly worked out the message:

Dated Feb 2, 1795
Dear Spymaster Washington,
I am pleased to inform you
that the scourge of our
existence, the Croatoan,
has been vanquished from our
young nation once and for all.

After weeks of intensive
searching, my men have
found no sign, nor heard
any tale of them. Thus, I
must conclude that our
recent efforts to eradicate
this menace have been
successful. The Croatoan
seems to have only been a
small, radical sect of
rapscallions, and I presume
that they will never bother
you again.
Your humble lieutenant,
Elias Hale

I considered the message for quite a while. Two things nagged at me:

The lesser one was the name "Elias Hale." I had never heard of him. Which made sense, given that I was living well over two hundred years after him; there were certainly lots of people from Washington's time who I hadn't heard of. But it was intriguing that Washington had a second spy with the last name Hale. The first being Nathan Hale. And of course, I knew of quite a few other Hales who were still working for the CIA. I figured that Elias must be a distant relative.

The more important issue was that the message wasn't nearly as helpful as I had hoped it would be. While it provided proof that the Croatoan had existed, it also claimed that the organization had been destroyed. Which indicated that it couldn't possibly be working now. That didn't mean there couldn't be a modern-day coalition of evildoers calling itself the Croatoan, but apparently, it wasn't the same coalition dating back to Washington's day.

Worse, besides stating that the Croatoan was wiped out, the message had no other helpful information. Nothing about who they were, or how they *had* been wiped out, or how many people had been in the group, or where their headquarters were. Not a word about their tactics, their methods, their cause, or their plans. The letter might have been of great historical import, but it was useless for my needs. It offered nothing that would help me clear Erica's name.

In my frustration, I almost crumpled the message and threw it into the compost pile. Only two things stopped me.

1) I couldn't bring myself to destroy a document of George Washington's. It was bad enough that I had broken into his house and totaled his carriage.

2) I felt I was missing something, although I couldn't think what it might be. But it was late. I was tired and scared and alone—not the best state of mind for solving problems.

And yet, there was no time to rest. I had things to do.

First, I had to regroup with my team. Fortunately, I knew how to do that.

Sort of.

Mike and I had established a burrow. And following proper security procedures, we hadn't shared its location with anyone else. So he and I were the only ones who knew where it was. In theory, he and Catherine had shaken the Croatoan and were heading there to regroup with me.

Unfortunately, it was more than twenty miles away.

Twenty miles was a long way to travel with the CIA, the police, and a subversive enemy organization hunting for you. Especially when you were a kid who was too young to drive.

I could no longer hear the police working the neighborhood around me. And it sounded as though all the homeowners had been calmed and returned to bed.

I folded Washington's letter, stuck it in my pocket, left the gnome garden, and used a knothole in the fence to case the street. No one was around. So I vaulted back over the fence and made my way through the neighborhood.

As I did, I heard faint voices in the distance. I returned to the corner where Catherine had shoved me into the landscaping, and then slipped back into the bushes to do some surveillance.

Several blocks down the road was the wreckage of

Washington's carriage. It had crashed into a tree and splintered apart. Six police officers surrounded it, diligently working the case. The scene had been cordoned off with yellow crime tape, and someone had actually drawn a chalk outline around the shattered carriage, like it was a murder victim.

While the police were distracted with that, I went the other way.

As I had noted before, several families had their bicycles on their porches, not even locked up. I noticed a nice, relatively new mountain bike that was the right size for me.

I felt terrible about stealing it. But there was a great deal at stake. I made a mental promise that I would return it after the mission was over.

Then I rode away into the night.

One of the nicest things about the suburbs of Washington was that they had an excellent system of bike trails. In fact, one ran along the Potomac directly from Mount Vernon all the way up to the city. I had ridden parts of it with my parents. It took me a few minutes to work my way over to it through the neighborhood, but once I found it, I was able to make decent progress. The path was mostly flat and, although it wasn't the most direct route to where I was headed, it was probably faster and certainly safer than going straight through the suburbs. I didn't have to avoid cars or navigate busy intersections. Although I was tired, as I rode, my endorphins started to flow, stimulating my brain. Despite everything that had gone wrong, I started to feel pretty good. And I had time once again to focus on Washington's letter.

Somewhere around the Pentagon, I realized what had been bothering me about it:

Washington had saved it.

As the nation's first spymaster, Washington must have received countless messages from his spies. Certainly, there would have been others about the Croatoan. And as president, he had surely seen plenty of classified documents as well. *So why had he taken such pains to hide this one?* After all, there was very little information in it, except for news that the Croatoan had been defeated. An argument could have been made that it was an important letter, perhaps one that Washington would cherish. But would that really make it worth enlisting Thomas Jefferson to build a secret hiding place for it? If anything, it would seem like Washington might want to keep that letter where people could see it.

I could come up with only two reasons for the concealment:

1) There was something in the letter that I had missed. Something more important than I had realized.

2) There had been many more important documents in the hiding place, but at some point, someone had discovered them all and made off with them.

The latter was the possibility that concerned me the most. It would explain why there had been only one letter in the cache—and a seemingly unimportant letter at that. It might have simply been overlooked and left behind. And if all the other documentation was missing, then I had a serious problem, because all the information I needed to help Erica was gone.

So I hoped it was the first possibility.

It had taken me a little over an hour of riding to get to the Pentagon, and from there, I had a decent idea of how to get to the burrow I had established with Mike. However, I now had to veer off the bike path and use bike lanes along major roads. Even though it was still quite early in the morning, traffic was already flowing. I had to focus more on not getting hit by a car and less on what Washington's letter might have been concealing.

After another hour, I found myself on streets that I was familiar with. I was back in the neighborhood where I had grown up.

In fact, my route to the burrow took me almost right past my home.

I couldn't help myself. I had to swing by.

I did it cautiously, of course. There was a decent chance that DADD or the Croatoan had it staked out, in case I tried to do something stupid. Which was exactly what I was doing.

I didn't go all the way home. I parked the bike a block away and then crept through some of my neighbors' yards until I could get a glimpse of my house in the distance.

The sun was now coming up, bathing my home in the first rays of the day. Dad and Mom usually started work early, so on a normal day, they would have been up, bustling about, making coffee, reading the paper, and eating breakfast.

But today wasn't a normal day.

The house was dark and quiet. My parents were no longer living there. They were off in a safe house somewhere. Or maybe they were already on their way to Florida.

I felt sad, seeing the house like that. Until I had gone to spy school, it was the only place I had ever lived. I had thousands of good memories there. Now I wasn't sure if I'd ever be back inside again.

A van was parked on the street in front of my house. The lettering on the side indicated it belonged to the gas company, but it seemed awfully early for the gas company to be out. Plus, I didn't see any gas company workers. Only the van. Which made me think that the van didn't belong to the gas company at all.

I didn't know *who* it belonged to, though. Agent Taco and her team at DADD? The Croatoan? Someone else?

I didn't wait around to find out. I slipped back through

the yards, recovered the bicycle, and continued on through the neighborhood.

Down the street from my old elementary school was a wooded park, a tiny patch of forest that had somehow avoided being paved to build homes or stores or roads. As elementary school students, Mike and I and our other friends had spent hours playing in that park.

We had even built a tree house.

It wasn't very well constructed, given that it had been built by fourth graders. It was made of plywood and two-by-fours we had scrounged from the dumpster when a new wing of our school had been added. The walls were all somewhat different heights, the roof leaked, and the floor tilted at a slight angle. There was no door, the windows were merely gaps in the walls, and the only way in was a ladder of wooden rungs we had nailed to the tree. Our original plans for it had been overambitious, as was the case with most of our schemes. We had thought it would be cool to wire it for electricity and put an old TV and a tiny refrigerator in there, then paint it and even install some windows.

We had never done any of that. But the basics of the tree house were still good. It was nestled in the crook of a century-old oak, big enough to hold six kids easily—although it could take eight if you didn't mind being crowded. We holed up in there on weekends and over summer vacation, using it as a place to play games, stash snacks . . . and pretend to be spies.

We all had spies on the brain and had spent hours reenacting scenes from James Bond and *Mission: Impossible* movies. We also formed our own imaginary spy force and went on missions around the neighborhood. The tree house was always our home base. We called it the Agency.

It was the perfect burrow for Mike and me. Close enough to spy school to be able to get to in an emergency, on familiar ground, and yet a part of our past that other people wouldn't know about.

I parked the stolen bike deep in the woods, then climbed up the rungs into the Agency.

It had held up well. Other kids had obviously been using it, probably for the exact same reasons we had. They had even stashed snacks there too. I found a cooler in one corner with a bag of chips and half a pack of Oreos.

I devoured them all. Stealing from kids again. I felt bad about this, too, but I was starving.

The fort trembled ever so slightly as someone started up the rungs. I turned to the open doorway, looking forward to seeing Mike again.

Only, it wasn't Mike who entered.

It was Zoe Zibbell. And she wasn't alone.

CONFRONTATION

"The Agency"
Vienna, Virginia
April 17
0700 hours

Chip Schacter and Jawa O'Shea climbed into the tree house behind Zoe. Mike and I had only built the place to accommodate kids, so a big teenager like Chip didn't fit inside very well. He had to cock his head sideways to stand up straight. His muscular body completely blocked the narrow doorway. Jawa and Zoe quickly moved to block off the open gaps in the wall that served as windows.

It suddenly occurred to me that the Agency had one fatal flaw as a burrow; it was easy to get cornered inside.

My friends were cutting off all the exits; I was trapped.

"I thought I'd find you here," Zoe said proudly.

"How did you know about this place?" I asked.

"I'm studying to be a spy," Zoe said. "It's my job to know things."

I looked to Chip and Jawa. Neither of them seemed quite as proud to have tracked me down as Zoe did. In fact, both seemed a bit ill at ease, as if they'd been hoping to not find me at all and avoid this confrontation. "So you've come here to capture me?"

"We've come to talk sense into you," Jawa said. "Aligning yourself with Erica is a mistake."

"She hasn't switched sides," I told him. "An evil organization is forcing her to work for them."

"Really?" Zoe asked skeptically. "How?"

I considered telling them about Trixie Hale, and how she was being used as leverage by the Croatoan, but I was quite sure that Erica and her family didn't want me to do that. The knowledge of Trixie's existence had already caused enough trouble. So I tried to get away with only telling part of the story. "They're threatening to kill someone she cares about."

"Who?" Chip asked.

"Her dog," I replied. It was the first thing that had jumped into my mind.

The three of them looked at me incredulously. "Erica Hale has a dog?" Jawa asked.

"Her family does," I said, making things up as quickly as I could. "His name is Gumbo and he's a golden retriever. And these bad guys have kidnapped the dog and told Erica that they'll kill him if she doesn't do their bidding."

"Oh no!" Chip exclaimed, horrified. I thought I saw tears welling in his eyes.

Zoe gave him a withering look. "You don't honestly believe this, do you?"

"Er . . . maybe," Chip said. "Erica could have a dog."

"She's never mentioned it," Zoe pointed out.

"She never mentioned that she had a mother who was a covert operative for MI6 either," I said.

"That was to protect her mother's secret identity," Zoe said. "Dogs don't have secret identities."

"They *could*," Chip argued. "Like maybe if there was a dog that worked for the government, sniffing out drugs, so all the drug dealers wanted it dead, but the dog wanted a normal life on the weekends, so it could go to the park and play fetch and stuff . . ."

"Erica doesn't have a dog with a secret identity!" Zoe snapped. "She doesn't have a dog, period! Ben is making all this up to protect her!"

"*Now* you think it's not nice to lie to your friends?" I asked.

"Because you seemed perfectly okay with lying to me yesterday."

"I was trying to protect you," Zoe argued.

"You pretended to believe me about Erica so that I would lead you to her!" I said angrily. "You used my friendship to get to her!"

"I thought she might be trying to kill you," Zoe replied, just as angry. "And you were too blind to see it! You've always been blind where Erica is concerned. Ever since you met her, she has consistently put your life in danger to further her own career."

"SPYDER put me in danger," I retorted. "Not Erica."

"Erica once got you kicked out of spy school just so that SPYDER would recruit you," Zoe said. "Without even telling you what she was doing. And she let you go to Mexico with Murray Hill when she knew he was plotting to double-cross you. She's been using you, ever since the beginning. But you've been too lovestruck to notice."

I felt my face flush in embarrassment. "Erica always had good reasons for what she did . . ."

"She tried to kill you yesterday morning!" Zoe exclaimed. "And yet you're still defending her! You're letting your emotions cloud your judgment here!"

"You're letting *your* emotions cloud your judgment," I shot back. "You've never liked Erica."

"That's not true," Zoe said.

"Actually, it is," Jawa noted. "You've always been a bit jealous of Erica."

"I meant the part about my emotions clouding my judgment," Zoe said, growing embarrassed herself. "Erica is working for the enemy, Ben. She is spinning a web of lies to confuse you . . ."

"And *me*," Chip said. "Does Erica have a dog or not?"

"Yes she does," I answered. "And he's adorable."

"Awww," Chip said.

"There's no dog, you idiot!" Zoe yelled. "Ben's *lying* to you!" Then she returned her attention to me. "I came here to give you a chance. If I really wanted to capture you, I could have brought Agent Taco . . ."

Jawa sniggered.

Zoe glared at him.

"Sorry," Jawa said. "Her name just makes me laugh. Something about it being a food. It's like being named Agent Marshmallow. Or Agent Turnip."

"Or Agent Kumquat," Chip added, and then both of them cracked up.

Zoe rolled her eyes, then looked back at me. "As I was saying, I could have brought Agent Taco and the rest of DADD and they could have arrested you right now. But I didn't want that to happen. I felt you deserved a chance to explain yourself."

"I've been trying to do that," I told her. "But you haven't been listening. Erica is innocent! This enemy group forced her to attack the CIA yesterday."

"An enemy group like SPYDER?" Jawa asked.

"Kind of. It's called the Croatoan and it's been trying to destroy the United States since even before it was founded. The Spanish created it to try to protect their interests in North America, but it went rogue a few hundred years ago. They were behind the American Revolution, the War of 1812, and every presidential assassination. . . ."

"You really expect us to believe this?" Zoe asked.

I looked from her to Chip and Jawa. Even they were looking at me as though I had suffered some sort of brain damage. "If I was going to make something up, do you think I would make up something this crazy? This organization is so ludicrous, it *has* to be real."

"Or maybe you just want us to think that," Zoe countered. "So you made up something as ridiculous as possible so that you could argue that you'd never make up something so ridiculous."

"Why would I do that when I could just make up something that was believable?" I asked.

Zoe said, "Maybe you thought that if you made up something believable, then we'd think it would sound *too* believable, which would be suspicious, whereas if you made up something ridiculous, then it would be *so* suspicious that it couldn't possibly be made up, so we'd believe it . . ."

"Ow," Chip said, wincing. "Zoe, your logic is making my head hurt."

"I have proof that the Croatoan exists," I said.

"What?" Jawa asked.

"This." I reached into my pocket and pulled out the aged message I had translated that morning. "It's a document from George Washington."

"*The* George Washington?" Chip asked. "The first president?"

"And the first spymaster," I clarified. "And it indicates that he knew about the Croatoan, all the way back when he was president."

Jawa squinted at the paper in my hands. "That just looks like a bunch of hieroglyphics."

"It's encoded," I explained. "But I translated it."

"You figured out how to translate George Washington's personal code?" Zoe asked suspiciously.

"It wasn't that hard. It was just a simple substitution cipher, where each symbol stood for a letter."

"Oh," Chip said. "Like the kind you find on the kids' menus in restaurants?"

"Exactly," I confirmed. "Apparently, coding things was kind of a new idea back then. I can show you what it says."

A stubby piece of chalk lay abandoned on the floor. I picked it up and wrote the translation of the message directly on the tree house wall.

Jawa looked from Washington's document to the wall as I wrote everything out. He was one of the smartest kids in our class, so it didn't take him long to realize that I had decoded everything properly. But once I finished writing, he frowned. "The message says the Croatoan has been defeated."

"Yes," I said.

"Then how could they still be operating now?" Jawa asked.

"I'm not sure, exactly. But the important thing is, they *did* exist . . ."

"You know what I think?" Zoe asked. "I think Erica's conning you. She drops a reference to this ancient group of bad guys to convince you that they're still active and manipulating her, then sends you off on a wild-goose chase to find this message, all to distract you from what she's really up to . . ."

"Which is what?" I asked.

"That's the million-dollar question, isn't it?" Zoe said. "Do you have any idea where Erica is right now?"

"Er . . . no," I admitted.

"Exactly!" Zoe cried. "She's probably off plotting some other evil scheme."

"She's probably lying low," I said angrily. "Because your

friends at DADD are hunting for her instead of the real bad guys. The Croatoan has *you* on a wild-goose chase. But if you help me, we can figure out what they're up to and stop them."

Zoe gave me a pitying look, like I was a child who still thought the Tooth Fairy was real. "Oh Ben. She really has you fooled, doesn't she?"

There was a tone of genuine concern to her voice, and my anger at her faded. It was suddenly clear to me that Zoe wasn't acting out of malice. She truly thought she was doing the right thing, and she was worried about me. I could even see things from her point of view: We *did* have a history of people who we had trusted defecting to the enemy, and Erica *had* fired a grenade launcher at the CIA while I was there that morning, and the whole Croatoan thing *did* sound ludicrous. For a moment, I even found myself wondering if Zoe was right. If Erica truly had manipulated me and I kept siding with her, then I would only end up in more and more trouble. I could wind up in jail for treason. Or dead.

But then I realized why I knew that Zoe was wrong.

I looked to my friends and spoke as earnestly as I could. "Zoe was right when she said Erica has put me in danger before. And I know that wasn't cool. But Erica has also been there for me when no one else was. When spy school recruited me merely as bait to catch a mole, Erica was the one who helped me catch the mole before I got killed. When I was accused of trying to assassinate the president, Erica risked everything to prove I was innocent. Erica has saved my life more times than I can count, and to be honest, she's saved all of your lives too. Not to mention the lives of thousands of other people. It doesn't make sense that she would do all that and then let herself be corrupted by the Croatoan. Erica might not have been the nicest person to you. Or the friendliest. At times, she's probably been a real jerk. But she isn't a traitor. And now she needs our help. So I'd really appreciate it if you'd give me a hand here. If you can't bring yourself to do that, then let me go help Erica on my own. At the very least, you owe her that."

Zoe, Chip, and Jawa looked to one another, mulling that over.

And then Zoe took a gun from her holster and aimed it at me. It was only a dart gun, but I still wasn't thrilled to be facing the business end of it. "I'm sorry, Ben. I can't do that."

Once again, I understood that she thought what she was doing was right. But now my anger at her returned. "Why not?"

"Because this is the only way I can protect you."

"By arresting me?"

"I'm preventing you from making a mistake. If we go

back to school now, you can probably patch everything up. We can explain that you weren't really in league with Erica. But if you run off to her again, you're only going to make things worse. I'm sorry, but this is for your own good. Are you going to come peacefully or not?"

"You're really going to sedate me?"

"I will if I have to. Just like Erica sedated me!"

"Please, Zoe," I pleaded. "I'm asking you as a friend. Let me go."

"And I'm telling you as a friend: no." There was sadness in Zoe's eyes. Her finger twitched on the trigger of her dart gun. "I'm only going to ask you one more time, Ben. Are you going to come peacefully or—"

Chip and Jawa both turned on Zoe at once. Chip gave her a light chop to the back of the neck that instantly knocked her out, while Jawa caught her before she hit the floor. The gun dropped from her hand and discharged, the dart embedding in the wall of the fort an inch to the right of my leg.

Chip, Jawa, and I faced one another, unsure quite where we stood.

"Sorry, Ben," Jawa said finally. He gingerly laid Zoe on the tree house floor. "I had no idea it was going to come to that. I thought she only wanted to talk to you."

"So . . . you believe me?" I asked.

"Honestly, I have no idea what to believe," Jawa replied.

"Yeah," Chip agreed. "All this stuff about the Chroma-zoan sounds totally cuckoo."

"Croatoan," I corrected.

"Whatever," Chip said. "It's bonkers."

"But it's evident that *you* believe it," Jawa told me. "And you've never been wrong before."

"So you're willing to help Erica and me?" I asked.

"No," Jawa said.

"What?" I exclaimed. "Why not?"

"Because there's still a decent chance you could be wrong on this one," Jawa replied. "And we've taken a big enough risk as it is."

"Zoe won't be out that long," Chip said. "And when she wakes up, she's gonna be angry. We'll have to cover our butts."

"We'll tell her you got the jump on us somehow," Jawa said. "Chip knocked her out so fast, there's a good chance she won't know what really happened. Then we'll buy you some time by feeding her some disinformation about where you were heading."

"Like Kansas," Chip suggested. "We can tell her the Pro-tozoan is plotting something there and that you and Erica went to join them."

I was disappointed that this was all they could give me, but still grateful that they'd protected me from Zoe. "Thanks. I appreciate it."

The tree house shook, signaling someone else was on their way up the ladder. We all turned to the doorway just as Mike's head popped into view.

Mike's eyes immediately locked on Zoe, probably because she was lying unconscious only two inches away from him. "Oh boy," he said. "This looks bad."

"She tried to arrest Ben," Chip explained. "We had to take her out."

Mike frowned. "She tried to arrest Ben now? But he's her best friend. I can't believe she'd do that."

It occurred to me that I had said something similar to Erica the day before. Which brought Erica's response back to my mind.

Not everyone thinks that way, she had said. *You can't only look at what's on the surface. You have to read between the lines.*

Which made me realize something else. "Whoa," I said. "I think there's more to Washington's message. And I also think I know how to read it."

CHEMISTRY

"The Agency"
Vienna, Virginia
April 17
0745 hours

Catherine Hale was waiting for us on the ground below the tree house. She had sent Mike up to see if I was there, while she stood guard down below, keeping an eye out for the Croatoan. It had never occurred to her that our burrow might have been compromised.

As I had hoped, she and Mike had managed to escape their pursuers on horseback, although Mike hadn't enjoyed it one bit. "I don't get why people like riding horses at all," he muttered to me as we climbed down from the tree house. "It feels like someone spent an hour kicking me in the crotch."

I noticed he was walking bowlegged due to his sore nether regions.

Jawa and Chip were excited to see Catherine; both had major schoolboy crushes on her. Suddenly, neither was in any hurry to leave. Instead, they stayed to hear what my revelation was, despite the fact that Chip had Zoe's unconscious body slung over his shoulder like a sack of potatoes.

"We need to read between the lines," I explained, holding up Washington's message so that everyone could see it.

"You mean, look for a hidden meaning?" Mike asked. "Because the message seems awfully straightforward to me. The Croatoan has been captured and destroyed."

I shook my head. "There's no hidden meaning. We need to *literally* read between the lines. I think there's another message here. An invisible one."

"Of course!" Jawa exclaimed, grasping what I meant. "It's like what we learned in History of Spying!"

"You learned something in History of Spying?" Chip asked blankly. "I fell asleep in every class."

"Me too," Mike agreed. "Professor Weeks is a bore."

Jawa gave Catherine a sly *Aren't these other guys idiots?* look and then tried to impress her with his knowledge of espionage. "Washington and his spies used invisible ink on a regular basis throughout the Revolutionary War and the early days of the country. Although they referred to it as 'sympathetic ink.'"

"But how do you know there's anything invisible written on this message?" Chip asked me. "Since it's, well . . . invisible."

"I can't guarantee there's anything," I admitted, "but it would explain why Washington went to so much trouble to hide this message. There's not too much to the part you *can* see. So maybe there's something important in the part that we *can't* see."

"Very clever, Benjamin," Catherine said in an admiring tone that made Chip and Jawa give me dirty looks. "If there truly is an invisible message here, then this document would be quite a clever bit of deception. If the Croatoan intercepted it, they'd mistakenly believe that Washington's spies thought they had been vanquished. Which would then trick the Croatoan into dropping their guard."

"And it would also explain why Washington used such a sucky code," Mike added. "Because he'd *want* the Croatoan to be able to crack it."

"Right," I agreed.

Chip snatched the message from my hands. "So how do we find out if there's anything invisible here?" He squinted at it, as if that would somehow make the words appear.

"A sympathetic ink had two parts to it," Catherine

explained. "An agent, which is the ink itself, and a counter-agent, which makes it visible."

"If I recall my history correctly," Jawa said, obviously trying to impress her again, "Washington's preferred method was to use gallotannic acid as the agent, which he made by soaking powdered nutgalls in water . . ."

"What the heck are powdered nutgalls?" Chip asked.

"It's what you get after riding a horse at high speed for an hour," Mike grumbled, gingerly adjusting the seat of his pants.

Catherine smirked with amusement, despite herself. "Actually, they're small growths that form on oak trees. Like those." She pointed to the branch of an oak that stretched above our heads, where some brown lumps the size of grapes were clustered.

"And ferrous sulfate would be the counteragent," Jawa continued proudly. "So all we have to do is whip up some of that."

Catherine frowned. "Unfortunately, that's a little tougher to do than gathering nutgalls. Plus, ferrous sulfate is corrosive and toxic. Unless anyone here is keen on having your skin flayed off, it'd be best to make it in a controlled setting. I don't suppose any of you know of a chemistry laboratory around here?"

Mike and I shared a look, struck by the same idea at once.

"There's one only a few blocks away," Mike said excitedly.

"Where?" Catherine asked.

"At our old middle school," I answered, with considerably less enthusiasm than Mike had shown.

Catherine immediately noticed this. "Is there a problem with your old middle school?"

"I didn't really enjoy my time there," I said. "In fact, it was pretty much the worst experience of my life."

"You do realize that people tried to kill you this morning?" Catherine asked.

"Yes," I replied. "Middle school was still worse."

"Well, let's go make some ferrous sulfate!" Jawa exclaimed enthusiastically. "Which way's this school?"

"I thought you had to deal with Zoe," Catherine reminded him. "That *is* what I overheard you telling Ben before, wasn't it? Right after he asked you to help him prove my daughter's innocence and you told him no."

Jawa's face fell. "Oh," he said embarrassedly. "Um . . . well . . . I . . . The thing is . . ."

". . . you weren't willing to stick your neck out at the time, but now you're willing to do it to try to impress me?" Catherine finished.

Chip broke into laughter. "Busted," he whispered.

Catherine shifted her gaze to him. "As I recall, Chip, you weren't willing to take the risk either."

Chip stopped laughing.

"Also busted," Mike said.

"School will be starting soon," Catherine pointed out, "which will make infiltrating the place rather difficult. Six people are far more suspicious than three, especially when one of them is unconscious. So Benjamin, Michael, and I shall take care of the ferrous sulfate while you two make good on your promise to return Zoe to spy school and feed the staff disinformation about where we've gone." She looked to Mike and me. "Which way is this middle school?"

Mike and I knew the route well, so we said our goodbyes to Chip and Jawa, then led Catherine through our neighborhood. Mike was moving a little slower than usual, due to his bowleggedness, but it still didn't take long to reach our old school. On the way, we hatched a cover story for our infiltration.

"This place doesn't look so terrible," Catherine observed as we headed up the front walkway. "A bit run-down, but not horrid."

"Looks can be deceiving," I told her.

I was feeling overwhelmed by bad memories of social alienation, chronic boredom, and menacing hordes of bullies. Plus, the last time I had visited, Joshua Hallal had surprised me there. I wondered if you could get post-traumatic stress disorder from middle school.

We arrived shortly after class had begun for the day, so we had to buzz the intercom at the front door and request admittance. Mrs. Khan, the school's administrative assistant, remembered Mike and me and automatically unlocked the door for us.

"Are you both re-enrolling here?" she asked as we entered the office, in the wary tone of someone who sensed a great deal of paperwork in her future.

"No," Catherine replied for us, flashing an ID card. "I'm Professor Hale from St. Smithen's Science Academy. I teach chemistry. The boys have been invited back today as part of an advanced education system to teach their old classmates about the wonders of covalent bonding."

"Oh," Mrs. Khan said, looking relieved. As an administrator, she had always been much more suspicious of students trying to leave the school than those trying to enter it. "I'm sure your old classmates will find that very interesting. Do I need to call Mr. Parivar?"

"There'll be no need for that," Catherine said confidently, filling out the visitors' log. "He's expecting us. And the boys know the way there."

That was good enough to convince Mrs. Khan. Catherine had a disarming personality—she appeared to be the least suspicious person on earth—and Mike and I had sterling reputations. I had never caused any trouble at school.

Mike had caused plenty of trouble—but never been caught.

"All right then," Mrs. Khan said. "Have fun." She printed out visitors' stickers for us and allowed us to pass into the school.

Since class was underway, the halls were virtually empty. The only person we saw was one of the girls' PE coaches. She might have questioned two students who were wandering the halls instead of in class, but since we were accompanied by an adult, she didn't give us a second glance.

My senses were overwhelmed as we passed through the school: the atonal clamor of students butchering Tchaikovsky in the music hall; the putrid stench of the boys' bathrooms; the distant chortle of Dirk the Jerk, the bully who had routinely shaken me down for my lunch money.

We made a quick stop at one part of the school that I'd never been inside: the teachers' lounge. This room had always held an air of mystery to me, but visiting it turned out to be very anticlimactic. There were only a few cheap tables and chairs, an ancient coffee maker, and a refrigerator filled with lunches in Tupperware containers, each of which had a name written on it or a threat warning everyone else to keep their hands off it. There was a faint haze of cigarette smoke, indicating that at least one of the teachers had been directly violating the school's non-smoking policy.

There was also a box of pastries. Which was what we'd

been hoping for. My parents had been on the PTA, which had funded breakfast every now and then for the teachers, a tradition that was, thankfully, still going on. We were starving. All the good pastries had already been picked through, leaving only things like bran muffins and danish with unidentifiable fillings, but we didn't care. Even Catherine dug in. We wolfed down everything that was left and then resumed our journey through the halls.

There were three science labs at the school, but due to break periods, one was always unoccupied. We found Mr. Parivar's to be empty. It was locked, but Catherine picked it within seconds. The cabinet where the more potent chemicals were all stored was also locked, following several incidents when troublemakers had used them to make cherry bombs and blow up the school plumbing. Catherine easily picked this lock too, and we quickly strapped on protective goggles, aprons, and gloves and set about making ferrous sulfate.

Catherine knew exactly how to do this, but it was a complicated process, involving dissolving steel wool in sulfuric acid, then filtering and heating the results. It took some time, but eventually, we were left with a greenish solution that billowed steam and smelled as though it might peel the paint off the walls.

"All right," Catherine said. "If we've done everything properly, I think a slight application of this should reveal the hidden message."

"You *think* it should?" Mike asked. "What happens if we've done this wrong?"

"It might dissolve that document and destroy any evidence of the Croatoan for eternity," Catherine replied. "So . . . let's hope this works."

I laid Washington's document on the lab table. As I did, something occurred to me. "Catherine, have you ever heard of a colonial spy named Elias Hale?"

She looked up from stirring the ferrous sulfate. "Of course. He was Nathan's brother—and thus, Alexander's great-great-great-great-great-uncle. Why do you mention him?"

"He's the one who wrote this letter to Washington."

Catherine gave the coded message on the paper a closer look. "Ah. That makes sense. Elias was the *good* spy in the family."

"Better than Nathan Hale?" Mike asked, surprised.

Catherine said, "Nathan was certainly brave and honorable, but he was a terrible spy. If you think about it, the reason we all know about him is because he got *caught*. On his first mission, no less. Meanwhile, Elias Hale was never captured—or even suspected of being a spy at all. He served as

Washington's top agent throughout the Revolution, Washington's presidency—and most of his life afterward." Catherine dipped a brush into the ferrous sulfate.

"So," Mike said, "Cyrus, Alexander, and Erica are all direct descendants of the bad spy in the Hale family?"

"There's far more to being a good spy than your ancestry," Catherine replied. "My parents weren't spies and neither were either of yours. But we're all doing a decent job at this." With that, she carefully dabbed the ferrous sulfate across Elias Hale's message.

The document didn't dissolve.

Instead, black lines began to emerge on the page. They formed slowly, as though they were nervous about appearing after so many years of being hidden. So at first, they were too faint to read.

"It worked!" Mike exclaimed.

"Mike?" someone asked behind us. "I thought I heard you!"

We all wheeled around to find Elizabeth Pasternak standing in the doorway. Back before I had met Erica Hale, I had considered Elizabeth to be the most beautiful girl I had ever seen. She was flanked by her closest friends, Chloe Appel and Kate Grant, who were also extremely attractive. I'd had crushes on all of them throughout much of my childhood. Meanwhile, the three of them hadn't known that I existed . . .

Until the last time I had seen them. I had been sent back to regular middle school for a day as part of a covert plot to convince SPYDER that I'd been booted out of spy school. During lunch, I had run afoul of Dirk the Jerk and his goons, who had tried to beat me up. I had knocked out Dirk in front of the entire school. Joshua Hallal had taken care of the other bullies, although no one knew that but me. Everyone else thought *I* had mopped the floor with them.

So the girls were all looking at me in a much different way than they had when I attended this school. First of all, they were looking at me, period, which was a change in itself. But there was also a coyness to Chloe's and Kate's gazes. Like they were intrigued by me.

Meanwhile, Elizabeth was focused on Mike. They had been hanging out regularly before Mike had been recruited to spy school and started dating the president's daughter.

"What are you doing here?" Elizabeth asked.

"Have you both transferred back to this school?" Chloe added, excitement evident in her voice.

"Uh . . . no," Mike said. "We're only here for the day. To teach our old classmates about inhalant bonding."

"*Covalent* bonding," Catherine corrected. "Hello, girls. I'm Professor Hale from St. Smithen's Science Academy. Aren't the three of you supposed to be in class right now?"

"No," Kate replied honestly. "We're excused so that we

can decorate the gym for the pep rally." She looked to Mike and me. "Do you guys want to come? It'll be a lot of fun."

"I texted you a couple weeks ago about a party," Elizabeth told Mike. "But you didn't respond."

"I'm sorry I couldn't make it," Mike said. "We were on a field trip."

"You chose a field trip over a party?" Elizabeth challenged. "Field trips are boring."

"This one wasn't," Mike said. "It was in Paris."

"Your school takes field trips to Paris?" Chloe asked us, amazed.

I wondered what she would have thought if she had known what we were *really* doing in Paris.

"Studying science has many rewards," Catherine said. "Now girls, I'm sorry, but we really need to get going. We're due back at school for physics lab soon." She plucked Washington's document off the lab table and led Mike and me toward the door.

The girls remained in the doorway, blocking our path. "I'm failing science," Kate told me. "I could use a tutor. Are you available?"

"I need one too!" Chloe said.

"Weren't you both A students in science when we were here?" I asked.

"We relapsed," Kate said quickly. "I need help. Especially

with my chemistry." She batted her eyes as she said this last word.

"Oh, for heaven's sake," Catherine said impatiently. "Girls, Benjamin will be happy to tutor both of you sometime soon. The boys won't be able to attend tonight's pep rally but will try not to miss your next party. Now, we really must go. If you don't get out of our way, I'll be forced to demonstrate the effects of chloroform on all of you."

Cowed, the girls promptly stepped aside, allowing us to pass through the door.

The bell was about to ring, signaling the time to change classes, so we hurried through the school.

"Sorry if I got a little testy with those girls," Catherine said, looking slightly apologetic for her outburst. "But my own daughter's safety is at stake here, and we don't have time to dilly-dally."

"We get it," Mike said, then gave me a playful punch on the shoulder. "Ben, Chloe and Kate were totally hitting on you! Man, you beat up a couple bullies and suddenly, you're Casanova."

I didn't feel like discussing this in front of Catherine, so I changed the subject. "Did the solution work? Can we read the words now?"

"They've just become legible," Catherine said enthusiastically. "Look." She held out the document.

However, I didn't get a chance to read it, as someone I had really been hoping to avoid entered the hall ahead of us.

Up until that point, I had feared that we might run into Dirk the Jerk or one of his goons. But the person we were now facing turned out to be worse.

My old middle school principal.

CONFLAGRATION

Robert E. Lee Middle School
Vienna, Virginia
April 17
0915 hours

Mrs. Festig was actually a decent administrator.
She had always done her best to make sure that we got a
decent education despite a paltry budget. But she was also a
tyrannical disciplinarian, operating under the fervent belief
that all teenagers were up to no good. In her book, tardiness
and roaming the halls without a pass were capital crimes.
The problem with this philosophy was that she often ended
up focused on the wrong people, accusing well-behaved kids
of plotting trouble while the real troublemakers were getting

away with murder—or at least the extortion of lunch money.

She was flanked by both of the school's security guards and faced us down, arms akimbo, with the self-satisfied smile of a detective who had just caught a trio of serial killers. "Mr. Brezinski," she said proudly. "I always knew you were trouble. And Mr. Ripley, I expected better from you."

I noticed a flicker of dismay cross Catherine's face. In that moment, I realized how worried she was about Erica. She had been doing an impressive job of remaining confident and collected, but her concern for Erica's safety was obviously wearing on her, and now we had yet another obstacle to confront. Mrs. Festig wasn't as daunting as enemy agents, but she was still preventing us from completing our mission of proving Erica's innocence and defeating the Croatoan.

And yet, Catherine still managed to stay calm. She plastered a smile on her face and spoke in her most pleasant voice. "I'm sorry, madam, but these young men haven't been up to any trouble at all. They've been under my supervision. I'm Professor Hale . . ."

". . . from St. Smithen's Science Academy," Mrs. Festig finished. "So I've heard. Only, I have no visit from St. Smithen's scheduled for today, and Mr. Parivar says he's never heard of you."

The smile on Catherine's face faltered, betraying her frustration. "I assure you, this is a simple misunderstanding."

"Let's see what the police have to say about that," Mrs. Festig said.

I heard sirens approaching. They sounded close by.

"Entering a school under false pretenses is a crime," Mrs. Festig told us. "As is stealing. So please hand over whatever you have in your hand." She pointed toward Washington's document.

The security guards strode toward us menacingly. Each pulled out a Taser.

I gulped, worried that things were going downhill fast. Mike seemed equally concerned. Even Catherine had to struggle to remain calm. Instead of responding to Mrs. Festig, she turned to Mike and me. "Michael and Benjamin, despite what this despotic troll thinks, I *do* know a thing or two about chemistry. For example, this substance that I borrowed from the lab is extremely combustible. So please take the appropriate precautions." She held up a test tube full of reddish fluid with a cork jammed into it, then casually tossed it onto the floor between us and the security guards.

The guards and Mrs. Festig gaped at this, which was completely the wrong response.

Mike and I turned away and shielded our eyes. There was a crack as the glass shattered on the floor, followed by a small blast. A wave of heat swept over me.

When I looked again, flames were roaring from a puddle of fluid in the middle of the hallway. Mrs. Festig and the guards were reeling, temporarily blinded by the blast.

"Well done, children," Catherine told Mike and me. "Now let's run."

We bolted down the hall in the opposite direction, just as the fire alarm came on. Within seconds, every classroom door burst open and students poured into the halls. Almost everyone was thrilled to see that there was a real fire, rather than a false alarm, as this meant that school was temporarily suspended, if not completely cancelled for the day. Most eagerly headed for the exits, although a few tossed their homework into the fire with the apparent hopes of fanning the flames and burning the school down.

Thus, we were quickly surrounded by a surge of other humans who covered our escape. Behind us, I could hear Mrs. Festig roaring in anger.

"What was that you just detonated?" I asked Catherine.

"Just a little incendiary device I whipped up in the chemistry lab. It always makes sense to have an extra explosive in case of emergencies."

"When did you make it?" Mike asked.

"While you were distracted by those three girls flirting with you. Speaking of which, here they are again."

Sure enough, Elizabeth, Chloe, and Kate were bearing

down on us. "Looks like school might be out for the day," Elizabeth said excitedly. "Are you guys busy?"

"Sorry, girls," Catherine said. "We really need to get back to our campus."

"Maybe we could go with you!" Kate suggested. "This science school of yours sounds really cool."

"Maybe some other time," I told her.

The crowd of students was surging toward the closest fire door. We passed through it with them, just in time to see three police cars screech to a stop in the parking lot.

"Oh bollocks," Catherine sighed.

The girls' interest in us ramped up even more. "Are they here for *you*?" Chloe asked us breathlessly. "Why?"

"It's all just a case of mistaken identity," I assured her.

Mike and I might have been able to blend into the crowd of our fellow teenagers, but Catherine stood out as the only adult. The police sprang from their cars and came our way.

"Do you have any more of those explodey things?" Mike asked her hopefully.

"I'm afraid not," Catherine said.

At which point one of the police cars blew up.

The explosion was significantly larger than the one Catherine had set off. It was the type of explosion you saw in movies, one that lifted the entire car into the air, flipped it over, and dropped it back into the parking lot. The police who had just climbed out of it were thrown to the ground by the blast. The students all gasped with amazement.

"You didn't do that?" I asked Catherine.

"No."

"Then who did?" Mike demanded.

"Me," said a familiar voice behind us.

I spun around to find Erica Hale.

Erica did this a lot. She was so naturally stealthy that she often seemed to materialize out of nowhere. I usually found this unsettling, but that day, I had a much different reaction: I was thrilled to see that she was all right. I wanted to grab her in a big hug, the way that normal people did when they saw their friends were safe, but I held back, because it didn't seem professional.

Catherine showed no such restraint. She threw her arms around Erica. "It's good to see you, Pookie."

"Please don't call me that," Erica groaned.

Catherine broke the hug, but only because we needed to get moving. While the police were distracted by their flaming car, Catherine led us through the crowd in the opposite direction. "Nice job with that explosion. What'd you use? C4?"

"Nitroglycerine," Erica replied. "It always makes sense to have an extra explosive in case of emergencies."

Catherine beamed at her proudly. "That's my girl."

Elizabeth, Chloe, and Kate were tailing us through the

crowd, fascinated by Erica—and a bit threatened by her too. I hadn't done a good job of hiding how happy I was to see Erica, and now I was obediently following her like a puppy. "Who's that girl?" Chloe asked me cattily. "Someone from your science school?"

"Best student there," I replied.

Elizabeth sized her up and put on a show of being unimpressed. "She doesn't seem that great. What's so special about her?"

"Just about everything," I said.

Two fire engines pulled into the parking lot nearby. Firefighters leapt out; some ran hoses to the closest hydrant, while others dragged hoses toward the school and the flaming police car. The explosion Catherine had set off in the school hadn't caused that big a blaze, but thunderclouds of smoke were billowing from the windows. No one seemed to have been hurt, but a fleet of ambulances was arriving as well.

"Where have you been?" I asked Erica.

Erica started to answer, but then cast a sidelong glance at the other girls. "Don't you have somewhere else to be?" she asked them.

"Normally, school," Kate answered. "But it's on fire. So . . . no."

"You three look like a savvy bunch," Catherine said. "I just got this new fragrance and I was wondering if you might give me your opinion on it." She took a small vial from her belt and spritzed a bit onto her wrist.

The girls looked at her curiously, but gave in and all sniffed Catherine's wrist. Each wrinkled their nose in disgust.

"Don't take this the wrong way," Elizabeth said, "but that smells terrible. What is it?"

"Chloroform," Catherine replied.

The girls looked at her in surprise, then collapsed in a heap on the lawn.

"I *did* warn them I'd have to use that if they didn't leave us alone," Catherine said to Mike and me. "My, they were a tenacious bunch. They certainly seem to have designs on the two of you."

Erica shifted her attention to me, looking the tiniest bit upset.

"I'm not interested in them," I said quickly.

Catherine waved to get the attention of a few paramedics as they climbed out of their ambulance. "Those three girls have just succumbed to smoke inhalation," she told them. "I think they could use some attention."

The paramedics rushed over to deal with Elizabeth, Chloe, and Kate, leaving their ambulance unattended.

So we stole it.

In all the mayhem with the smoking school and the flaming police car and the hundreds of students eagerly fleeing the grounds, no one even noticed. We simply climbed in, Catherine took the wheel, and we drove away.

"Did you make any progress on the Croatoan while I was gone?" Erica asked as we exited the school parking lot.

"Quite a bit," Catherine said, presenting Washington's document.

I took it from her hands, relieved to finally have a second to read it. The ferrous sulfate had worked perfectly. In the blank spaces between the lines of code, the hidden words were now visible:

Croatoan Headquarters located. 750 paces northwest of the Great Falls of the Potomac. Beneath the old mill.

"Hold on now," Mike said, sounding a bit suspicious. "That's completely straightforward and helpful. There's no riddle to solve? No clue that just leads to another clue?"

"Were you hoping for one?" Catherine asked him.

"No!" Mike exclaimed. "But every time we've found a lead so far, it's only led to another puzzle. This says exactly where we're supposed to go. It's too easy."

"I'm fine with easy," I said.

"So am I," Mike agreed. "In fact, I'm freaking thrilled with easy. But do you think we can trust it? Could this just be a code for something else?"

"I think this is on the money," Catherine said. "We've had to work through several layers of codes to get this far already—and the directions make sense. The Great Falls of the Potomac is a national park now. Since the land has been protected, there's a chance the Croatoan might still be operating from there."

"Still?" I asked. "It's been over two centuries since this message was written."

Catherine said, "If you find a location that works, why change it? Your government has been using the same Capitol building for two centuries, while our royals have been using Buckingham Palace for even longer. Why shouldn't the Croatoan do the same? The Great Falls of the Potomac would have been an inspired location for the Croatoan to operate from even then. They're close to Washington, but not *so* close that they'd fall under scrutiny. I believe we're not too far from them right now."

"They're only half an hour away with traffic," Erica reported, fiddling with the ambulance's GPS system.

"Traffic won't be an issue," Catherine said, flipping on the siren.

The cars ahead of us quickly pulled to the side of the road to let us pass. Catherine floored the accelerator and we raced by.

I watched our old middle school disappear behind us. More police cars and fire engines were pulling into the parking lot, students were crowding the lawns, and smoke was blackening the sky above.

Mike said, "Have you ever noticed that, wherever we go, we leave a trail of chaos and destruction?"

"Yes," I said. "That had occurred to me too."

"It's awesome, isn't it?" Mike asked, grinning from ear to ear.

We sped on down the road, heading for what we hoped was still the headquarters of the Croatoan.

CONSPIRACY

Great Falls Park
Maryland/Virginia border
April 17
1000 hours

With the siren on, it only took us fifteen minutes to get to the falls, during which Erica updated us on where she had been: protecting her sister.

"I figured the Croatoan would consider you going to Mount Vernon a breach of trust," Erica explained. "So I had to make sure Trixie was safe."

"Didn't you tell me it was a bad idea to do that?" I asked.

"Yes," Erica admitted. "But only because I didn't want you to know that was what I was actually going to do. In case the Croatoan captured you and tortured you for information about where I was."

I swallowed hard at the thought of that. "You really thought that was a possibility?"

"Definitely. So it made sense to play things safe. While all of you were getting that document, Dad, Grandpa, and I went up to Trixie's boarding school in Connecticut."

"Your father went along?" Catherine asked, looking worried. She knew better than anyone how incompetent Alexander was. She had once told me that she barely trusted Alexander to use a stapler, so relying on him to protect their daughter would have been a concern.

"Don't worry," Erica assured her. "Grandpa and I did all the dangerous stuff. Dad just stayed in the car and kept watch."

"Thank goodness." Catherine heaved a sigh of relief, which I recognized as the opposite reaction most mothers would have had to the statement Erica had just made. "Did you have any trouble?"

"None. I think the Croatoan was too busy keeping an eye on you guys."

"So where is Trixie now?" I asked.

"With Grandpa. He's taking her on a tour of Revolutionary War battle sites."

"Ugh," Mike said. "Why didn't he take her to do anything fun?"

Erica looked at him curiously. "That *is* fun. Who doesn't like visiting Revolutionary War battle sites?"

"*Everyone*," Mike said.

"Well, Trixie loves it. She's having a great time. And she doesn't have the slightest idea how much danger she was in."

"She's *still* in danger," Catherine reminded Erica. "Just because you didn't have any trouble with the Croatoan this time doesn't mean we're out of the woods yet. Until we can figure out what they're up to and defeat them once and for all, your sister's life hangs in the balance."

"I know, Mom. You don't have to be so dramatic." Erica rolled her eyes, the way a normal teenage girl might have.

There were only three cars in the parking lot of Great Falls Park when we arrived. It was still somewhat early on a weekday, and the park usually attracted only a tiny fraction of the tourists that visited Washington, DC; it wasn't easy to get to without a car, and even a lot of locals didn't know about it.

However, I had been to the falls dozens of times, since they were close to where I had grown up and were free to visit. It struck me as strange that our mission was leading there; after traveling all over the world in pursuit of bad guys, I was now looking for an evil organization in my own backyard.

The falls were surprisingly extensive. While the Potomac was wide and slow-moving near Washington, DC, only fourteen miles upstream, it narrowed significantly and thus flowed much faster. At the park, it churned through a maze of small islands, resulting in dozens of separate cataracts that dropped nearly a hundred feet over a quarter mile. Repeated flooding had stripped the banks bare, so the falls were flanked by jagged rocks that jutted high into the sky. A sheen of mist hung over it all, and the morning sunlight refracted through it, creating rainbows. It was all quite breathtaking.

Unfortunately, we had to focus on what was probably the least attractive section of the park.

The old mill still sat exactly where Washington's message had indicated, 750 paces northwest of the falls, tucked into the forest between a hiking trail and the riverbank. Despite visiting so many times, I had never really noticed it, which was exactly what the park service wanted. The old mill was an eyesore, and due to a lack of funding, it had fallen into decay over the past two hundred years. Furthermore, the forest had practically swallowed it so it was almost invisible from the trail. It had probably never been much to look at, but now it was folding in on itself and was overrun by foliage. The mill was surrounded by a chain-link fence on three sides and a steep cliff overlooking the river on the fourth. The fence was bedecked with signs warning visitors not to trespass on the premises under penalty of prosecution—or, more likely, death by an old mill collapsing on you.

Despite this, the grass in front of the gate was scraped bare, indicating that the gate had been swung open on a regular basis, and a faint path led to the mill's door. As usual, Catherine picked the lock easily, and then we followed the path to the mill.

There was another lock on the door, a surprisingly new one. It looked as though it was at least two centuries younger than any other part of the building.

Catherine picked this one too and led us inside.

The mill was the spookiest place I had ever been in my life. On a previous mission, I had found myself in a cave filled with insects and skeletons—and on another, I had ended up in an underground tunnel lined with human skulls. But the mill made both those places look as innocent as a petting zoo.

For starters, there was the noise. The whole building creaked and groaned ominously, and there were dozens of other unsettling sounds as well: wind whistling through the gaps in the walls; dripping water; the scuttle of rodent feet; the high-pitched squeaks of what I presumed were bats. It was also dark, the only light coming from faint sunbeams that made it through the forest canopy and then holes in the roof. Not that I *wanted* to see anything inside the mill: Everything in there was straight out of a horror movie. The floor was covered in a gelatinous slick of ancient leaves, mud, and what I feared were long-decayed animals; rats the size of small dogs glowered at us from the shadows; the walls were hung with sharp, rusting objects like pitchforks and scythes. I couldn't even fathom *why* anyone would have wanted a pitchfork or a scythe in a mill, except for thinking that someday, a few centuries in the future, they would freak out any visitors who broke in.

Or maybe a modern-day evil consortium had put them there, hoping to scare the pants off anyone who came poking around.

"Spookiest place ever," Mike muttered, echoing my thoughts.

"It *is* an evil lair," Erica informed him, then thought to add, "We think."

"I get that it's an evil lair," Mike replied. "But don't evil people care about interior decorating? If someone's bent on world domination, do they really need their hideout covered with rats and slime? What's wrong with carpeting? Or curtains?"

"This *does* look a bit too grotty," Catherine observed. "I don't think anyone's been operating out of *this* room. However . . ." She paused by the northern wall of the mill and looked down at the floor. ". . . this area has a bit less detritus on it than the rest."

"Does 'detritus' mean 'rat poop'?" Mike asked.

"It means disgusting stuff in general," I said. "So if there's less there . . ."

"Then maybe someone's tried to keep this area a bit cleaner," Catherine concluded. "In fact, it looks like someone *has* tidied up this area, then dirtied it once again to make it appear as if it wasn't cleaned at all. Aha!" She kicked aside a wad of something wet and gooey to reveal a brass ring that had been hidden beneath it. The ring was affixed to the floor with a hinge. Catherine took a monogrammed handkerchief from her pocket, gingerly wrapped it around the ring so she wouldn't have to touch it with her bare skin, and lifted up.

A trapdoor that had been concealed beneath all the gunk popped open. Below it, an ancient wooden staircase descended into the darkness.

"This looks promising," Catherine said cheerfully.

"And still really spooky," Mike grumbled.

Catherine headed down the stairs. It seemed terribly unchivalrous to let her go first, but she didn't seem to have any problem with it, while the idea of heading down into a dark room *underneath* a room that was already making my skin crawl terrified me.

I really hoped that the next sound I heard wouldn't be a scream of horror. Or a cry of pain.

I was *not* expecting a gasp of delight.

That was followed by Catherine exclaiming, "Children! Come quickly!"

We hurried down the stairs after her . . . and found ourselves in what looked like a tastefully decorated rec room.

The difference between the horror show upstairs and the room downstairs was so stark, it felt as though we had gone through a portal into another dimension. Someone—or more likely, a team of people—had gone through a great deal of trouble to keep the downstairs clean and nicely maintained over the years.

First of all, there was lighting. Modern, energy-efficient fixtures had been installed in the ceiling, indicating that the lair had been used a lot recently. The electricity came from a portable hydroelectric generator, which was powered by a small stream of river water coursing through an underground tunnel. This would have kept the hideout off the main electrical grid and thus, hard to detect. It also meant there wasn't a lot of power, so the lights were somewhat dim, but still, this created a pleasant, homey glow from the lamps, which was a nice contrast to the shiver-inducing gloom upstairs.

Then, the rock walls had been plastered and painted a soothing shade of light green. Some framed posters with inspirational sayings hung on the wall. And there was furniture. It wasn't expensive furniture, given that it was in a hidden room underneath a death trap, but it was still somewhat tasteful and comfy-looking. A couch and two armchairs were arranged around a coffee table while a few filing cabinets and storage shelves lined the walls.

The room wasn't that big, so it didn't take Catherine and Erica long to case it and determine that no bad guys were lurking in the corners, waiting to ambush us.

"This is what I'm talking about," Mike said, looking over the room with visible relief. "Lights, chairs, a little paint, and . . . No way! Foosball!"

Sure enough, there was a foosball table off to one side. Mike raced to it and yelled, "I call red team!"

"We're not here to play foosball," I told him. Catherine and Erica were now searching the room for clues, so I joined them.

"It won't take long," Mike said. "Because I'm gonna kick your butt. I *rule* at foosball."

I ignored this challenge. "We need to see if this is the lair of the Croatoan."

"Of course it's the lair of the Croatoan," Mike said. "Who else is gonna hide their headquarters underneath a spooky three-hundred-year-old mill? The Shriners?" He dropped the ball onto the table. "Come on. Just one game."

"Why is this so important to you?" I asked. "We have a foosball table at our dorm."

"The foosball table at our dorm stinks," Mike argued.

"All the legs are different sizes, the players barely spin, and a raccoon got in and ate all the foosballs."

"Oh my," Catherine said, sounding extremely surprised. She had found something in the filing cabinets.

"Tell me about it," Mike agreed, misunderstanding her concern. "We haven't been able to play a decent game of foosball in weeks."

"She's not talking about the foosball table," I chided him, joining Catherine at the cabinets. The moment I saw what she was looking at, I couldn't help but say "Oh my" as well.

She was holding a piece of paper that was brown and brittle with age. The handwriting on it had faded to the point where it was barely legible, but I could still make out some of it:

. . . Mr. Booth has been completely hoodwinked and truly believes his actions will be perceived as part of the play . . . he thinks he will be using a prop gun, rather than a real one . . . insists upon shouting "Sic semper tyrannis" *instead of the line we wrote for him. Believes the Latin will make him sound more erudite . . .*

"These are plans for assassinating Lincoln," I said with a gasp. "They tricked John Wilkes Booth into doing it."

"There's a whole file full of assassination plots alone." Catherine leafed through more ancient papers. "Kennedy, McKinley, William Henry Harrison . . ."

"William Henry Harrison wasn't assassinated," I said. "He died after getting a cold while giving his inaugural address."

"It seems that's simply what the Croatoan wanted everyone to think," Catherine said. "In truth, they slipped him some brandy laced with arsenic."

Erica now held up an old document she had found in another filing cabinet. "Here's the plans for a plot to throw all the tea into Boston Harbor to provoke the British into retaliation."

"The Boston Tea Party wasn't thrown by Americans?" Catherine asked, shocked.

"Apparently not," Erica said. "The Croatoan framed them. And the Brits bought it hook, line, and sinker."

"Oh." Catherine grew embarrassed. "I suppose we owe you an apology for that."

Mike had forgotten all about foosball and was now leafing through an armload of documents. "Here's a contract with pirates to raid American settlements in the 1820s. And plans to crash the stock market in 1929. And a scheme to capture a giant gorilla and let it wreak havoc on New York City. . . ."

"That's the plot of *King Kong*," I told him.

"I guess not all their plans worked out," Mike said. "It seems they couldn't find a giant gorilla. But they *did* sell the idea to Hollywood for a lot of money."

Catherine was looking over all the files, appearing amazed and horrified at once. "There must be evidence of a hundred different diabolical conspiracies here. After all these years, we finally have proof that the Croatoan exists and has been actively plotting against this country."

"But there's nothing in these files about what they're plotting *now*," I observed sadly.

"Because it's over here," Erica said.

The rest of us turned to her.

Erica was standing before what had looked like a normal wall, but was really a secret panel. Now she slid it aside, dramatically revealing a small alcove.

Inside were a drafting table and a bulletin board. They were covered with plans for a new evil scheme.

Whoever had been plotting wasn't very well organized. The drafting table was a mess, covered in piles of scratch paper, sketches, surveillance photographs, and books full of dog-eared pages. Crumpled soda cans, stubby pencils, and other garbage was strewn about. Everything was spackled with modeling clay and stippled with bright blue paint. It looked like someone had hosted art class for a bunch of kindergartners.

However, despite the clutter, it wasn't hard to determine what the Croatoan's target was: the Washington Monument.

There were dozens of surveillance photos of it, taken

from every angle imaginable. There were maps of the National Mall with the monument circled and routes to it plotted out. There were several clay models of the famous stone obelisk, in various states of demolition. Some models had been toppled, some had been sheared in half, and others had simply been blown apart. It appeared that someone had been working out the most dramatic way to destroy it.

"Looks like they're going after the Washington Monument," Mike observed.

"Thank you, Captain Obvious," Erica said. "The real question is why?"

"The Croatoan despises America," Catherine answered. "And the monument is a great symbol of this country. Destroying it would make a big statement."

"But it wouldn't *do* anything," Erica argued. "It won't take down our government. It won't destroy America. SPY-DER was at least plotting to get rich. These guys are just going to make a mess."

"Sometimes that's all people want to do," Catherine explained.

"That's crazy," I said.

"There's plenty of crazy in this world," Catherine told me. "And it's the worst kind of dangerous." She picked up the shattered base of one of the models of the monument, sniffed it, and grew deeply concerned. "They used an RDX explosive on this. It's extremely powerful. They've only used a minuscule amount here, but a truck full of this wouldn't just topple the Washington Monument. It'd leave a crater the size of the Rose Bowl and level every building nearby."

"The monument is smack in the middle of the National Mall," Mike noted. "There's a dozen museums and other monuments around there. . . ."

". . . and the White House," I added.

"If the Croatoan attacked in the middle of the day, the whole place would be crawling with tourists," Mike concluded. "Thousands of them, maybe."

"Then we need to figure out when they're planning to do this," Catherine said. "And fast."

"I'll bet they're going to attack at ten a.m. tomorrow," Erica said.

"Why do you say that?" I asked.

Erica held up a crumpled memo that she had pulled from the trash can. "Because it says right here, 'The attack is scheduled for ten a.m. on April eighteenth.' That's tomorrow."

I took the memo from her and read it. Despite the fact that it had smears of bright blue paint on it, it was surprisingly corporate:

To: All Operatives
From: El Capitan

Re: Operation Downfall

The attack is scheduled for 10am on April 18.

Let me not die ingloriously and without a

struggle, but let me first do some great thing

that should be told among men hereafter.

Remember: Any moment might be our last.

But everything is more beautiful because

we're doomed.

"Sounds like they're plotting a suicide mission," I said.

"Sounds like they're a bunch of lunatics," Mike scoffed. "Who talks like that?"

"Zealots," Catherine answered. "Fanatics. Extremists. People who are willing to die for a cause, no matter how bizarre we might consider it."

Something suddenly occurred to me. "The ceremony rededicating the Capitol is tomorrow at ten a.m.!"

"That's right!" Catherine exclaimed. "It's the perfect time for the Croatoan to strike!"

"How so?" Mike asked. "The city's going to be crawling with police and Secret Service agents."

"The *Capitol* is going to be crawling with police and Secret Service," Catherine corrected. "All their attention will be focused *there*, where the president and Congress and all the dignitaries are."

"The Washington Monument is in a direct line of sight from the Capitol steps," I said. "If they blow it up during the ceremony, it will happen right in front of everyone in our government. And on live TV."

"That's a heck of a statement," Mike said.

Erica was looking over the drafting table, frustration etched on her face. "There's so much here about *what* the Croatoan is plotting, but there's nothing here about *who* they are."

"So?" Mike asked. "We know where and when they're going to strike tomorrow. So we can stop them when they try."

"It'd be nice to stop them *before* they try," Erica said. "Like today. So we catch them by surprise and not while they're driving a truck loaded with RDX through Washington, DC. If something goes wrong then—or if they decide to simply detonate the truck and martyr themselves anyhow— they'll take out a good chunk of the city."

"Oh," Mike said. "Good point."

"And yet," Erica went on, rifling through the piles of paper, "they've been smart enough to never use their names on any of these documents. Only code names like 'El Capitan,' who must be the leader."

"They never even call themselves the Croatoan," Catherine noted, looking over the drafting table herself. "There's not a single phone number or an address . . . Michael! Be careful with that! It's an explosive!" She wheeled on Mike, who had picked up a Hot Wheels car.

Mike immediately held the car at arm's length. "I thought it was just a toy!"

"They've been using it to model their attacks," Catherine explained. She took it from Mike, then used tweezers from her utility belt to gingerly pick a small bit of gunk off it. It was the size and color of a blob of earwax. "If you're not careful with this, it could bring this whole building down on our heads."

Mike grimaced. "Sorry."

Catherine plucked a plastic evidence bag from her belt as well. "If you wouldn't mind holding this open, we can handle this explosive properly. I apologize if I was a bit curt with you just now. I was just worried you were going to reduce us all to tiny pieces."

"No need to apologize," Mike said graciously. "It makes sense to be cautious. I like having all my body parts attached."

Or at least he said something like that. I had stopped paying attention to them, even though they were dealing with a highly reactive and powerful explosive. Catherine's comment about being reduced to pieces had triggered something in my mind. A thought had been nagging me all day, and now I began to make sense of it.

I ran to the drafting table, found a piece of scratch paper with only a tiny bit of blue paint on it, and tore it apart.

"Careful!" Erica warned me. "This is all evidence . . . What are you doing?"

"Reducing something to pieces." I grabbed a pen and wrote letters on eight separate scraps of paper:

C R O A T O A N.

Then I placed them all on the table and shuffled them around.

"You're anagramming them?" Erica asked, intrigued.

"Yes." I kept moving the letters about, looking for new patterns. It didn't take me long to find one. And when I did, everything quickly fell into place, revealing a name:

N O R A T A C O.

Erica looked at me, amazed—and concerned.

"I knew there was something weird about that name," I said.

"Whoa," Mike said. He was staring at the letters I had anagrammed, still clutching the tiny plastic bag with the RDX explosive in it. "Agent Taco's a mole?!"

Catherine's watch suddenly began beeping ominously. She glanced at it and grew extremely worried. "We have to go. *Now*," she said, and ran for the staircase. As she did, I caught a glimpse of her watch screen. There was some grainy video playing on it.

Catherine explained everything as we raced up the stairs. "I set up a perimeter camera on the path leading to this mill. Someone just tripped it."

"The Croatoan?" I asked.

"I can only assume so. They're coming for us."

WATER SAFETY

Great Falls Park

Maryland/Virginia border

April 17

1100 hours

The first shot pierced the wall of the old mill just as I ascended the stairs from the secret lair. It left a relatively large hole by the front door and an even larger one on the opposite side of the building. Which meant the Croatoan was firing on us from the front.

So we went out the back.

The fact that there wasn't a back door didn't stop us. Our muscles were supercharged with adrenaline, and the wooden walls of the mill were weakened by time, the elements, and several thousand generations of termites.

Catherine led the way, throwing her shoulder into the wall, which broke open like a saltine cracker, leaving a human-size hole. Sunlight poured through the gap, sending the rats and bats scurrying.

Another shot tore through the front door of the mill.

Mike, Erica, and I followed Catherine.

Since the mill was now between us and the bad guys, we couldn't see them at all. I had no idea how many there were, or what they looked like. All I knew was that they had weapons and weren't hesitating to use them.

And if all that wasn't bad enough, we had one other problem: We were running toward a cliff.

It was the edge of the gorge closest to the mill. I saw it coming as we ran through the woods. Not far ahead of us, the trees suddenly stopped and there was only daylight behind them, as though the world had ended. I could hear the rush of water and see the billowing clouds of mist beyond.

In the brief time it took to get there, I thought of several arguments against running off the top of the cliff. Things like "This is dangerous" and "This is crazy" and "This looks like it could be very painful." But I realized that all of those could be countered by the argument "If we stay here, the bad guys are going to kill us."

The others all jumped before me. Not because they were

braver, but because they were faster. Catherine, Erica, and Mike disappeared before my eyes in rapid succession.

I hesitated for a brief moment before jumping—because it was a *cliff*. Despite how much danger I was in, the rational part of my brain still wanted me to slow down, even for a few milliseconds, just to make sure I wasn't going to miss the river and splatter onto some rocks.

There was a gunshot from behind me. A bullet ricocheted off the rocks by my feet. I leapt off the cliff before anyone could shoot again.

This wasn't the first time I had jumped from a great height into a river while on a mission. In fact, I had jumped from significantly bigger heights before. So in this case, I didn't have much time to panic on the way down. I hit the water relatively quickly.

The water seemed to grab me and yank me downstream before I was even submerged in it. It was like I had jumped onto a moving train, if trains were cold and wet and wound through mazes of rock and were full of debris.

The cold, the wet, and the rocks were bad enough, but the debris was a major concern.

Since the river was running high and fast, all sorts of things were being dragged along in the current. Some were things you might expect to find in rivers, like logs. Others were things that had no business being in a river at all but which thoughtless people had tossed in upstream, like plastic bags and fast-food packaging and sheets of plywood. Only seconds after I leapt in, a good-size tree trunk came flying toward me with a shopping cart spiked on the end of it. I had no idea how this had happened, and there was no time to figure it out. I simply flailed wildly to get out of the way and let it barrel past.

Before me, I saw Catherine, Erica, and Mike bobbing up and down as they were sucked through the gorge. To my right, atop the cliff, I caught a glimpse of the three Croatoan members who had been chasing us, silhouetted against the sky. I saw the sunlight glint off a shotgun in one's hands, and then there was another boom and wood splintered off the tree trunk ahead of me. After that, I was pulled into the gorge, where the rock walls were steep enough to block me from their sight.

I was moving too fast for the Croatoan to keep up by running along the bank, although due to the jagged rocks and the forest at the edge, the bank wasn't really possible to run along anyhow. I was also quite sure that the Croatoan wouldn't jump in the river after us, because jumping into the river was insane . . . unless people with guns were chasing you. So for the time being, I figured I was safe from the Croatoan and only had to worry about drowning and hypothermia and being smashed to death on the rocks.

In front of me, the river forked into several different

channels amongst a maze of small islands. Catherine was dragged one way, Erica another, and Mike yet another.

I pointed my feet downstream; it was far better to encounter a rock with your feet than your skull. Then I fought to keep my head above water and hoped for the best.

A human body suddenly popped up in the water next to me.

I screamed. Which, in my defense, was a completely normal reaction to having a body suddenly emerge next to you in a river. Especially a body missing half of its limbs and with a coat of slime where the face should be.

It took me a second to realize it was a department store mannequin that had also been tossed in the river upstream. It was wearing only the top of a bikini, because the bottom half of its body was gone.

Being made of plastic, the mannequin was buoyant. So I grabbed on to it and used it to stay afloat.

I arrived at the maze of islands and was pulled into a different channel than any of my friends had gone through. Mine turned out to be narrow and quick-moving, and my mannequin and I were bounced between the rocky sides like a Ping-Pong ball. I kept moving the plastic woman back and forth so she would take the impact. Thus, she protected me from the rocks, although it was tough on her. With each hit, there was a sickening crunch of plastic.

Then came the main falls.

I fired out of my narrow chute and found myself rushing toward them. A few tourists were gathered at the scenic lookout point. I waved desperately to them for help and saw all their faces go white with horror, not so much because I was going over the falls but because I was doing it with what appeared to be only half of another human being.

I clung tightly to my mannequin as I tumbled over the lip, using her as a humanoid life preserver. We dropped fifty feet, plunged into the roiling water at the bottom, and were churned like socks in the washing machine. Every time I thought I was about to surface, I'd get yanked back down again. I was on the verge of blacking out when I finally managed to break through.

I desperately sucked in a few deep breaths of air as I was tossed through more rapids.

Then the river widened and calmed dramatically. It was still flowing fast, but I could now maneuver a bit and was in far less danger of being slammed into a rock. Soon the steep cliffs gave way to muddy beaches.

To my relief, I saw Catherine, Mike, and Erica on one of these. They were wet and bedraggled and Catherine had a good-size branch tangled in her hair, but they seemed to be otherwise okay. In fact, Catherine and Erica looked surprisingly calm and collected, as though they had just had a refreshing dip in the pool. They came to the water's edge to help me stagger ashore with my mannequin.

"I see you made a friend," Mike said.

"She might have saved my life." I dropped the plastic torso on the ground. "Is everyone all right?"

"Yes," Catherine said. "Although we'd best get moving. We've gained some ground on the Croatoan, but they could make it up fast."

"No one's going anywhere," someone said.

We all turned around to find five DADD agents standing slightly uphill from us, pointing guns our way. And right in front of them, grinning proudly, was their leader.

Agent Nora Taco.

INTERROGATION

Undisclosed location
Somewhere near Langley, Virginia
April 17
1700 hours

"You have caused us a great deal of trouble,"
Agent Taco told me. "So let's put an end to that, shall we?"

I was lying on a cot in a holding cell. It was nicer than a jail cell but not nearly as nice as a hotel room. Besides the cot, there was a table with a few chairs and a small selection of books and sudoku puzzles to help pass the time of incarceration. There was no private bathroom; instead, there was one down the hall, and you had to ask the guards for permission to use it.

I had been brought there—along with Catherine, Erica, and Mike—right after our capture on the riverbank. There had been no way to escape; we were outnumbered, outgunned, and exhausted after our time in the river. The DADD officers had blindfolded us and bundled us into a paddy wagon. The driver had taken us on a looping, indirect route to mess with our senses of direction so we couldn't tell where we were, but we still hadn't driven for that long, and we hadn't gone over any bridges—there was a telltale sound when a car drove over a bridge—so that meant we were still somewhere in northern Virginia.

DADD had split all of us into separate cells, so I didn't know where anyone else was. I hadn't heard any of them, which indicated that the building was soundproofed. It was also large enough to have at least four separate cells.

I had originally intended to spend my time plotting to escape . . . but I fell asleep instead. I was exhausted. I'd had very little rest in the past twenty-four hours, so I passed out almost immediately upon being locked in the room. It happened so quickly, I didn't even have any memory of it. One moment, I had been sitting on the cot, and the next, it was hours later and Agent Taco was standing over me.

Zoe Zibbell stood next to her. I suspected that Zoe had been asked to come along because she was my friend, the idea being that I would open up to her in a way that I might not with Agent Taco alone. But that wasn't going to work. I was too upset with Zoe.

Instead, I gave her a hard stare and said, "Just so you know, Agent Taco here isn't who you think she is. She's a mole for the Croatoan."

Agent Taco laughed at this, like it was the most ridiculous thing she'd ever heard. But then, any good double agent would have trained themselves to laugh when someone accused them of being a double agent. She waved to one of the chairs and said, "Why don't you put yourself together and have a seat?"

I sat up in the cot. On the wall across from me was a one-way mirror, meaning that it allowed me to see my own reflection, but allowed people standing on the other side to watch me.

I was a mess. I had terrible bedhead. The bedcovers had left a ribbed pattern on my cheek, so I looked like I'd been hit in the face with a waffle iron. Plus, I hadn't been allowed to change clothes, so I was dirty and grimy and had the musty smell of a damp rag that had been forgotten behind the washing machine for three months.

I smoothed out my hair the best I could and shifted to the chair. Agent Taco and Zoe sat down across the table from me.

"Agent Taco isn't working for the bad guys," Zoe informed me. "*You* are."

"I am not."

"You are too . . ."

Agent Taco held up a hand to silence our debate, then looked to me calmly. "Ben, there is no evidence that the Croatoan even exists. It's only a rumor . . ."

"That's exactly what I would expect someone who is working for the Croatoan to say."

Agent Taco sighed. "And why do you think I'm working for them?"

"Your name," I said.

Agent Taco blinked at me, confused. "My name?"

"'Nora Taco' is an anagram of 'Croatoan,'" I replied, beaming with satisfaction.

I had been expecting Agent Taco to give me a look of surprise that I had figured it out. Or maybe a sly smile, impressed that I had seen what no one else had. Instead, she groaned. "Oh, for Pete's sake. As if this name wasn't embarrassing enough already."

Her response was so genuine, I believed it. "You mean . . . it's just a coincidence?"

"Of course it's just a coincidence!" Agent Taco shouted. "Do you honestly think that if I was really a covert Croatoan agent, I'd pick a fake name as blatantly obvious as an anagram of the evil organization I worked for? Or if I *was* cocky enough to do such a thing, do you really think I'd pick *Nora Taco*?! Not Nora Coat? Or Nora Cato? Or Ron Acota?"

"Ron's a man's name . . . ," I pointed out.

"It'd be less conspicuous for me to have a sex change than to have the last name Taco! Do you know what it's like to go through life with a last name that's also a food? Do you realize how much I've been teased? Do you have any idea how much fun people have made of my name?"

"Children can be awfully cruel," Zoe said sympathetically.

"I'm not talking about children!" Agent Taco exclaimed. "I'm talking about my fellow agents! They're the worst. Just once, I'd like to be able to go out for Mexican food and not be accused of cannibalism. And when this gets out, I'm never going to hear the end of it." Agent Taco rubbed her temples, like the mere thought was giving her a migraine headache.

Zoe patted her arm supportively. "I promise, we won't say anything to the other agents."

"They already know." Agent Taco waved around the room. "This whole conversation is being recorded. Half the team is watching through that mirror. The director of the CIA probably knows about this by now." She groaned again and buried her face in her hands.

"Nice going," Zoe whispered to me. "Look how much you've upset her."

"Upset *her*?" I whispered back. "She captured me and locked me up all day!"

"And you accused her of being a double agent based on shoddy evidence."

"That's still plausible. What if she came up with a ridiculous fake name on purpose, knowing that if anyone ever pointed it out, she could just say that no double agent would ever pick such a ridiculous name, so she'd deflect attention from herself when, in fact, she has really been a double agent all along? It's kind of brilliant."

"It's not," Zoe told me. "In fact, that theory is the complete opposite of brilliant."

I realized she was probably right. The simpler explanation was that I had accused someone of being a double agent due to nothing more than coincidence. Although I didn't feel that bad for Agent Taco. And I still had some suspicions. "If you're not with the Croatoan, then how did you find us at the falls?"

"I placed a tracking device on you at your tree house," Zoe replied. "Before Mike snuck up on Chip, Jawa, and me and knocked us all out, that jerk."

I realized that must have been the story Chip and Jawa had told Zoe so she wouldn't realize that *they* had knocked her out. I wasn't pleased that they had pinned the blame on Mike, but this wasn't the time to defend him. I had something much more important to discuss. "Okay, so you guys aren't Croatoan—"

"There's no such thing as the Croatoan," Agent Taco interrupted. "It's just a crazy myth concocted by conspiracy theorists."

"It's not," I insisted. "We found evidence they exist."

Agent Taco still looked like she didn't believe me. "And what would that be?"

"We found the Croatoan's secret hideout, no thanks to you guys. They've been using the same place since the American Revolution."

"That's what you were doing at the falls?" Agent Taco asked.

"What'd you think we were doing? Going for a swim?"

"It looked like you were trying to get away from us."

"We were trying to get away from the Croatoan. Which was trying to kill us because we'd found their secret plans. Everything they've plotted for the past few hundred years— *and* the plans for their current scheme. They're going to blow up the Washington Monument at ten o'clock tomorrow morning."

Agent Taco and Zoe shared a concerned look—although I couldn't tell if they were concerned about the monument or my sanity. "Why?" Zoe asked me.

"To make an anti-American statement, I guess. It's going to happen right during the ceremony at the Capitol, for the whole world to see."

"And you found *real* evidence of this?" Agent Taco asked skeptically. "Not some weird anagram of 'Washington Monument' like 'Summon a Newt Nothing' or 'Stout Minnow Hangmen'?"

I gaped at her, astonished. "You're very good at anagramming."

"It's a gift."

"Then why didn't you know your own name was an anagram of 'Croatoan'?"

"I *did*. I was just hoping no one else would notice. So what's your evidence for this attack?"

"This." I dramatically pulled the memo Erica had found in the Croatoan's trash can out of my pocket and slapped it on the table.

Unfortunately, the memo had been in my pocket during my time in the river, and had thus turned into a soggy mess. Most of the ink had blurred into smears. The quotes about sacrifice were still somewhat visible, but the important part, about the planned attack, was completely illegible.

Agent Taco eyed it with disgust, as though I had just placed a booger-laden Kleenex on the table. "Exactly what is that?"

"Er . . . ," I said. "It *was* a memo from El Capitan . . ."

"Who's that?" Zoe asked.

"The leader of the Croatoan. I think. And he or she was saying that their mission, Operation Downfall, is scheduled for tomorrow morning at ten a.m. I also have a letter of George Washington's which states that the Croatoan exists and then gives directions to their hideout in invisible ink." I searched through my pockets, but came up empty. "Only, I might have lost it in the river."

"You had a message of Washington's in invisible ink?" Agent Taco asked me dubiously.

"I know how that sounds, but it's true. Washington was the first spymaster for the United States. His message led us to the hideout in the first place. I'm sorry I lost it, but"—I pointed to the remains of the soggy memo—"I can assure you, this was serious evidence."

"It doesn't *look* like serious evidence," Agent Taco said. "It looks like a joke. I'm growing tired of your shenanigans, Ripley. This has all gone far enough—"

"Ben doesn't joke," Zoe said suddenly.

Agent Taco glared at her, obviously unhappy to have been interrupted. "What was that?"

Zoe was still staring at the soggy paper on the table. "Ben doesn't joke. I mean, he *does*. About things that are funny. Like ducks wearing hats. But not about something like this."

"So . . . you believe me now?" I asked her.

"I believe that *you* believe it," Zoe admitted. "I understand that Erica could trick you into thinking the Croatoan was manipulating her, but . . . I can't imagine you ever fabricating evidence. And even if you *did* fabricate it, why would you ruin it before showing it to us? That doesn't make any sense." She tried to meet my eyes, but couldn't bring herself to do it, as though she was embarrassed by how she had doubted me. So she turned to Agent Taco instead. "Maybe we should follow up on this."

"At least go check out the old mill at the falls," I said. "There was plenty of other evidence for the attack there. And for all their other schemes as well. There's a whole room full of it in the basement."

Agent Taco looked back and forth between us. Then she took out her phone and made a call.

I could hear the other person answer. "Hello?"

"Agent Rao, this is Agent Taco."

"Nora Taco?" Agent Rao asked, laughing. "Or do you mean Agent Croatoan?"

Agent Taco winced and looked to me accusingly. "Thanks a lot."

"Sorry," I said.

Agent Rao stopped laughing. "What's up?"

"I'm still in the interrogation room with Ben Ripley. He

truly seems to believe that the Croatoan exists and is plotting to blow up the Washington Monument tomorrow at ten a.m."

There was a pause at the other end. Then Agent Rao said, "Catherine Hale, Erica Hale, and Mike Brezinski have all independently claimed the exact same thing in their interrogations. We've been monitoring them all. Their stories match up perfectly."

"That wouldn't happen if they were all lying, right?" Zoe asked.

"It's possible, but highly unlikely," Agent Taco told her, then said to Agent Rao, "Ripley claims the Croatoan was using an old mill near the falls as a base . . ."

"Ripley's accomplices claimed the same thing," Agent Rao said. "So we have a team on-site to investigate."

"And . . . ?" Agent Taco asked.

"The mill's been burned down. The fire started only minutes after you pulled these guys out of the river."

Agent Taco frowned. "Sounds like someone's trying to cover their tracks."

"That's our assessment too," Agent Rao said. "So we're considering this a credible threat. Cease your interrogation at once and convene in the hub."

"Will do." Agent Taco hung up and looked to me. "Agent Ripley, it appears that I may have misjudged you.

Please accept my apologies." She sounded more businesslike than apologetic, as if this was something she just wanted to get out of the way as quickly as possible.

Still, I was relieved to hear it. "Apology accepted," I said.

Agent Taco stood abruptly and headed for the door. "Both of you, come with me."

Zoe and I snapped to our feet and followed her.

The moment we were out the door, it became evident that we were in the basement of the CIA. I recognized the hallways from the previous day.

Agent Taco walked at such a brisk pace, we practically had to run to keep up with her. "Agent Zibbell, you'll accompany me back to my office. We have a lot to follow up on."

That single statement confirmed what I had been suspecting throughout my interrogation. "So . . . you've offered Zoe the position as junior DADD agent?"

"Yes. She has shown the determination and skill necessary for the position. I *did* tell you there was only a limited time to accept my offer."

"I know," I said, still feeling a pang of jealousy. "So, are you taking me to whatever division is helping defeat the Croatoan?"

"No." Agent Taco looked at me as though I was missing something that should have been incredibly obvious. "If your intelligence is credible, this is now a domestic terrorist group planning an attack on American soil. It's no longer CIA jurisdiction."

My spirits sank as understanding descended on me. "You mean . . . ?"

"Your services are no longer required," Agent Taco said coldly. "You're off the mission."

WITNESS PROTECTION

CIA headquarters
Langley, Virginia
April 17
1745 hours

"How can I be off the mission?" I asked angrily, following Agent Taco through the bowels of the CIA. "There wouldn't even *be* a mission without me."

"For starters, you're off the mission because you're a *child*," Agent Taco said.

"So?" I demanded. "I've been on plenty of missions already."

"Those were extreme circumstances. And not all of those were officially sanctioned. On quite a few, you'd gone rogue, which is generally frowned on at the Agency."

"I only went rogue because the Agency couldn't be trusted," I pointed out. "And I succeeded where the Agency had failed."

"Even so, you are still only a student," Agent Taco said.

I pointed at Zoe. "She's only a student too! And yet, you're still keeping her working on this!"

"Agent Zibbell is helping me wrap up our mission at DADD," Agent Taco reminded me. "She is not going up against a terrorist cell."

"Tracking down undercover agents could still be dangerous," I argued.

"It usually isn't," Agent Taco said. "When you catch a mole, they tend to give up very quickly and often cry a great deal. To be honest, yesterday was the most action I've seen at this job."

"Really?" Zoe asked, now looking disappointed.

"Really. I've never been shot at once in all my years here."

"Oh," Zoe said sadly.

"That's generally regarded as a *good* thing," Agent Taco told her, then looked to me. "Meanwhile, counterterrorism can be far more hazardous. You may have had some success before, but you are still only in your second year of training. You have much to learn yet—and our enemies can be deadly."

Agent Taco had a point. It struck me that I was arguing to be placed in danger, to confront a fanatical organization that had already tried to kill me twice that day alone. A year before, I would probably have been arguing the opposite; I would have been perfectly happy to sit on the sidelines and let someone else risk their life. But things had changed during my time at spy school. Not only was I more competent but I was also less sure of the competence of other people.

Agent Taco gave me a hard stare. "You're worried that, if you're not involved, this mission won't succeed, aren't you?"

"Of course not," I said, but in truth, Agent Taco had read my mind. That was exactly what I feared. Although I also felt that we should bring Erica and Catherine in as well, wherever they might have been.

Agent Taco knew I was lying, and she bristled at it. "There are thousands of extremely qualified, capable, and accomplished people at this agency. I realize you have had some unfortunate experiences with a few corrupt agents, but I have worked hard to eradicate all those bad apples . . ."

"I'm the one who found that list of corrupt agents in the first place," I reminded her. "Along with Erica and Mike and Catherine Hale. So wouldn't it make sense to have all of us helping out with this mission?"

"No." Agent Taco led us into an elevator and we began

to ride upward. "This agency generally works in a very different way than what you have experienced. In fact, the entire intelligence community works differently from that. Each agency is tasked with separate directives, and within those agencies, there are specialized divisions with specific areas of expertise. When one agency comes across a threat that is the jurisdiction of another agency, we pass that intelligence along and trust the other agency to take care of it. That's what is happening now. A domestic terrorist group like the Croatoan plotting an attack on American soil falls under the jurisdiction of the FBI and Homeland Security, not the CIA. So it's their job to handle it, not ours."

"So . . . you're going to just step aside as well?" I asked.

"My job is weeding out covert agents, not counterterrorism. So, yes, I'm going to let others handle this. Speaking of which . . ."

The elevator doors slid open, revealing Agent Heather Durkee. "Hello!" she exclaimed cheerfully. "It's so nice to see you again!"

We emerged into an underground parking garage. However, it appeared to be a secret underground garage, designed so that people could come and go from the Agency without being seen. There was no employee parking. The only vehicles in it were of the type that the CIA used for covert operations, designed to look like they were not CIA vehicles at all: floral delivery trucks, airport shuttles for hotels that didn't actually exist, and . . .

Gas company vans. Like the one I had seen parked in front of my own house that morning. Which made me realize it was DADD who had been parked there, keeping an eye out for me, and not the Croatoan.

That wasn't quite as surprising to me as Agent Durkee's presence. I quickly grasped what that meant—and I wasn't happy about it. "I'm being put under federal witness protection?"

"Your life *has* been in constant peril," Agent Durkee told me pleasantly. "The Agency believes that it's too dangerous to send you back to school for the time being. So you get to hang with me for a bit!"

I frowned, despite myself.

"Oh, come on!" Agent Durkee said, looking slightly offended. "It won't be that bad. So let's turn that frown upside down!"

"It's nothing personal," I said. "It's just that . . ."

". . . you feel like you've just been given a babysitter," Agent Durkee concluded correctly. "I understand. But this is nothing to be ashamed of. Agents are placed under temporary protection all the time. And you won't be alone. All your friends are coming, see?"

She led me to a shuttle bus with tinted windows. On the side were the words "Happy Acres Home for the Aged and Infirm." Agent Durkee opened the door to reveal that Mike, Erica, and Catherine were already seated inside, waiting for us.

The three of them didn't look happy to be there either. Even Catherine was surprisingly sullen. Only Agent Durkee seemed pleased; she had the unbridled glee of an entertainer at a toddler's birthday party. "All aboard!" she announced exuberantly, then made a train whistle. "Wooo-wooo! The shuttle is about to leave the station!"

Zoe hadn't met Agent Durkee yet. She gave Agent Taco a *You've got to be kidding me* look.

Behind Agent Durkee's back, Agent Taco gave Zoe an *I know what you're talking about* look in return. Then she pointed me toward the shuttle. "Agent Ripley, you have your orders."

There didn't seem to be any point in arguing with her. So I climbed inside the shuttle and took my seat.

Zoe stayed outside, standing by Agent Taco, looking quite pleased that she wasn't being shipped off with the rest of us.

Erica immediately grasped what was going on. "You made *her* your junior agent?" she asked Agent Taco angrily.

"She betrayed her friends!" Mike exclaimed.

"That's exactly the sort of person we're looking for at DADD," Agent Taco said. "The kind of person who doesn't show any loyalty to their friends at all."

Zoe grimaced at this.

"Quite often, our friends *are* the ones who turn out to be double agents," Agent Taco clarified. "So I need people on my team who won't let friendship get in the way of their work."

"Then DADD is the last place I'd ever want to work," Mike grumbled.

Erica sank back in her seat, glaring at Zoe so irately, I felt I needed to say something in Zoe's defense. "You *have* said yourself that friendships are liabilities," I pointed out to Erica.

"That was before I had friends," Erica said quietly.

Even though a great number of startling things had happened that day, hearing Erica admit this out loud might have been the most startling thing so far.

Agent Durkee hopped into the driver's seat and did her best to try to lift everyone's spirits—although she used a tone that would have been far more appropriate with children who were still being toilet-trained. "Cheer up, everyone! Federal Witness Protection doesn't have to be a downer. Lying low can be lots of fun. You'll see!" She made another train whistle noise and started the engine.

The shuttle doors slid closed and we headed through the parking garage.

I looked back out the window at Zoe. She waved goodbye, looking upset about how things had worked out, then turned and followed Agent Taco back into the building.

"I can't believe *we're* being forced into this," Erica muttered under her breath. "Zoe's the one who ought to be in Witness Protection. Because next time I see her, I'm going to punch her lights out."

"Erica," Catherine said sternly. "Violence is never the answer to our problems."

Erica asked, "What about back in Paris, when Dane Brammage was trying to kill you, and you had to throw him off the Eiffel Tower in order to survive?"

Catherine frowned at this. "All right, violence is *occasionally* the answer to our problems. But I think this one could be solved with a good, honest talk over a nice cup of tea."

We arrived at an underground guard booth. Beyond it, a steel garage door blocked the exit. Agent Durkee handed her ID and some paperwork to the armed guards, who perused it carefully.

"Why are we even trusting Agent Taco?" Mike asked me. "I thought you said she was Croatoan."

"Turns out, the whole thing with her name being an anagram of Croatoan was only a coincidence."

"Her name is *really* Nora Taco?" Mike asked. "That's terrible."

"I've encountered worse," Catherine said. "There was an agent at MI6 whose name was honestly Winnifred Von Tootlepants."

The guards at the gate seemed to be satisfied with the paperwork and pressed a button that opened the steel garage door. It lowered into the ground, revealing a long tunnel ahead.

Agent Durkee drove us down it, happily singing show tunes.

Despite this, the mood in the back of the shuttle remained glum. In fact, the show tunes probably made it worse. Erica was already in a foul mood, and there were few things she hated more than cheerful people singing show tunes. I had once seen her threaten to disembowel a street busker if he so much as *thought* about starting another verse of "Seasons of Love."

Hoping to change the subject, I looked to Catherine. "They're not letting you work this mission either?"

"I work for British Intelligence, not American Intelligence," she explained. "So I have even less jurisdiction here than all of you do. This isn't the first time something like this has happened, and I'm sure it's far from the last. So rather than make waves and fight the system, I might as well direct my talents elsewhere, such as helping keep an eye on all of you."

"You don't trust the Federal Witness Protection Program to do that?" Mike asked.

"Of course I do," Catherine said, although the look in her eyes said that might not be the case. She obviously didn't want to offend Agent Durkee. "But it can't hurt to have an extra hand around, can it?"

"My thoughts exactly!" Agent Durkee agreed. "The more the merrier, I always say."

Ahead of us, the tunnel ended at another garage door. This one also slid open as we approached, and daylight streamed in.

We emerged from underground at the back of what looked like a normal suburban shopping center, in an alleyway filled with dumpsters and rear entrances to businesses. Two men who were dressed to look like low-rent shopping center security guards were on patrol, but given the way they made eye contact with Agent Durkee, it appeared they were really undercover CIA agents, keeping watch over the tunnel entrance.

We came out of the alley into the shopping center parking lot. It appeared to be a real, working shopping center, which allowed it to provide the perfect cover for a covert entrance to the CIA. It was the kind of place where it made sense for the occasional gas company truck or floral delivery van or eldercare shuttle to be passing by or parked in front of. There was a Thai restaurant, a delicatessen, an ice cream parlor, an office supply store, and, of course, a coffee shop.

Agent Durkee parked in front of the ice cream parlor. Then she turned around to face us. "No need to be alarmed, folks. We're just picking up another agent here. As you know, I'm only the CIA liaison to Witness Protection. The real deal's joining us right now. And then we'll head out to the safe house to meet your parents, Ben."

I sat up, startled. "I thought my parents were already in Florida."

In response to my surprise, Catherine and Erica went on the alert, but before they could do anything, Agent Durkee fired a Taser gun, striking them at close range. Both women jolted uncontrollably as electricity coursed through them, and then collapsed unconscious in their seats.

Mike and I gaped at Agent Durkee, terrified. I expected her to drop the cheerful act and shift into a more menacing persona to match her duplicitous nature. But she still remained surprisingly upbeat and chipper. "Oopsy. I was really hoping I wouldn't have to do that. I guess I've spilled the beans."

"You're with the Croatoan?" Mike asked.

"Oh, I'm not just *with* the Croatoan," Agent Durkee said proudly. "I'm in charge of it."

"You're El Capitan?" I gasped. "But you were in the room with me when Erica attacked the CIA! If she had really tried to kill me, you would have been killed too."

Agent Durkee said, "When I blackmailed Erica here into killing you, I didn't realize she would do something as reckless as firing an RPG at the CIA. I thought she'd just poison your chocolate milk or something subtle like that. But being present at the scene of the attack *did* make me look like a victim, rather than the mastermind, which kept me above suspicion. So I guess everything worked out just peachy."

I had a memory of Agent Durkee going pale at the sight of the blast at the CIA. At the time, I had thought she was concerned for me and my family, but now I realized that she'd been shaken by how close she had come to getting killed by her own evil scheme.

I suddenly felt myself overcome with anger. Agent Durkee hadn't only put my life in danger—she had endangered my parents as well. I glanced at the Taser in her hands, wondering if I had the skill to overpower her before she could shoot me.

Agent Durkee sensed this and pointed the Taser directly at me. "Don't get any ideas, or I'll zap you, too."

"You can't drive and keep that aimed at us," Mike said.

"I know that, silly," Agent Durkee said. "I really am picking up someone else here. Only, he's not with the Federal Witness Protection Program. That was just a little fib. He's a partner in crime. In fact, I believe you know him."

The passenger door opened and someone else got in, holding a gun in one hand and a triple-scoop ice-cream cone in the other.

My nemesis, Murray Hill.

INCARCERATION

Virginia suburbs near the CIA

April 17

1800 hours

"It's nice to see you guys again," Murray said gleefully, his mouth full of ice cream. "How have you been?"

The last time I had seen him had been a few weeks earlier, in Paris. He had been in relatively good shape then, the result of being incarcerated in a spy school holding facility where he had little to do but work out and nothing to eat but healthy food. Since then, his typically horrendous eating habits had quickly caught back up with him. His face was undergoing what was most likely a chocolate-induced profusion of pimples, and he had already developed a startlingly large potbelly, which bulged beneath his sweat-shirt.

I ignored Murray and looked to Agent Durkee, who was now driving us through the suburbs. "Where are my parents?"

Murray frowned. He didn't like to be ignored. "Don't you want to hear what I've been up to since Paris?"

"Not really," I said, then shifted my focus to Agent Durkee once again. "Are they all right?"

"For now," Agent Durkee said. "And you'll see where they are soon enough. I'm taking you there too."

"But I've been doing some *really* cool things," Murray said, sounding a little desperate to be noticed.

"Let me guess," I said. "The whole time you were with us in Europe, acting like you were working with the CIA to help get rid of SPYDER, you were secretly working with the Croatoan. Because getting rid of SPYDER would allow the Croatoan to become more powerful. And you were really cheesed off at SPYDER for trying to kill you."

Murray frowned again, now upset that I had ruined his dramatic revelation. "Er . . . yes. That's basically the gist of it." He turned to Agent Durkee. "Ben has a way of figuring out everything ahead of time. It can be really annoying."

"We've figured out what you're plotting as well," Mike said defiantly. "We know all about your plans to blow up the

Washington Monument. And you won't get away with it. The CIA knows everything."

Agent Durkee laughed. Although, instead of being a menacing, evil villain laugh, it was more of a high-pitched titter. She sounded like a cartoon squirrel. "The CIA can't stop us. Operation Downfall will succeed tomorrow. An example must be made. This country is the rightful property of Spain and it always has been!"

Mike said, "I think there's a few hundred thousand Native Americans who might question that."

Agent Durkee swerved into another parking lot. We hadn't gone very far from the strip mall where we had picked up Murray, which meant we were still quite close to CIA headquarters—not to mention close to where Mike and I had grown up. In fact, we were at a place that Mike and I had visited quite a lot in our lives: our local bowling alley.

"We're going to Bowl-a-Rama?" I asked, confused.

"Guess you don't know everything after all," Murray said proudly. "This is the perfect place to hold hostages. There are cheap rooms upstairs, and it's so loud, no one can ever hear your cries for help."

"Plus, it's near the CIA," Agent Durkee said. "So I don't have to waste too much time in traffic going between my day job and my incarceration center." She pulled into the alley behind the building, which looked very much like the one that covered the secret entrance to the CIA garage. There were loading docks and dumpsters and two big men disguised as security guards. Although, rather than being undercover CIA agents, these guys were Croatoan thugs.

They yanked open the van doors right after Agent Durkee parked. Both had guns, although they probably didn't need them. The men were big enough to snap us like toothpicks if they wanted to.

"Take them upstairs," Agent Durkee ordered in Spanish.

I could speak Spanish fluently, but Erica had always advised me it was better to not let my enemies know that I could understand them. So I didn't let on.

"Sí, El Capitan," the thugs replied. They yanked Mike and me out of the van, then grabbed the limp bodies of Catherine and Erica, slung them over their shoulders, and motioned us toward the bowling alley with their guns.

Murray's point about the noise of the bowling alley was immediately made clear. Even through the wall of the building, the rumble of the bowling balls, the clatter of the pins, and the clanking of the pinsetting equipment was extremely loud. There wasn't anyone around to shout to for help, but even if there had been, they wouldn't have heard us.

"This is so weird," Mike said to me. "I had my ninth birthday party here. And now it's a secret evil lair."

Since the thugs had us at gunpoint, Murray no longer

needed to train his own gun on us. So he stuck it back in its holster, took another mouthful of ice cream, and said to Agent Durkee, "You and I have some business of our own to take care of."

"Do you have what I asked for?" Agent Durkee asked.

"It's in a safe place," Murray replied cryptically. "Do you have my money?"

"It's upstairs." Agent Durkee led the way through the back door of Bowl-A-Rama.

This took us into a narrow hallway behind the pinsetting equipment at the end of the bowling alleys. It seemed to be designed to allow maintenance workers access to the machinery. The noise was now as deafening as front-row seats at a rock concert.

I was hoping that Catherine and Erica were only pretending to be asleep. The narrow alley seemed like the perfect place for them to catch the thugs off guard, quickly knock them out, and then help us escape.

Instead, they remained stubbornly unconscious.

A staircase headed up to the floor above the bowling alley. Agent Durkee and Murray led the way up it, while the guys with the guns stayed at the rear.

As Murray started upstairs, a small black pebble that had been wedged in the sole of his shoe came loose and clattered onto the step in front of me. I pretended to stumble on the stairs, dropping to my knees, and quickly palmed the pebble. Then I got back to my feet and kept going up.

The thugs didn't seem concerned by my behavior, thinking I was merely being a clumsy kid, but Mike whispered, "What's so special about that rock?"

In the din of the bowling alley, it seemed safe to speak. Even though there were bad guys only a few feet from us on either side, they couldn't hear us. "There's a forensic geology division of the CIA," I explained. "They can analyze a rock and tell you what part of the world it came from. Erica and I used it once before. Which means we can tell where Murray's been since Paris . . . maybe."

As garrulous as Murray was, I was pretty sure he was hiding something—because Murray was *always* hiding something. I knew that examining the pebble was a long shot to finding out what that was; forensic geology had its limitations. But at the moment, I was willing to take any clue I could get.

Although, before I could get to the forensic geology lab, I still had some other things to do. Like escaping the Croatoan and defeating their evil plans.

Mike looked as though he had many more questions to ask about forensic geology, but we arrived at the floor above the bowling alley and the noise of the pinsetters lessened. Not by much, but still enough that we had to watch what we said.

A hallway led between two rooms, both of which had an imposing steel door. Agent Durkee unlocked one door, revealing a room that was entirely empty save for a briefcase.

Agent Durkee took the briefcase and handed it to Murray while the thugs laid Erica and Catherine down on the floor of the room.

Erica and Catherine still remained unconscious. I was finding this quite annoying.

Agent Durkee shut the door again, locking Erica and Catherine in the room.

Murray polished off his ice-cream cone, wiped his hands on his shirt, and then opened the briefcase. It was full of cash. Neat stacks of hundred-dollar bills.

"Now, where's what you owe me?" Agent Durkee asked.

"Right here." Murray hiked up his sweatshirt, revealing that what I had thought was his potbelly was actually padding. A large canvas bag was strapped around his abdomen. He cautiously unfastened it and handed it over. "Be very careful with that," he warned. "I packed it as safely as I could, but still . . . there's enough explosive there to put the Washington Monument into orbit." He gave Agent Durkee a wink and giggled.

Agent Durkee laughed as well, the same high-pitched, cartoon-squirrel titter as before. "Nice doing business with you, Murray."

"You too. Best of luck tomorrow." Murray looked to Mike and me. "Nice seeing you guys, as always. Tell Erica I'm sorry we didn't get to chat on account of her being unconscious and all." With that, he headed back down the hall with his briefcase full of cash, whistling happily.

Agent Durkee opened the door to the second room. "Get in there," she told me.

Normally, it would have been depressing to walk into a holding cell while one of my enemies was escaping with a briefcase full of cash and the others were plotting a massive terrorist attack, but this wasn't so bad. Because my parents were in the room.

They were seated at a spindly card table, playing Parcheesi. Not because they really liked Parcheesi all that much, but because it was the only thing they had been given to do.

They cried out when they saw me and leapt from their seats. I ran to them and gave both a big hug at the same time.

"Have you come to rescue us?" Mom asked.

"Uh . . . no," I said. "The people doing the rescuing usually aren't being held at gunpoint."

"Oh, right," Mom said. "Sorry. This is my first hostage situation. I'm still learning how it all works."

"Mike!" Dad said warmly. "How'd you get mixed up in all this?"

"I've been recruited to spy school too," Mike told him. "I was working with Ben on this mission when everything went south."

"Really?" Dad didn't seem to know whether to be impressed or concerned. "Well, that's very nice to hear—about the spy school. Not the getting captured."

"Are you guys all right?" I asked.

"To be honest, no," Mom said. "I mean, they haven't hurt us or anything, but . . . things have taken a really bad turn since we met that traitor over there." She glared at Agent Durkee.

For the first time since I'd met her, Agent Durkee's cheerful disposition faded. "Traitor?" she repeated. "I am *not* a traitor. I am still loyal to the country of my ancestors, the country that had claim to America first!"

"Are you Native American?" Dad asked honestly.

"I am *Spanish*!" Agent Durkee exclaimed proudly. "Like my parents and their parents and *their* parents. And like them, I am a warrior. A warrior devoted to the noble cause of destroying America so that Spain can once again take its rightful place as the ruler of this land."

"Doesn't look like you've done such a good job," Mike said. "You've been at this for a couple centuries and the United States is still here."

I knew exactly what he was doing. He was following

Berloff's First Rule of Provocation: If you want to get a bad guy to talk, act like you're not impressed by them.

It worked. Agent Durkee flushed angrily. "We have struck many great blows against this country! We have brought America to its knees time and time again. But tomorrow, we will finish the job once and for all! We will finally decapitate the horrendous beast that is America, leaving this country in ruins—and all the world will rejoice in our victory!"

It was quite a dramatic speech. I got the sense that Agent Durkee might have practiced it in front of a mirror. She seemed very pleased with herself at the end of it.

"I'm sorry," I said. "I didn't hear any of that over the bowling alley. Could you repeat it?"

"What?" Agent Durkee gave a groan of exasperation, then launched into the entire speech once again. I had heard it all perfectly the first time, but I just wanted to annoy her. She said it louder this time, but every word and inflection were exactly the same. She had definitely practiced it. She wasn't just doing it for our benefit but for the two thugs who worked for her as well. This time, she finished with a great theatrical flourish.

"Sorry," I said. "I still didn't get that."

"Me either," Mike agreed, fully aware of what I was doing. "It's crazy loud in here."

"Oh, for crying out loud!" Agent Durkee shouted. "I'll

say this one more time, but listen closer, will you?" And with that, she launched into the speech a third time, yelling at the top of her lungs and gesticulating like she was performing *Hamlet* onstage.

By this point, my parents had caught on that I was only making her do this for fun, and they were doing their best not to laugh at the performance, putting their hands over their mouths to cover their giggling. But I had another agenda as well. While Agent Durkee was distracted, I cased the room, trying to figure out a way to escape.

Unfortunately, I couldn't find one. The walls were thick and windowless, and the single doorway was blocked by two armed men the size of young elephants. The rest of the room was empty, save for the folding chairs my parents had been sitting in, the card table, and the Parcheesi game. The table and chairs were so flimsy, they looked like they would shatter if I banged them against the wall.

Agent Durkee wrapped up her speech once again.

"I really have to apologize," my mother said. "But I still missed a lot of that."

The rest of us all chimed in in agreement.

"You have got to be kidding me!" Agent Durkee exploded.

"Don't be upset with us now," Dad said. "We didn't ask to be held captive over a bowling alley. If you wanted us to hear your dramatic speeches, you should have held us hostage someplace quieter. Like a library or a day spa."

"I'm only going to say this one more time," Agent Durkee said. "So listen closely . . ." She paused, realizing that my parents and Mike were now giggling uncontrollably. "You guys are messing with me, aren't you?"

"Not at all," Mike said, snickering into his hand. "Please, go right ahead. But try to be loud this time."

Agent Durkee steamed at all of us. "You're all a bunch of jerks, you know that?"

"*We're* jerks?" I asked, incredulous. "You have started wars and crashed the stock market and assassinated presidents!"

"To rid the world of a country that doesn't deserve to exist!" Agent Durkee proclaimed. "And tomorrow, it *won't* exist anymore."

"Sorry," Mom said. "Could you speak louder?"

"All of you think you're really funny, don't you?" Agent Durkee asked. "I bet you won't think it's so funny when I leave you to rot in this room for the rest of your lives." With that, she led her goons out the door and then threw all three locks on the other side.

Mike immediately started laughing again.

"This part isn't really that funny," I told him.

"It *is*," Mike insisted. "The look on her face when she realized we were pranking her? That was priceless. Oh, and also, I still have this." He reached into his underwear and pulled out a plastic evidence bag that appeared to be empty.

"You've been carrying a plastic bag in your underwear all day?" my father asked, concerned. "Why?"

"And why should we be happy about that?" Mom added.

I came closer to Mike, looking into the bag. It *wasn't* empty. It held the tiny flake of RDX explosive Catherine had pried off the toy car earlier that day. "You still have the explosive?" I asked excitedly.

"I crammed it in my underwear before we jumped into the river," Mike said. "And no one thought to frisk me down there all day."

"You've been carrying a sample of one of the most powerful explosives known to man in your undies all afternoon?" I asked.

"It wasn't exactly my idea of a good time, but yes."

Mom came closer, peering intently at the flake in the bag. "That little thing is an explosive?"

"Yes," Mike said.

"So we can use it to blast our way out of here?" Dad added.

"Yes," Mike said again.

"How?" Mom asked.

Mike pursed his lips thoughtfully. "Er . . . I'm not really sure. I haven't studied explosives yet." He looked to me. "Any ideas?"

"Some," I said. "But they're not very good ones."

"That's still better than what I have," Mike admitted. "Spill them."

So I told Mike what I was thinking. Mike concurred that it wasn't a very good idea, but he still didn't have anything better, so we decided to try it.

We cautiously placed the tiny flake in the keyhole of one of the locks on the door, so that a slight bit was sticking out. Then we took the only thing we could find to throw at it, which was one of the folding chairs. I advised my parents to curl into balls with their arms over their heads.

"How big an explosion do you expect that tiny little thing to make?" Mom asked skeptically.

"Hopefully big enough to blast the locks off the door," I told them.

Mike was the better athlete, so we decided he should throw the chair. We went to the other side of the room. Then I counted to three and Mike whirled around and flung the chair as hard as he could.

Both of us turned and shielded our eyes, just to be on the safe side.

As I had hoped, Mike's aim was spot-on, although the explosion wasn't as big as I had hoped.

It was about a hundred times bigger.

RDX turned out to be much more powerful than either

Mike or I had expected. The resulting blast sounded like a rocket launch and flung both of us into the wall.

When we looked back at the steel door, it wasn't there anymore. It had been blasted out of its frame so hard that it had knocked the door across the hall off its hinges as well. Also, a good portion of the floor was now missing, letting us see down into the bowling alley below.

My parents were staring at the hole, stunned.

Dad asked Mike, "You had an explosive that powerful by your private bits all day?"

"I did not know it was that powerful," Mike admitted. "Otherwise, I would really have reconsidered hiding it in my underwear."

Catherine and Erica peered out of the room across the hall. Both still looked a bit groggy from their time being unconscious, as though perhaps the explosion had just woken them up. "What did you do?" Catherine asked.

"We used the RDX we found," I said.

"It was only a tiny bit," Mike explained. "And it did all this!"

"I warned you it was powerful," Catherine said. "So imagine what a good amount could do to the Washington Monument."

I imagined it—and it gave me the shivers. But as I thought about the Croatoan's plans, something even more frightening occurred to me.

I had made a terrible mistake. I had gotten something very wrong about the Croatoan.

However, I didn't have time to say anything. Both of the Croatoan henchmen were coming for us. They had heard the blast and were charging down the hallway—or what was left of the hallway. Each was holding a weapon.

We did not have any weapons. So we had to run.

Luckily, there was a nice, new, gaping hole in the floor for us to flee through.

Catherine and Erica led the way, jumping down onto the bowling lanes below. Mike and I hung back to make sure my parents could handle it. It was a twenty-foot drop through the hole, and I thought my parents might be reluctant to do it—but having two heavily armed enemy agents running toward us was a very good motivation for action. Mom and Dad didn't hesitate for a second. They ran right past me and leapt down to the lower floor.

Mike and I followed them. We landed in one of the center bowling lanes, close to the end where the pins were.

No one was bowling at the moment. They had all stopped when the explosion had torn the hole in the ceiling and were now watching with surprise as we jumped down into the lane. (In addition, it seemed that the explosion had knocked all the pins down at once, giving everyone simultaneous strikes, so they all had to wait for the pins to reset anyhow.)

In the aftermath of the explosion, it was unusually quiet for a bowling alley. The pinsetters were still whirring and clanking, but the clamor of the rolling balls and falling pins was gone. All the bowlers just stared at us silently.

Catherine and Erica were already racing down the lanes in the direction of the bowlers, heading for the exit. Mom, Dad, Mike, and I followed.

Since it was my local bowling alley, I recognized a few people. There were a couple of kids from school, and some folks who lived near us, although the person who was most agog was Bob Peterson, our boastful neighbor. He gaped at my parents as we ran past them.

"Ronald? Jane?" Bob gasped. "What are you doing?"

"Oh, just running away from some evil henchmen!" Dad exclaimed, thrilled to have Bob see him doing something cool.

Erica and Catherine each grabbed a few bowling balls and heaved them down the lane we had just come up.

Behind us, the Croatoan thugs jumped down through the hole in the ceiling. The moment they landed, the bowling balls arrived, cracking them in the shins and knocking them off their feet. Then the next wave of balls clonked both of them in the head.

"Did you say evil henchmen?" Bob asked, thrown by everything that was happening.

"Yes I did!" Dad yelled. "The family and I are just helping save the country! Sorry I don't have time to talk! Nice seeing you!"

We raced for the exits.

My mother gave my father a stern look. "I don't think you're supposed to be boasting to the neighbors about this."

"Aw, come on," Dad said. "The guy talks about his stupid golf club membership every chance he gets. This is *way* cooler than that."

Back in the bowling lane, the Croatoan thugs staggered to their feet. Neither had been knocked unconscious, but both were seriously dazed. One attempted a shot at us, but was reeling so badly that it went wide and annihilated a neon beer sign, which exploded in a spray of sparks as we ran past it.

We shoved out the doors into the parking lot. A local mom was herding a group of fourth graders into her minivan after a birthday party. The kids were hopped up on cake and ice cream, their faces smeared with icing.

Catherine flashed her badge at the mom. "I'm terribly sorry," she said, "but due to national security issues, I'm afraid I'll have to commandeer your vehicle. Have a nice day."

She said it so sweetly that the harried mother simply handed over the keys. The rest of us piled into the van and deposited the startled fourth graders back in the parking lot. Catherine leapt into the driver's seat and punched the gas. We roared through the parking lot and swerved into traffic.

"Seat belts, everyone," Mom and Catherine told all of us simultaneously.

I realized that introductions still needed to be made. "Mom and Dad, this is Erica Hale and Erica's mom."

"Call me Catherine," Catherine said pleasantly, veering through traffic at seventy miles an hour. We quickly left Bowl-a-Rama and the Croatoan far behind.

"Erica is at school with me," I explained. "Catherine is an agent with MI6."

"Oh, hello," Dad said, looking slightly shell-shocked by everything that had happened. He smiled at Erica. "I've met your father. He seems like a very good spy."

"He's not," Erica said. "He only looks like one."

"On behalf of the entire intelligence community, I apologize for what has happened here," Catherine said, skidding around a corner. "It appears that the very people tasked with protecting you were corrupt, and so you've been plunged into a very dangerous situation. I'm afraid we'll have to find somewhere safe for all of us to lie low until the proper authorities can take care of the Croatoan."

"I don't think we can trust the CIA to take care of the Croatoan," I said.

It was the first chance I'd had to speak since my revelation back at the bowling alley, where I realized that I had made a serious mistake.

Everyone looked to me, concerned.

"Why is that?" Erica asked. "Do you think the Agency has been corrupted again?"

"No, I think the Agency is fine," I replied. "But they're not going to catch the Croatoan tomorrow. They're going to be looking in the wrong place. The Croatoan tricked us. They're not going to attack the Washington Monument at all."

"Then what are they planning to do instead?" Mike said.

"I have no idea," I admitted.

FRUSTRATION

The Pancake Shack

Vienna, Virginia

April 17

2000 hours

I explained everything over pancakes.

We were all starving. My friends and I had barely eaten a thing all day, and my parents had only been given stale bowling alley pizza while being held prisoner.

So we went to my favorite all-day pancake place and ordered a ton of food.

"It doesn't make sense that the Croatoan would blow up the Washington Monument," I said. "That's not the kind of thing that they do."

"They hate America," Catherine countered. "And this would make a great statement against this country."

"You said that before. But the Croatoan doesn't make statements. Ever since Roanoke, they've been working behind the scenes, manipulating events without anyone knowing it was them."

"Ooh!" Dad said, his mouth full of banana nut pancake. "Like evil puppeteers."

"Exactly," I agreed. "They've started wars and crashed the stock market and had presidents killed. Which are all things that directly affected this country in a negative way. But what would blowing up the monument do?"

"It'd make a big mess," Mom suggested, tucking into her waffles.

"Yes," Erica said, pondering this, "but if anything, an attack like that might actually strengthen America. Nothing brings people together like uniting against a common enemy."

"That's a good point," Catherine admitted. She had ordered only plain nonfat yogurt with berries and seemed to be regretting the decision. She was looking hungrily at everyone else's pancakes and waffles.

"Plus," I went on, "did you notice how Murray and Agent Durkee acted when we said the Croatoan was going to blow up the monument? Both of them seemed to think it was funny."

Mike paused, thinking back to this, a forkful of chocolate chip pancakes halfway to his mouth. "Didn't Agent Durkee say the plans to blow up the monument were going to proceed?"

"No," I reminded him. "She said *Operation Downfall* was going to proceed. And then she laughed."

"Oh yeah," Mike said, remembering it now. "She did. And then when Murray said he had enough explosive to send the monument into orbit, he winked at her and both of them laughed. They weren't doing that just to be evil; they were mocking us!" He turned to Catherine. "I think Ben's onto something here."

"So . . . this is all just a hunch?" Catherine asked, gloomily poking at her yogurt. "You don't have any concrete evidence?"

"No," I admitted.

"Then how do you explain what we found at the old mill?"

"It was a ruse," Erica said, understanding what I was thinking. "The Croatoan played us. They knew you were on their trail after finding you at Mount Vernon. So they used that to their advantage. They built a pile of evidence at their hideout that made it *look* like they were planning to hit the Washington Monument, knowing that you'd take it to the CIA and send them off on a wild-goose chase."

"And then they decided to burn down their hideout with

all the evidence in it?" Catherine asked skeptically.

"What self-respecting criminal organization would leave their hideout standing after it was discovered?" Erica asked.

Catherine tapped her fingernails on the table thoughtfully. After a while, she said, "All of you have some valid points, but this is still only a hunch. We just used up every bit of credibility we had getting the CIA to believe that the Croatoan not only exists, but that they're plotting to blow up the monument tomorrow. Now imagine what will happen if we go back to them and say we were wrong, but that we think the Croatoan is plotting to hit something else, only we don't have any evidence to back that up—and we have no idea what the real target is."

"You'll sound like a bunch of nincompoops," Dad said.

The rest of us nodded in agreement sadly, realizing Catherine was right.

"What if we turn in Agent Durkee?" Mike asked. "We know she's working for the Croatoan! We caught her breaking the law!"

"No, you *saw* her breaking the law," Catherine corrected. "And then she got away. If you'd caught her, things might be different."

"Then let's find her," I said.

"Do any of you have the slightest inkling where she might be?" Catherine asked.

"No," I conceded.

"Then tracking her down is going to be very difficult," Catherine said. "And even if we did find her, you don't have any proof to back up your claims that she's a double agent for the Croatoan. It'd just be your word against hers."

"And your word too," Mike said. "That has to mean something, doesn't it? She shot you with a Taser!"

"And thus, I was unconscious for your entire confrontation with her. So I missed out on all the parts where she incriminated herself. Except for the part where she hit me with the Taser, and she could always claim that was an accident. Which happens. Alexander has accidentally shot me with a Taser several times."

"He did?" Dad asked, surprised.

"I told you he wasn't a good spy," Erica said.

Catherine said, "It certainly makes sense to try to track down Agent Durkee and bring her to justice. But it's probably not the fastest way to stop the Croatoan."

"Then what is?" Mom asked.

"Figure out what the Croatoan is truly plotting," Catherine said.

"It must have something to do with the ceremony at the Capitol," Erica said definitively. "The president and most of the government will all be gathered there. It's the perfect place for the Croatoan to strike."

"And, thanks to us, a lot of the security will now be diverted toward the Washington Monument," I added.

"They really ought to cancel the ceremony," Mike said, concerned.

"They won't," Catherine said. "Not until we can produce some concrete evidence. And we need to find some—fast."

She laid out her plans while we polished off our food. She would try to track down Agent Durkee, while Mike, Erica, and I would return to school and do our best to deduce what the Croatoan was really plotting. Although first, we had to protect my parents.

Alexander Hale would take care of that. He had a hidden lair at the academy that he referred to as the Eagle's Nest. I had been there once before, shortly after arriving at spy school. Catherine called Alexander, and he immediately agreed to shepherd my parents to the Eagle's Nest and keep watch over them. Alexander wasn't my ideal bodyguard—as he wasn't that competent and had rendered himself unconscious while trying to fend off enemy assailants on more than one occasion—but I didn't have much choice. Besides, he wasn't corrupt, which was more than I could say for the last agent who had been placed in charge of protecting my parents.

Then Catherine set off to find Agent Durkee, and Erica called Chester Snodgrass.

After all, I still had the pebble from Murray's shoe.

Chester Snodgrass was a specialist in forensic geology in the Department of Evidence Assessment. He had helped us determine the provenance of a specific rock before, and he listened attentively as Erica told him about the pebble and how we were trying to discover where Murray had been, hoping it would give us a clue to what the Croatoan was plotting. Unfortunately, Chester didn't feel he could be of much help.

"Forensic geology takes a great deal of time," he warned on the phone. "You only have hours, while this will probably take *days*. And even then, there's a good chance it will be inconclusive."

"It's better than nothing," Erica said. "And right now, this is virtually the only lead we have." So she headed off to deliver the pebble to Chester while Mike and I returned to our dorm to ponder what the Croatoan might be up to.

We even brought Jawa aboard, since he was so smart. We brainstormed, we spitballed ideas, and we scrutinized the one piece of evidence we had left: the ruined, damp memo from the Croatoan's hideout. But we came up empty. By midnight, we were all bleary-eyed with exhaustion and even more frustrated than before. Finally, Mike pointed out that this wasn't doing any of us any good and suggested everyone should retire to their rooms and take a nap.

I followed his first suggestion but ignored the second. Instead, I sat at my desk, staring in vain at the memo, struggling to come up with some plausible plot of the Croatoan's. But my brain was fried. I kept nodding off, dreaming up schemes, and then snapping awake, thinking I had cracked the case, only to realize that what I had come up with was delirious, such as the Croatoan attacking Washington with giant robot wombats—or plotting to airdrop millions of mice on Wisconsin to devour our national cheese reserves. Eventually, fatigue won out and I passed out facedown at my desk.

I woke several hours later with the disturbing sensation that someone was in my room.

I sat up quickly, fearing an assassin . . .

"It's only me," Erica said.

Since I was still at my desk, seated in the only chair in the room, she was sitting on my bed. If she was tired, she wasn't showing it. Instead, she looked like her usual, competent, perfectly composed self. And yet, I couldn't conceive of any possible reason she could be there that wasn't an emergency situation.

"What's wrong?" I asked.

"Nothing," she said. "Well, apart from a Colonial Era group of fanatics plotting to overthrow our government. But that's not why I'm here."

"Then why . . . ?"

"You never doubted me through all this. When other people did."

"Look, I know you're upset with Zoe, but—"

"I'm not just talking about Zoe. I'm talking about *everyone*. The entire CIA. Probably every other branch of the government too. And I'm not blaming them. I even understand why Zoe did what she did. I just don't like how she used you to do it. But you . . . I fired a grenade at the room where you were supposed to be at the CIA, and you still had faith in me."

"If I had been the one shooting at you, you would have had faith in me."

"Not necessarily."

My jaw dropped slightly. "Really?"

Erica broke her gaze from mine. "Maybe. With anyone else, I would think the bad guys had gotten to them. That they were won over with promises of money or power. It happens all the time. I would never have thought Joshua Hallal would have turned—but then he did. So after that, I figured anyone could be corrupted. And then you came along. You're the kind of person I thought Joshua *was*. . . ."

"And you're still worried I might betray you someday?"

Erica turned to face me again. There was a sadness in her eyes that I had never really seen before. "You know, when I was a kid, I used to feel bad about my sister."

"Because she got to have a normal life and you didn't?"

"No." Erica looked at me like I was crazy. "Who wants a normal life? I felt bad because I was being groomed to be a spy and she wasn't."

"Oh."

"Trixie will never get to stop an assassination—or uncover a massive conspiracy to overthrow the government—or prevent Antarctica from being melted and flooding the world. But now I realize there might be something good about her life."

"She'll never have people try to kill her?"

"I said *good*. Not boring." Erica paused a moment, then said, "She won't ever have to worry about who she can trust. Or fear that her friends will become liabilities. Or run away from relationships because they're dangerous in this business."

I didn't really know what to say to that. The only time Erica had ever opened up to me like this before was when she had been under the influence of truth serum. For a moment, I wondered if I was still asleep; this conversation seemed like something I might have dreamed.

Erica said, "According to my mother, the girls back at your old school today were flirting with you like crazy."

I felt myself turning red. "Back when I was in school with them, they didn't even know I existed."

"And now they do. Mom says they were all really pretty."

"I'm not interested in any of those girls," I said.

I wasn't sure, but I thought that, for the briefest moment, a smile played across Erica's lips. Then she said, "Why not?"

"They're all too normal for me."

Erica nodded at that. "Anyhow. I just wanted to thank you for having faith in me today. And to let you know that I don't take that lightly."

"Sure thing," I said. "And, for the record, I know you've always had faith in—"

I didn't get to finish the sentence, because Erica suddenly lunged at me.

REVELATION

Armistead Dormitory

The Academy of Espionage

April 18

0815 hours

I hate to admit it, but for a moment, I actually thought Erica was attacking me. I was still tired and groggy, and it had been an extremely long day, during which I had been asked to question the loyalty of my friends over and over. So when Erica sprang toward me, the idea crossed my mind that I had gotten everything wrong and that she really was a Croatoan double agent, and that I was now in serious trouble.

But instead of kicking my butt . . . Erica hugged me.

I probably would have been less surprised if she had attacked me.

I wasn't sure if the hug was romantic or merely thankful, but I wasn't going to question it. Erica generally had the aura of someone who would need an instruction manual for giving a hug, but she turned out to be quite good at it.

It ended far sooner than I hoped it would. After a few seconds, Erica released me and took a step back, looking slightly embarrassed about what she had done.

"I've owed you that for a while," she said.

I looked at her blankly. Between the lack of sleep and the sudden hug, my brain wasn't functioning so well.

"Right after you came here," Erica explained. "On our first mission. We infiltrated the principal's office, and you couldn't remember a key piece of information, so I promised you a hug if you could remember it, and then you did."

"That was four hundred and thirty days ago!" I exclaimed, then added quickly, "Not that I've been counting."

Erica smiled, amused. "This seemed like an appropriate time to give it to you."

I thought about trying to explain that there had been *lots* of appropriate times to give me a hug over the last 430 days, but then decided that might seem thankless. And then I got distracted by the fact that, even though Erica was no longer hugging me, she was still standing somewhat close to me, so maybe what I *should* have been thinking about was kissing her.

However, I didn't make a move right away.

I was confused, thinking that Erica might have changed her mind about dating me—but I still wasn't 100 percent sure. And one thing you didn't want to do around Erica was make any sudden, unexpected movements. Not unless you wanted to find yourself curled in the fetal position on the floor, racked with pain.

So I just sat there, looking into her eyes, wondering if she wanted me to kiss her or not. And then I gathered my nerve, thinking, to heck with it, I would kiss her anyhow.

But before I could make a move, Erica ducked away from me, sat on my bed, and began speaking as though we were in the middle of a completely different conversation. "The thing about the Croatoan is that they're extremely unpredictable . . . ," she began.

I couldn't understand what was going on.

Until Chip Schacter burst into my room a second later.

Now I got it. Erica had heard him coming and had not wanted to be caught doing anything that appeared even remotely romantic. She had done such a great job of looking normal—or at least as normal as Erica got—that Chip didn't suspect a thing.

I had never been a particularly violent person, but at that

moment, I gave serious thought to throttling Chip for interrupting us. Or knocking him unconscious so that Erica and I could be alone together again.

". . . so we can't possibly guess what they'll do next," Erica finished, then looked at Chip. "What are you doing here?"

"I hear you're all figuring out what the Croatoan's up to," Chip said.

"We're *trying*," I clarified. "We haven't had any success."

"Well, why'd you ask Jawa for help but not me?"

"Because you're an idiot," Erica said.

Chip appeared to take this as teasing, unaware that Erica had really meant it. He noticed the ruined memo lying on my desk and picked it up. "Is this your evidence?"

I realized, to my chagrin, that Chip wasn't going to leave anytime soon—and that whatever moment I'd had with Erica was ruined. "Yes."

Chip squinted at the blurred words on the page. "What's this say? I can't read it."

"It got ruined when we jumped in the river," I explained. "It was a memo telling everyone that Operation Downfall was to proceed at ten a.m. tomorrow . . ."

". . . which would be *today*," Erica put in.

". . . and then there were some weird quotes about how they had to be ready for sacrifice," I went on. "Something like 'Any moment might be our last and everything is . . .'"

"'. . . more beautiful because we're doomed,'" Chip finished. Although he wasn't looking at the memo at all. He was saying it from memory.

Erica narrowed her eyes at him suspiciously. "How do you know that?"

"It's from the *Iliad*," Chip said.

"I knew I'd heard that somewhere before!" I exclaimed. The *Iliad* was the ancient Greek poem that told the story of the Trojan War. I had tried reading it in sixth grade, though I had ended up skimming most of it to get to the good parts, like where the Greeks scammed the Trojans with the Trojan horse. Now I sat at my desk and ran a quick search on my computer. It only took a few seconds to find what I was looking for. "The other quote in the memo is from the *Iliad* too: 'Let me not then die ingloriously and without a struggle . . .'"

"'. . . but let me first do some great thing that shall be told among men hereafter,'" Chip said.

I turned to him, astonished. "Wow. You know that poem really well."

"The *Iliad* was a poem?" Chip asked, surprised. "I thought it was just a graphic novel."

Erica was so intrigued, she didn't even think to insult Chip for this. "One quote from the *Iliad* would make sense," she said, pacing back and forth in my tiny room. "But two indicates a bit of an obsession. El Capitan has the *Iliad* on the brain. So . . . why would that be?"

"What's all the excitement about?" Mike was standing in my doorway with Jawa, both looking like they had just stumbled out of bed.

"Chip realized the quotes from the memo were really from the *Iliad*," I said.

"Chip knows the *Iliad*?" Mike asked.

"Chip knows something, period?" Jawa asked.

"Why's everyone always surprised when I know stuff?" Chip asked, sounding hurt.

Erica said, "When something only happens once every few years, it's considered a special occasion." She had to stop pacing, because with five people in it, my tiny room was now as crowded as a subway car at rush hour. "There might be something meaningful about the *Iliad* for Agent Durkee beyond those quotes. What's significant about that story?"

"The Trojan horse, obviously," Mike said. "The most ridiculous military tactic of all time."

"Ridiculous?" Jawa asked. "That was a historic victory!"

"The Greeks hid inside a giant horse!" Mike said. "And the Trojans fell for it like a bunch of morons. There they are, fighting a war for ten years, and then one day, all of a sudden, there's a giant wooden horse sitting outside the city and all the Greeks are gone. So the Trojans just bring it inside their city and don't even think, 'Hey, maybe we should check this thing to see if any of our enemies are hiding inside it'? If you're going to be that dumb, you deserve to lose the war. It's the worst ending to a story ever."

"Except for *The Wizard of Oz*," Chip said.

Jawa looked at him, shocked. "What's your problem with *The Wizard of Oz*?"

"The Wicked Witch was made out of sugar!" Chip exclaimed. "All they had to do to kill her was pour water on her! How is that possible? Did the witch never take a shower? Or get caught in a rainstorm? Or have a drink of water? How much of a threat can you be if someone can kill you by spitting on you?"

"I can't believe this," Mike said. "But Chip's actually making sense."

"I can't believe we're talking about *The Wizard of Oz*," I said. "We're supposed to be figuring out why the *Iliad* is important to the Croatoan."

"I think I might know," Jawa said solemnly. He was staring at the Croatoan's memo. He pointed at the smear of bright blue paint on it. "Tell me about this. Was this the only paint in the room?"

"No," Erica said. "There was quite a lot, splattered everywhere."

"All this color?" Jawa asked.

"Almost," I said, doing my best to remember. "There were a few splotches of a blue that were close to this . . ."

"Like someone was fiddling with the paint, trying to get the color exactly right," Erica said. "Is something important about the color?"

"This is a very specific blue," Jawa said. "And I know where I've seen it before." He got on my computer and brought up some images.

They were of a sculpture. A sculpture of a giant rooster. It was exactly the same color blue as the smear of paint on the memo.

"It's called *Hahn/Cock*," Jawa explained. "It was displayed in Trafalgar Square in London at one point, but now . . ."

"Oh no," Erica and I said at once.

Both of us were focused on the same photo of the sculpture. It was on the roof of a building. And in the distance behind it was the dome of the US Capitol.

". . . it's on the rooftop viewing area of the modern art wing of the National Gallery of Art," Jawa concluded.

"That building has a direct line of sight to the Capitol dome," Erica said, sounding gravely concerned. "And it's not far away. From up there, the Croatoan could launch a good chunk of RDX at the ceremony today and blow everyone to bits."

"The Secret Service must know about that spot, though," Chip pointed out. "They lock down every rooftop within a mile radius hours before an event like this. I'll bet no one's been able to access this area since last night."

"But what if the Croatoan has had agents on the rooftop since *before* last night?" I asked.

Everyone stared at the image of the giant blue statue.

"You think they built a Trojan rooster?" Mike asked.

"Sort of," I said. "The sculpture was already there. So they wouldn't have to build anything at all. Or trick the museum into bringing it inside. They'd only have to visit ahead of time, cut a hatch in the statue, get inside, and then have someone on the outside seal them in."

"Which explains why they were working so hard to find the exact right color of blue paint," Erica said. "So they could cover up the damage to the sculpture and not have anyone notice."

"Let me get this straight," Chip said. "You're thinking that agents from the Croatoan visited the museum yesterday and sealed themselves inside this giant rooster? And now they're going to sneak back out and use their position on the roof to attack the ceremony at the Capitol?"

"It could work," Jawa said thoughtfully. "I've spent a lot of time at that museum . . ."

"'Cause you're a nerd," Chip teased.

"Liking art doesn't make you a nerd!" Jawa said testily. "It makes you cultured!"

"Guys, focus," Erica said.

"Right," Jawa agreed. "Like I said, I've spent a lot of time at that museum. That statue is easily big enough to hold a few people and a device big enough to launch the RDX."

"But how would they get the launcher into the museum in the first place?" Mike asked. "There's security at the museum, right?"

"Easy," Erica answered. "The rooftop is wide open. So they could have parachuted in last night and then hidden in the rooster."

"I'm sure the Secret Service has swept the museum twenty times today," I added. "But they'd never expect someone to be *inside* the sculpture. So once the building is declared clear, the Croatoan would have free rein to do whatever they wanted up there."

Mike asked, "Won't the Secret Service have someone stationed up on that roof today?"

"Definitely," Erica said. "But only one or two agents. And they'll be focused on everything around the museum, not the chicken itself. So the Croatoan could take them by surprise."

We took a few moments to consider all of this.

"It could work," I said finally. "The Croatoan is calling

this Operation Downfall. I thought that meant they were going to knock over the Washington Monument—but it could also mean toppling the US government. The president and most of Congress will be at the Capitol today. Murray sold Agent Durkee a big chunk of explosive last night. Enough to take out most of our government in one shot."

"Last night, Agent Durkee said the Croatoan was going to decapitate the horrendous beast that is America," Mike added. "That sounds like a metaphor for wiping out all our heads of state at once."

"So we're in agreement," Jawa said. "The Croatoan is using a Trojan rooster. Now what do we do about it?"

I looked at my watch. It was just past eight thirty in the morning. "We tell the FBI, Homeland Security, and the Secret Service. They've got almost ninety minutes to act on this. That should be plenty of time."

Everyone nodded, thinking that made sense.

There was only one problem:

No one believed us.

AERIAL ASSAULT

Armistead Dormitory

The Academy of Espionage

April 18

0845 hours

"A Trojan chicken?" Zoe asked incredulously.
"You honestly think that's what the Croatoan is up to?"

"Yes," I said. "Although technically, it's a Trojan rooster."
We were in Zoe's dorm room. Zoe was still in her pajamas
and had obviously been asleep when I had urgently knocked
on her door. Her hair was piled on her head at an odd angle,
making her look slightly lopsided.

Erica, Mike, Chip, Jawa, and I had split up to try to
reach someone at the FBI, Homeland Security, or the Secret

Service with our ideas. We figured Erica had the best shot, as several of her family members were highly respected agents with strong connections in intelligence. Mike was trying to reach Jemma Stern, the president's daughter. Jawa and Chip were seeking out some professors, while I had been sent to see if Zoe could use her newfound connections at the CIA.

I had told her about everything that had happened over the past few hours, from Agent Durkee's betrayal to our escape to our discovery of what the Croatoan's plot really was. "I know it sounds crazy . . . ," I continued.

"It sounds far worse than that," Zoe said bluntly. She caught a glimpse of herself in the mirror, seemed to grow self-conscious about her hair, and grabbed a brush.

"Still, if you could tell Agent Taco about it, then maybe she could alert someone at the FBI."

Zoe shook her head. "I can't go to her with this, Ben."

"Sure you can. We know Agent Taco has contacts at the FBI. She already alerted them about the Croatoan attacking the Washington Monument . . ."

"That's the problem. It was already a hard-enough sell convincing people that the Croatoan exists. And that they're going after the monument. But now, after we've done that, you want us to go back to them with some cockamamie story about a Trojan chicken?"

"Trojan rooster."

"I don't care if it's a Trojan platypus," Zoe snapped. "They'll never believe it. And we'll look like a bunch of idiots."

I stared at her, shocked, as I grasped what was happening. "You don't believe I'm right about this, do you?"

Zoe set her brush down and turned to face me. "It's nothing personal. But it was already hard enough to believe this whole Croatoan thing . . ."

"They exist, Zoe. They tried to kill Mike and me last night while you were busy cozying up to Agent Taco."

Zoe's gaze hardened. "That's not fair, Ben."

"Fair?" I repeated. "You betrayed my trust yesterday to make yourself look good!"

"I was trying to protect you!"

"Well, I'm trying to protect the president and Congress and thousands of other people. But you won't help because you care more about your reputation at the Agency than them."

"This isn't about my reputation," Zoe said testily. "This is about doing what makes sense. And this Trojan chicken thing makes no sense at all."

I had already said a few things I regretted in anger, and I was tempted to say more. But I took a deep breath and tried a different tactic. "Zoe, when I first came to this school, you were pretty much the only one who believed in me. In fact, you believed in me so much, you thought I was a far better spy than I really was. That's how we became friends. Well, now I've finally become a better spy. I know this plot sounds insane, but I believe I'm right about it. So now I need you to believe I'm right about it too."

Zoe looked into my eyes and calmed herself. A long moment passed. Finally, she said, "I'm sorry, Ben. This just can't be correct."

"But the evidence . . ."

". . . is some quotes from the *Iliad* and a few specks of blue paint. Which is laughable. Now, thanks to you, the FBI, Homeland Security, and the Secret Service are already focusing on the Washington Monument. If the Croatoan goes for that, they'll stop them, and you'll be a hero. But they'll never buy the Trojan chicken thing. And if you try to convince them of it, they'll start to doubt what you've already come to them with—and instead of being a hero, you'll be a laughingstock."

"And what if I'm right, Zoe? What if the Croatoan really *is* using the Trojan rooster?"

"Do yourself a favor, Ben. Get some sleep. Maybe when you wake up, you'll realize how ridiculous this all sounded."

I considered staying there and arguing longer, but there didn't seem to be any point. All it would do was escalate into a major fight—and time was running out. So I simply left the room and went to track down the others.

Unfortunately, they hadn't had any better luck. Jemma Stern was still blocking Mike's calls, Jawa hadn't been able to convince anyone he was right, and Chip had been actively ridiculed by his professors.

Even Cyrus Hale had failed. He was visiting Fort Ticonderoga with Trixie when Erica called him with the update. Cyrus always trusted Erica, so he immediately accepted our assessment of what was going on. Sadly, he had far less success convincing others. His contact at Homeland Security told him it was in poor taste to play practical jokes on the morning of a major security event. His friends at the FBI had suggested he might be going senile in his advancing age. And his liaison at the Secret Service laughed so hard at the idea of a Trojan rooster that his back went into spasms and he had to go lie down.

Meanwhile, Catherine Hale hadn't been able to locate Agent Durkee; the leader of the Croatoan had vanished without a trace. I suspected this was because Agent Durkee was now hidden inside the rooster, but I had no way to prove it.

So that left all of us with only one option:

"We're going to have to go with Plan B," Erica said. "Taking care of this ourselves."

Chip and Jawa were thrilled by this prospect, as they had missed our previous few missions and, thus, hadn't experienced the unadulterated terror of having the enemy trying to kill them repeatedly.

However, I had serious concerns. "That's Plan B? That ought to be Plan C or D at best. The Secret Service and Homeland Security have the museum surrounded. We're never going to be able to get in there without authorization."

"That's why we're not going through the front door," Catherine said. "We'll have to parachute onto the roof. The same way the Croatoan probably came in."

"An aerial assault?" Chip exclaimed. "Awesome!"

"Oh no," I said, remembering my last aerial assault; it had taken place over Paris and had not been an enjoyable way to arrive in the city. "That ought to be Plan Z. The National Mall is a no-fly zone to begin with. With the ceremony, they'll have military patrols on high alert. Anything entering the airspace is going to be shot down on sight."

"That will be my father's problem," Erica said. "He's going to be flying us in."

"Alexander's doing the drop?" I asked.

"Do you know anyone else with a helicopter?"

I didn't. Alexander had recently been given a vintage Russian military helicopter as a gift. It had been owned by an incredibly wealthy British computer programmer named Orion, who couldn't even remember why he'd bought it in the first place. Alexander had proven quite adept at flying it and had used it to help us escape a SPYDER assault on Orion's mansion. So Orion had let him have it. Alexander had parked it at an airstrip right outside the city and had been practicing flying it on weekends.

This still didn't make it a good plan, in my opinion. But I couldn't come up with anything better.

Which was how, forty-eight minutes later, I once again found myself strapping on a parachute inside a Russian helicopter, racing toward the restricted airspace over the capital city of a world power. Alexander was at the controls while Catherine, Erica, Mike, Jawa, Chip, and I suited up for our airdrop.

"Y'know what would be nice?" I asked Mike, who was putting on his chute next to me. "To ride in a helicopter and *not* jump out of it for once."

"You *did* enroll in spy school to become a spy, didn't you?" he asked me. "You wanted adventure, right?"

"Yes," I conceded. "But we've had a lot more adventure than I was expecting. When most kids our age go to a bowling alley, they actually *bowl*. They don't get held hostage and then have to fend off terrorists with bowling balls."

Below us, the suburbs of northern Washington were racing past in a blur. Directly ahead, approaching quickly, the spear of the Washington Monument stabbed into the sky.

"I kind of liked blowing that door off the hinges," Mike

said. "Most kids don't get to do things like that. Or hang out with girls like her." He subtly nodded toward Erica.

I looked her way. Erica was suiting up for action. She was acting like our hug had never even happened. This made some sense, given the circumstances; ideally, we should have been focused entirely on the mission and not our social lives. But I worried that Erica was already regretting showing me any affection and was going to return to being her usual, aloof self—or worse, she might withdraw and become even more aloof.

Which wasn't what *I* should have been thinking about before a dangerous mission. But I couldn't help it—and neither could Mike.

"I know you've been wavering between Erica and Zoe," he said quietly, aware the others wouldn't hear us over the roar of the rotors, "and I understand they both have their pluses. But Zoe used you yesterday, which wasn't cool."

"Erica has used me too."

"For the sake of a mission, where she was trying to do something good. Zoe only used you to get that position at DADD."

"That wasn't her original intention, I don't think. She thought she was helping me."

"Then she should have been honest about . . . Whoa!" Mike tumbled to the floor as the helicopter banked suddenly.

"Sorry about that!" Alexander yelled. "I need to do some maneuvering here. We've got company!"

As we had all expected, the government was on high alert. But they had responded even faster and more aggressively than we had hoped. Two F-16 fighter jets were racing toward us.

I grabbed the wall of the helicopter to keep from being thrown off my feet. Jawa wasn't so lucky. He was tossed out of his seat and ended up sprawled on the helicopter floor.

Chip managed to stay in his seat, but he paled when he saw the jets. "That's not good."

Catherine watched the approaching F-16s, then turned to Alexander with sadness in her eyes. "Abort the mission."

"What?" Erica exclaimed. "You can't do that!"

"It's more dangerous than I had anticipated," Catherine explained. "I thought they'd only send other helicopters to chase us off. Those jets are capable of blowing us out of the sky." She looked to Alexander again. "I said abort! Why haven't we aborted?"

"I think I can shake them," Alexander said, although not quite as confidently as I would have liked. He began weaving through the air so that the jets couldn't lock in on us, which made the helicopter pitch back and forth wildly. It was like trying to stand on a rowboat in a hurricane.

"We can't jump out of a helicopter while we're under attack!" Catherine protested. "It's far too perilous!"

"But what about the Croatoan?" Jawa asked, struggling back to his feet. "If we leave, they win."

"If we stay, we're gonna die!" Chip told him. "Those jets are gonna blow us out of the air!"

Mike frowned at him. "I thought you were excited to go on a mission for once."

"A mission where I *survive*," Chip corrected. "I don't want to be a farter."

"A martyr?" Jawa asked.

"Right. One of those."

"So we'll jump out of the helicopter before they shoot it down," Jawa argued.

"You want to jump under these circumstances?" Chip asked fearfully. "We've only done simulated jumps before. If anything goes wrong now, we're gonna end up as splotches on the sidewalk."

"I can't believe I'm saying this, but Chip is right," Catherine said remorsefully. "If this mission ends in disaster, the Croatoan will win anyhow. You're only children. This was risky enough before. But now—I can't ask you to do this . . . Erica! Stop!"

Erica had made her way to the sliding side door of the helicopter. Now, defying her mother, she threw it open. A gust of wind blasted through it, nearly taking me off my feet again.

"We're almost over the drop zone!" Erica yelled over the wind.

Through the doorway, the National Mall was below us, a slash of green through the heart of the city, but then it slipped from view as Alexander banked wildly once again, and all I could see was sky.

"Erica Daisy Hale," Catherine said, in the stern voice that my own parents had used on me when catching me breaking the rules. "Close that door and sit down right now or you're grounded."

Mike looked at me, stunned. "Her middle name is 'Daisy'?"

"Mother!" Erica exclaimed, exasperated. "I can do this!"

"Erica, if you don't listen to me, you're not going on any more missions for a year!"

Erica gave Catherine the sort of glare normal teens used on their parents when told they had to skip a party and stay home to mow the lawn. "You never let me do anything!"

"I let you overthrow SPYDER last month!" Catherine argued. "But I am not just your mother here. I'm the mission commander. So what I say goes. Now close that door right now, young woman."

Despite Alexander's maneuvering, he still hadn't radically changed his course, so we were now almost over the museum. But this had also allowed the F-16s to home in on him. They were flanking us now, coming in from both sides. I knew they wouldn't shoot us down over the city unless it was the last resort, as a flaming helicopter plummeting into the middle of the Mall would be dangerous for anyone below. But that would still be preferable to a terrorist attack on the Capitol, which was what it probably looked like we were attempting.

Erica looked out the doorway at the approaching drop zone, then turned back to Catherine and sighed. "All right, Mom. You win."

I saw Catherine visibly relax, at once pleased that her daughter had listened to her—but also saddened by the call she'd had to make.

However, I wasn't the slightest bit relaxed.

In that moment, I was quite sure that Erica hadn't caved at all—and that she was only lying to get her mother to back down. I wasn't sure how I knew this when Catherine didn't; perhaps Erica had manipulated me enough times to get her way on missions that I could now recognize the signs. So while Catherine dropped her guard, mine went up—and I lunged across the helicopter to grab Erica before she could jump out the door.

I was a little too late. I caught Erica's parachute, but she had already committed to jumping. I knew the math: Her strength and the force of gravity were too much for me to hold back, but I wasn't thinking rationally. I couldn't allow Erica to place herself in such grave danger if I could help it.

And maybe I *could* have held her back, if Alexander hadn't banked at exactly that moment, veering to confuse the F-16s. The sudden tilt of the helicopter threw me forward, and so, instead of me pulling Erica back, she pulled me out . . .

The next thing I knew, I was falling.

ART APPRECIATION

1,500 feet above the National Mall
April 18
0959 hours

I had the presence of mind to cling as tightly as I could to Erica as we plummeted toward earth, which certainly saved my life.

I had only jumped from a helicopter once before, and that had been a tandem jump with Erica, who did all the hard work, even though she had been partially blinded at the time. Erica had trained for things like this far more than I had. Before coming to spy school, the most dangerous thing I had ever done was trying to jump my skateboard off Mike's front steps. (And for the record, I had repeatedly failed at that, resulting in plenty of bumps, bruises, and a fractured arm that needed to be in a cast for six weeks.)

So I held on with all my strength as we cartwheeled over each other, which allowed Erica to grab on to me as well. She pulled me in close so that we were face-to-face and said, "For a smart person, you can be a real idiot sometimes."

I didn't say anything, because I was doing my best not to throw up. The ground and sky kept rotating around us as we fell, so the world was a blur. I had glimpses of the helicopter banking away quickly before anyone else could jump out after us and the F-16s correcting course to pursue it and the earth getting disturbingly closer and closer to us as we fell.

The only plus to all this was that we were apparently too small and moving too fast for the F-16 pilots to have spotted us. Instead, they were focused on the chopper.

Through it all, Erica stayed amazingly calm, as though we had merely stepped out for a stroll. "I'm not going to deploy your chute yet," she explained, "so that the government and the Croatoan have less time to shoot us out of the air."

"Good idea," I managed to say. I really wanted to ask *when* Erica was going to deploy my chute, but I didn't want to mess up her concentration—or puke on her. So I waited.

I now experienced one of those situations that had occurred with disturbing frequency in my life since I had come to spy school, where my fear made time feel like it was stretching out. Every second we fell felt like hours, and while I normally would have enjoyed the prospect of being face-to-face with Erica Hale for hours at a time, it would have been far preferable to do that on a romantic beach, or perhaps on a picnic blanket at the park, rather than while dropping like a pair of stones toward the National Mall.

And then, after what seemed like an eternity but which was probably only two or three seconds, Erica said, "Aim for the highest part of the roof," reached behind me, and yanked my ripcord.

It felt like I was in a speeding car that had suddenly slammed on the brakes. It seemed as though I had stopped dead, but this was only relative, because I had really just stopped plummeting, and it took me another moment to realize that I was still coming down quite quickly and wasn't really in control—the equivalent of avoiding wrecking your bike but then careening wildly across a crowded highway.

Below me, the roof of the modern wing of the National Gallery of Art was approaching fast.

I was close enough to see what had happened there. The Croatoan's plot had, indeed, used a Trojan rooster. The giant blue statue stood on the rooftop viewing area—it was hard to gauge the exact size from my vantage point, but it looked to be at least fifteen feet tall—and a hatch hung open directly beneath the tail. At some point, not much earlier, it would have looked as though the rooster had pooped out two enemy agents.

There had been two Secret Service agents stationed on the roof to keep an eye on the surrounding area, but they had apparently assumed the building was secure and been caught by surprise. Both lay sprawled unconscious at their posts, while the Croatoan was now preparing for their attack.

The ultramodern design of the museum was a jumble of geometric shapes. The patio where the giant blue rooster sat was a rhombus beside a significantly larger triangle of glass—the massive skylight over the central atrium. It glinted in the sunlight so brightly I could feel the heat from it.

I also saw why Erica had told me to aim for the highest part of the roof. That was where the Croatoan was set up. It was a diamond-shaped tower that rose above the skylight and provided a direct, unobstructed shot at the Capitol.

I could see Agent Durkee and one of her henchmen on the roof. Agent Durkee must have come directly there from the bowling alley the night before to get inside the rooster. They had erected what looked like a supersize version of a grenade launcher to fire a lump of RDX at the Capitol ceremony. Although they were now looking up at Erica and me. Agent Durkee's face was filled with a mixture of surprise and anger.

The henchman merely looked confused, as though he couldn't quite figure out what was happening.

Our helicopter was racing off toward the horizon with the F-16s in pursuit.

Meanwhile, thousands of people were gathered at the Capitol. The dignitaries were all arranged in the bleachers on the western balcony, while a great crowd of onlookers filled the lawn and stretched all the way back to the Mall—although the presence of the helicopter and the F-16s had seriously spooked everyone. The fringes of the crowd were starting to scatter for cover. The Capitol was too far away for me to see clearly, but there seemed to be some activity there, too, possibly the Secret Service leaping into action to spirit the president away.

The problem was, the Croatoan could fire the RDX much faster than the president could run. And there were still thousands of other people in the line of fire.

"Get to the launcher!" Erica yelled, and then pulled her own ripcord.

"I'll try!" I had seen that the RDX would detonate after a good-size impact—like Mike hitting it with the chair. In theory, the launcher would be designed to protect the explosive and keep it from going off accidentally, or else the Croatoan would run the risk of blowing themselves up, rather than their targets.

Agent Durkee looked to her henchman and shouted, "Shoot them, you idiot!" although even now, her voice was so chipper and friendly, it sounded like she was telling him to give us a hug. Then she returned her attention to the launcher, preparing to fire it.

The henchman pulled out a gun, but Erica already had the drop on him. She had deployed her chute at the last possible moment, so she was still moving with considerable speed. She swung in feet-first, delivering a kick to the henchman's face that sent him flying backward into the supersize launcher. It tumbled off its tripod and clattered across the roof.

Agent Durkee cursed and ran after the launcher.

Erica couldn't go after it too, as she was busy fighting the henchman. Although Erica was an adept fighter, the henchman was an enormous hunk of muscle, and Erica was trying to wrest the gun from his grasp and unfasten her parachute at the same time.

So I went after Agent Durkee and the launcher myself.

Only, I didn't really have any idea how to control myself in the parachute. On my previous jump, Erica had steered us down. I realized there were pulls to my left and right that could adjust the angle of the parachute and thus my direction, but I was literally learning on the fly. I fumbled with the pulls as I dropped, frantically shifting left and right.

Agent Durkee reached the launcher.

I managed to hit the correct section of the roof— which was a small victory in itself—but biffed the landing. I stumbled and went down on my face, after which my parachute, still fully deployed, caught the wind and dragged me along. All I could do was grab on to the launcher as I was swept by and yank it from Agent Durkee's grasp. She cursed again and ran after me, catching hold of the other end of the launcher.

At which point, my parachute dragged me off the edge of the roof.

I would have sailed away with the launcher had Agent Durkee not been holding on to the other end, but her weight and that of the launcher were too much for my chute. We all dropped . . .

Right onto the skylight.

The glass shattered beneath us and we tumbled through it, crashing down onto the giant Calder mobile that hung from the ceiling. The mobile looked like the sort of thing that would be hung above the crib of a giant baby to amuse it, a series of large blue and red metal shapes, all delicately suspended by a network of metal struts. Agent Durkee and I both lost our grip on the launcher as we fell. I bounced painfully off two of the big metal mobile pieces and dropped again, only to have my parachute get tangled in the struts and catch me, so that I was left dangling like a marionette five stories above the ground floor. Meanwhile, Agent Durkee belly flopped onto the largest metal piece and clung to it like a bug on a lily pad, while the launcher snagged on another parachute cord and ended up penduluming ten feet away from me.

A host of new problems immediately presented themselves. To begin with, the struts of the mobile were all designed to move separately. Upon our impact, they careened about wildly, which resulted in Agent Durkee, the launcher, and myself all being swung about in different directions at once.

Next, the mobile hadn't been designed for people to use it as a carnival ride. It was only anchored into one spot in the ceiling, and as we whirled about, I could hear the giant screw groaning under our weight. If it tore loose, we would all go crashing to the floor below.

Also, the launcher looked like it might snap off at any moment. Hitting the floor far below seemed like it would be a big enough impact to detonate the RDX and level the whole block.

And finally, Agent Durkee was really, really angry. Her cheerful persona was gone. It seemed as though she had spent her entire life repressing her anger, and now several decades of it had all volcanically erupted to the surface at once. "Do you realize what you've done, you putrid little scuzzball?" she shrieked at me. "I've been working on this plot for years and now you've ruined it! I'm going to kill you!"

I tried to keep my wits and focus on how to survive my current predicament. In theory, with my math skills, I could calculate how to swing myself over to the launcher before Agent Durkee could get to it, but there were too many moving parts of the mobile, each going an entirely different way, and I was dizzy and my head hurt. So I decided to wing it. I grabbed on to the parachute cords above me and tried to climb them like a monkey on a vine.

This didn't work so well. It was difficult enough to climb a stationary rope hanging from the ceiling of a gymnasium (which I knew from experience), but shimmying up a rope that was whipping around was considerably harder, especially since every move I made sent a ripple effect through the mobile, changing the movements of everything else. At the same time, Agent Durkee was scrambling up toward the anchor in the ceiling, setting off her own chain reaction of movements, while still venting angrily.

"I worked so hard for this day!" she raged. "All those years of plotting and scheming—and you undid it all in just a few seconds!"

I realized that Agent Durkee wasn't trying to get to the launcher. She was only trying to get off the mobile before it snapped free and dropped. And given her fury at me, it seemed she was hoping the mobile would snap and drop with me on it. In her enraged state, it didn't seem to have occurred to her that if the RDX exploded, it would kill her, too—or maybe she was willing to have that happen. If her attempt to destroy the US government had failed, maybe she was willing to settle for taking out one of its museums.

The mobile was trembling violently, its various pieces careening about. I was swinging around like a tetherball on its string while Agent Durkee screamed and the parachute ropes began to fray and the screw holding the whole mobile into the ceiling began to tear loose from its mooring. Little bits of metal sheared off and clattered down onto my head.

But I was making progress, ever so slowly. And I began to hatch a plan.

The central atrium of the museum wasn't a completely empty void. A walkway bridged the gap one floor down, but off to the side. As the mobile spun, the launcher occasionally swung out over the walkway. I started to work out the math and the timing, trying to ignore the fact that Agent Durkee had almost made it to the anchor in the ceiling, and that she was still spewing invective at me. "And then I had to spend the night inside that stupid giant chicken with Fernando! Do you have any idea how awful that was? It was humid and cramped and Fernando smells like bad cheese! But I suffered through it—just like I've suffered through so many other things in my life—knowing that my moment of glory would finally come! But noooooooooo! You had to mess everything up!"

"I'm very sorry!" I yelled up to her. "I know you worked

very hard on all this! But your plan *was* to kill a whole lot of people!"

"People who didn't deserve to be here! People who stole this country from its rightful owner, Spain!"

She had reached the anchor in the ceiling. She climbed up it, then hung on to the beam that the mobile was suspended from and began to kick at the giant screw, trying to knock it loose.

The mobile trembled with each jolt and began to swing about even more violently. I focused on the launcher as it whirled about, dangling on its loop of parachute cord.

The cord was on the verge of snapping and dropping the launcher.

And Agent Durkee was doing everything she could to knock the mobile free from the ceiling.

Which meant I didn't have much time.

I put my math skills to the test, doing the calculations as well as I could—then realized the moment had come and threw myself into action.

As a big metal piece of the mobile wheeled past me, I kicked off it as hard as I could, then swung across the atrium on my parachute cord like Tarzan. The launcher, on its own cord, twirled into my path, and I opened my arms wide as I slammed right into it.

It hurt. A lot. But then, I wasn't expecting that colliding with a large metal object at high speed would tickle and had steeled myself for the pain. I hugged the launcher tightly as my own force of motion changed its trajectory. I swung out over the bridging walkway with it.

The cord holding the launcher snapped. But I had been expecting this, too. In fact, I'd been counting on it. I dropped to only a few feet above the walkway and released the launcher. It skidded along the floor and came to a gentle stop resting against a railing.

It did not blow us all up. So far, so good.

I still had problems, though.

Up at the ceiling, Agent Durkee kicked the mobile's anchor with everything she had. There was a screech of rending metal, and the entire thing tore free.

I was still swinging through the air beneath it, connected to it by my parachute.

I desperately fumbled with the buckle holding my parachute on. It popped open, and the centrifugal force of my arc sent me flying over a railing into a gallery full of confusing modern art. I hit the floor much harder than the launcher had and tumbled painfully across it.

At the exact same moment, the mobile dropped through the void.

The harness from my parachute whipped around a statue by Constantin Brancusi, then yanked it off its base and over the railing.

The mobile smashed into the ground floor several stories below, and then the Brancusi impaled it.

I was quite sure both works of art were extremely expensive and probably irreplaceable. But the loss of them seemed relatively small compared to the devastation we had just avoided.

I lay on the floor of the gallery, exhausted, my body racked with pain, and looked over at the launcher.

It sat there calmly, still not exploding.

"Are you kidding me?" Agent Durkee screamed, apoplectic with rage. "You had to thwart this, too?" A strand of parachute cord dangled near her, and she slid down it to the walkway, then stormed toward me with fire in her eyes. "Well, now I'm going to do to you what you've done to my scheme! I'm going to destroy you if it's the last thing I . . . unnngghhh." She gave a groan of pain and collapsed, unconscious.

Erica Hale was standing at the other end of the gallery, by the stairway from the roof, holding a dart gun. "Man," she said, "I thought she'd *never* shut up." She came to my side. "Are you all right?"

"Not really," I replied. "I mean, I'm happy to be alive and all, but I'm in a tremendous amount of pain."

Erica knelt and looked me over. "Looks like you might have broken something. Maybe lots of things. Sorry I couldn't get here sooner. That henchman was really hard to knock out."

"Any chance you know first aid?"

"I know exactly how to make you feel better." Even though Erica said this clinically, there was a hint of something else behind it. I had the distinct sense that, maybe, she was thinking about kissing me.

But before she could do that—or even reach into her utility belt for some aspirin—a horde of Secret Service agents burst into the gallery. They came through every door at once, ready for action, guns pointed directly at us. "Hands in the air!" the head agent shouted. "You're under arrest for threatening the leadership of this country and for the destruction of several very expensive works of art!"

Erica obediently raised her hands. "You've got the wrong people. We're the good guys here."

"You don't look like good guys to me," the Secret Service agent said.

"Trust me," Erica said, nodding in my direction. "This guy is as good as they get. While you were all dorking around outside, he just saved every last one of us."

In that moment, all the trouble I had been through was instantly worth it. Getting praise from Erica Hale was the best reward I could ever ask for. Even though it hurt to even smile, I did it anyhow.

And then pain and exhaustion overwhelmed me and I passed out.

RECUPERATION

Good Samaritan Hospital
Washington, DC
April 22
1200 hours

"I hate to bother you, but . . . Is your name Benjamin Ripley?"

The words startled me in the quiet of my hospital room. I was sitting upright in my bed, staring out the window at the Capitol dome, thinking about how it would have been destroyed if things had gone differently four days before. I was recovering from some badly bruised ribs and a nasty sprain in my left shoulder. My arm was still in a sling, but other than that, I was able to get around with only moderate pain. I was supposed to be released the next day.

I had never heard the voice before, but I instantly recognized the face of the girl standing in the doorway of the room.

Trixie Hale.

She was even prettier than her photo, in part because I could now see that she looked a great deal like her sister. And yet, in the way she presented herself, she seemed almost like the anti-Erica. She wore a floral sundress and had a pink scrunchie in her hair. She was immediately friendly and cheerful. And she had brought me cookies. She held a plate of them in her hands, and they looked homemade.

"That's me," I said. "Are you Trixie?"

A smile spread across Trixie's face. The type of big, warm smile that I had almost never seen on Erica. "You've heard of me?"

"Erica's mentioned you," I said.

"Oh. I can never be too sure about things like that. Erica can be awfully secretive."

"Yeah, I've noticed that."

Trixie flashed another smile, like we were in on a joke together, then came to the side of my bed. "Erica's mentioned you, too, obviously. Would you like a cookie? I made them myself."

One of the cardinal rules of spy school was to never

accept a cookie—or any food, really—from someone you had just met. But Trixie was a Hale, I was hungry because the hospital food was atrocious, and the cookies smelled incredible. So I took one. As I did, it occurred to me that my presence in the hospital was supposed to be a secret. The CIA had checked me in under an assumed name and was covering the bills with a fake insurance account. "How'd you find me?"

"It wasn't that hard. I followed my father here."

"Ah." I suppressed a grimace. Alexander had come by earlier to pass along the word that the Federal Witness Protection Program had set my parents up in a nice seaside town in Florida, and they seemed to be adjusting very well. My mother had already found work at a veterinary clinic and joined a book club while my father was learning how to make ice cream. I could only hope that the Witness Protection Program was being more careful with them than Alexander had been with me.

"I can be pretty sneaky sometimes," Trixie said proudly. "Sometimes I think I might make a pretty good spy."

It runs in your family, I thought, but didn't say it. Instead, I asked, "So what brings you here?"

"I just wanted to meet the boy my sister's always talking about."

I was still wired to a heart monitor. It began beeping

wildly, signaling how excited I was to hear this, although thankfully, Trixie didn't seem to notice. "Erica talks about me a lot?"

"Well, she's only mentioned you three or four times, but for Erica, that's plenty. There was some guy she liked before . . . Joshua something . . . She only brought him up twice. She hasn't mentioned him in years, so I'm guessing that ended badly."

"That's kind of an understatement." I took a bite of cookie and gasped. The only time I had ever eaten anything that tasted so good was when Catherine had baked it. "Oh wow. This is amazing."

Trixie blushed, looking flattered. "Thanks. The secret is I add a dash of Himalayan sea salt. Anyhow, I just came to town to see my family and, well, word slipped out that you were in the hospital, so I figured I ought to meet you. I can be a little overprotective when it comes to my sister."

"Yeah, she can be protective of you, too." I was doing my best to try to calm myself, so that my heart monitor wouldn't keep beeping furiously and make the medical staff think I was having a heart attack, but I couldn't. I had spent much of my stay in the hospital thinking about Erica and Zoe. Zoe had come to visit me a few times. She had felt terrible for not trusting me about the Trojan rooster. She had asked for my forgiveness and wanted to know if we could go back to being friends again. I had agreed. After all, she had thought she was doing the right thing, she was trying to help me—and she was a good student who deserved to be a junior member of DADD. Although sadly, I felt that something was now off between us. That no matter how much I wanted our friendship to return to normal, it would never quite be the same again.

Meanwhile, Erica hadn't visited me in the hospital at all. I knew Erica had a fear of getting close to people—this wouldn't be the first time she had shown me some emotion and then pulled away. But I also knew *why* Erica had a fear of getting close to people. She obviously cared greatly about Trixie, and that had been used as leverage to force her into doing the Croatoan's dirty work. Plus, it was possible that Erica hadn't visited me in the hospital in order to protect me. After all, Alexander's visit had allowed Trixie to find me; it was possible that enemies could have followed him too.

But still, it was upsetting that Erica hadn't come. Or even sent a card. It had made me question how much she liked me. So now, hearing that she had actually discussed me with her sister meant a great deal. I desperately wanted to interrogate Trixie about it, to learn exactly what Erica had said, and was wondering how to do this without looking foolish when Mike burst into the room.

He barreled through the door, clutching a piece of paper,

panting as though he had run all the way there from school. "Ben!" he exclaimed. "I've got big news . . . Oh." He froze upon seeing Trixie. For a brief moment, he was thrown by her presence, but then, being Mike, he immediately changed his behavior. In an instant, he went from frantic to debonair, flashing her his most charming smile. "Hey there," he said suavely. "I'm Mike. Ben's friend."

Trixie smiled back. "Hi. I'm Trixie. Would you like a cookie?" I could tell that she liked him, which wasn't an advanced work of deduction; most girls liked Mike.

"Sure." Mike took a cookie, but kept his eyes locked on Trixie. "Are you friends with Ben? Because if you are, Ben's in trouble for never mentioning you."

Trixie giggled, flattered.

"Could you give us a few minutes alone?" I asked Trixie quickly, before she could tell Mike who she *really* was.

"Sure," Trixie said. "It sounds like you have something important to discuss."

"No!" Mike said quickly. "It's not that serious. Hang out for a bit."

"Sorry," Trixie said, and she really seemed to mean it. "But I have to go." She set the cookies on the table beside my bed and told me, "It was very nice to meet you. I hope it won't be the last time." She gave me a wink that Mike couldn't see.

"I hope we get to see each other again too," Mike told her.

"That'd be nice," Trixie said, then slipped out the door.

"She is *gorgeous*," Mike said. "Though she looks a little familiar."

"She volunteers here," I said, as convincingly as I could. "Maybe you've seen her around here before."

"No way. If I had seen that girl before, I would have remembered her."

"Didn't you have some big news to tell me?" I asked, desperate to distract him. Mike getting into a relationship with Erica's sister would be a recipe for disaster.

"Hmmm?" Mike asked absently, still staring off in the direction that Trixie had gone. "Oh. It's just a lead as to what Murray Hill might be plotting next."

My heart monitor spiked again. "You just told Trixie you didn't have anything important!"

"Well, what was I supposed to tell her, that we're covert junior spies and I had a lead to what your nemesis is plotting?" Mike shut the door to my room, then said, "I should have gotten her number. When you see Trixie again, can you get her number for me?"

"Mike. Focus."

"Oh. Right. We heard back from Chester Snodgrass in Forensic Geology."

My heart monitor began to speed up once more, registering my excitement. "And he found something?"

"That pebble had a rare concentration of elements in it. There's only two places on earth that have anything similar: Nicaragua and Antarctica."

I stiffened at this, intrigued. "What was Murray doing in Nicaragua?"

"Or Antarctica," Mike added. "The CIA is interested in that too. Like I said: suspicious."

"Is this something they want us to investigate?" I asked, but Mike didn't get a chance to answer me, because Trixie Hale opened the door and reentered the room.

She no longer had a smile on her face. Instead, she had a look of shock and defiance, as though she had just discovered something amazing and unsettling at once. "Who do you both work for?" she asked.

"You were eavesdropping on us?" I replied, upset with her—but also upset with Mike and myself for letting our guard down.

"Like I said, I could make a pretty good spy. But apparently, not as good as both of you."

"We were only joking," Mike said quickly. "We're not really spies."

Trixie Hale checked the hallway to see if anyone else had overheard, then locked the door. "I didn't only come looking for you because of Erica," she told me. "For years, I've suspected something strange was going on with my family, but no one would ever tell me the truth. And now it appears you might know what that is." She leveled a steely gaze at us, and for the first time, I could see part of Erica's personality in her. "There's a hard way to do this and an easy way. Which would you prefer?"

"Easy," Mike and I said at once.

"Good." Trixie Hale smiled brightly. "I'm all ears, boys. So start talking."

April 23

To: ████████████████

Director of Central and South American Affairs
Central Intelligence Agency

From: Special Agent ████████████████
Re: Operation Sneaky Monkey

Just a heads-up that our team has begun operations in Nicaragua,
following up on the evidence recovered by ████████████████ as
part of the recent actions against ██████████. We are attempting to track
down ex-████████ agent ████████████████ and determine what
brought him to this area. Evidence indicates that he may be involved
with a new (or previously unknown) evil organization. Hopefully, we will
have further updates soon.

However, while Agency protocol does advise against utilizing agents-
in-training except for worst-case scenarios, I feel that, in this case,
we might need to consult agents-in-training ████████████████
████████████████, or even ████████████. After all, they
know ████████ personally, and thus far better than any adult
agents here. Of course, we would take steps to make sure that these
young agents were used only in an advisory capacity and do everything
we could not to put them in harm's way. (Although, should they end up
in harm's way, they *have* proven themselves to be relatively hard to kill.
Certainly harder to kill than most other children their age. So hopefully,
we could weather such events with minimal casualties.)

I defer to your judgment on this delicate issue.

Sincerely,

P.S. ████████ wants a pet squirrel monkey for her birthday. Any chance
you can help me export one through diplomatic channels? If not, I think I
might be able to get her to settle for a lizard of some sort.

author's note

How much of what I said about George Washington is true?

After I published *Charlie Thorne and the Last Equation*, I got a lot of letters and emails asking me the same question about Albert Einstein. That book centered around a secret equation discovered by Einstein, and readers wanted to know how much of the information I shared is true. (If you've read *Charlie Thorne and the Last Equation*, you know what I'm talking about; if you haven't read it, what are you waiting for? Go read it!) Seeing as this book uses George Washington as a reference point, I figured I might get a similar question. So I figured I'd answer it before you could ask it.

Basically, just about everything I say about Washington in this book that doesn't have to do with the Croatoan is the truth. Washington really was our first spymaster, and his spy network was integral to his victory in the Revolutionary War. His spies really did use invisible inks made from powdered nutgalls and revealed with gallotannic acid. His spies also used the very simple code that I use in this book (although, according to historian John A. Nagy, it was really known as Major General Braddock's Cipher). My description of

Mount Vernon is based as accurately as possible upon my visits to it, and Washington really did spend as much time as possible there. (Once he stepped down as president, he returned to Mount Vernon and rarely left it again.)

I should also point out that Thomas Jefferson really was a man of many talents, including architecture, and that he did really have a pet prairie dog that Lewis and Clark sent to him during their expedition (although it was not named Fluffy).

As for the Croatoan, however, I made all of that up. Except the part about the word "Croatoan" being left on a tree outside Roanoke. (To this day, no one really knows what that meant or what happened to the Roanoke colony.) There has not been a secret society plotting against America since its inception—and thus, they did not attempt to assassinate Washington or pull off any of the other conspiracies in this book. Washington did not have his spies investigate them, and Jefferson didn't create a hidden safe in Mount Vernon to hide documentation about the Croatoan. All that is written in jest, the same way that all the other plots in this series have been.

To that end, a brief word on conspiracy theories: Don't believe them. Most conspiracy theories that you hear about these days are based on as few facts as the ones in this book. (Maybe even fewer facts.) Please note that there is a difference between something that our intelligence agencies claim and something that a bunch of people on the Internet claim. Although I sometimes make the members of our intelligence community out to be less than competent, once again, that's all in fun. In reality, our intelligence agents are some of the bravest, smartest, hardest-working people there are. So if the FBI or the CIA claims something happened, you can assume it did. If someone claims there's a massive conspiracy, and that the FBI, the CIA, and every media outlet (except one or two)—and maybe even the rest of our government and perhaps 99.9 percent of the scientists on Earth—have been working together to manipulate you, then I wouldn't believe it any more than I'd believe a book in the fiction section of your local library.

That said, here's Major General Braddock's Cipher for your enjoyment, just in case you want to use it to send some coded messages to your friends. (And if your teacher catches you doing it, you can always claim it's an extra-credit project for history class.)

MAJOR GENERAL BRADDOCK'S CIPHER

a ... ⊓   t ... ⊕
b ... ⊔   u ... ⊃
c ... ℭ   v ... ⊇
d ... ⊐   w ... ℏ
e ... ✳   x ... 𝕃⊐
f ... ⌐   y ... ⧈
g ... ⚓   z ... 8
h ... ⊢⊣
i ... △
k ... ⧻
l ... ℓ
m ... ▷
n ... △
o ... ♂
p ... ⬜
q ... 𝒳
r ... e
s ... o

acknowledgments

Readers are always asking me where ideas come from. The best I can say is you have to always be curious about the world and open to new experiences, because you never know what might inspire you. The story of how this book came to be is a good example.

This series is particularly popular in the Washington, DC, area, which might not be surprising, since that's where much of it takes place. Plus, the schools in that area are great supporters of authors and I am often invited there to speak. I always enjoy these trips for two reasons: (1) They allow me to do research in addition to visiting the schools, and (2) I have lots of friends in the area.

In February of 2018, I was visiting schools in the Virginia suburbs and was scheduled to do a reading at wonderful bookstore in Alexandria called Hooray for Books! On that day, I was being driven around by a media escort named Paul Peachy who has become a friend. Paul pointed out that my last school of the day wasn't too far from Mount Vernon, and I had an hour to spare before the bookstore event, so maybe we should drop by Washington's home.

At that very moment, I was checking my email—and found a message from a woman named Diana Cordray, who was manager of the education center and youth programs at . . . Mount Vernon. She had learned that I was in the area and was inviting me to come over.

It seemed that fate wanted me to visit Mount Vernon. So Paul and I dropped by and Diana met us there.

It was the end of a cold, wintry day, but I was absolutely stunned by Mount Vernon. It is certainly one of the most gorgeously located homes in the world, and it is a testament to the Mount Vernon Foundation—and the states of Virginia and Maryland—that the home and its incredible view have been so well preserved. Diana pointed out to me that George Washington wasn't just our first president but also our first spymaster—and that was the spark for the story. So huge thanks to Diana and Paul for that.

I didn't have quite as much time as I would have liked to explore the grounds that day, but fortunately, I had a return trip to the DC area planned for August—along with my favorite research team: my children, my niece, and my parents. We returned and spent a day there. (For the record, Mount Vernon in August is much more humid than Mount Vernon in February.) So thanks to Violet, Dashiell, Ciara, and Mom and Dad.

And now, for the usual round of thanks to everyone who helps to make my life easier and advises me on how to do my job better:

First, there's my incredible team at Simon & Schuster: Liz Kossnar, Justin Chanda, Kendra Levin, Dainese Santos, Anne Zafian, Milena Giunco, Audrey Gibbons, Lisa Moraleda, Jenica Nasworthy, Chrissy Noh, Anna Jarzab, Brian Murray, Devin MacDonald, Christina Pecorale, Victor Iannone, Emily Hutton, Caitlin Nalven, and Theresa Pang. I'm going to single out my cover designer, Lucy Cummins, here, whose covers for this series are unbelievably good. And massive thanks to my incredible agent, Jennifer Joel, for making all this possible.

Thanks to my amazing fellow writers James Ponti, Sarah Mlynowski, Julie Buxbaum, Leslie Margolis, Julia Devillers, Christina Soontornvat, Adele Griffin, Karina Yan Glaser, Michael Buckley, Chris Grabenstein, and Rose Brock.

Thanks to all the school librarians and parent associations who have arranged for me to visit, all the bookstore owners and employees who have shilled my books, and all the amazingly tireless festival organizers and volunteers who have invited me to participate.

Thanks to the home team: Barry and Carole Patmore, Alan and Sarah Patmore, Andrea Lee Gomez, and Georgia Simon.

Dash and Violet, one last shout-out. You're the best kids in the universe. I love you.

A Reading Group Guide to
Spy School Revolution
by Stuart Gibbs

About the Book

Superspy middle schooler Ben Ripley faces the Croatoan, a new evil organization that's so mysterious, the only proof it exists is from the American Revolution. With SPYDER defeated, Ben is looking forward to life returning to normal, or as normal as possible when you're a superspy in training. For once, everything seems to be right in Ben's world . . . until someone bombs the CIA conference room next door. To Ben's astonishment, the attacker is none other than Erica Hale, the spy-in-training he respects more than any other. Ben refuses to believe Erica is working for the enemy, even if the rest of the CIA does. His mission: prove Erica is not a double agent working against the US, locate a fabled colonial-era insurgent group, figure out what their devious plot is, and thwart it. But this time, Ben finds himself up against opponents he has never encountered before: his own friends. They're not as ready to trust in Erica as he is, and Ben is forced to rely on his wits and skills more than ever before. How can he succeed when he doesn't even know who he can trust?

Discussion Questions

1. After defeating SPYDER in his last adventure, Ben is looking forward to life resuming some normalcy. Do you believe a return to some sort of routine is a possibility for him? If so, what might that look like for a kid like Ben? What do you think he enjoys most and least about being a spy?

2. In a classified document, readers learn that due to a previous European mission, Ben's family is in danger; the CIA will need to implement a "domestic reassignment procedure" to secure their safety. What might be the greatest challenges to participating in such a relocation procedure? Do you see any benefits?

3. Ben's parents finally learn the truth about his education and secret spy life. Ben's father states, "'We thought you were just going to some boring science school! But you're training to be a spy! My son, a spy!'" Consider his parents' reactions to this shocking news. What do you think Ben is feeling? How might your family react if they found out you were involved in similar training and missions?

4. As he reflects on his family learning his secret, Ben thinks, "Lying to them had been one of the worst things about being a spy." Like Ben, do you find keeping secrets from the people you love to be difficult, even if it is to protect others? When do you think it's okay to keep secrets? When is it not? Explain your answers.

5. When the CIA discovers that Erica Hale is responsible for the bombing of a CIA conference room, she is instantly believed to have been working for an enemy and becomes the CIA's most wanted. Why does Ben feel so confident that Erica isn't to blame? What does his faith in her indicate? How do you feel about his choice to risk his own reputation to try to prove her innocence?

6. When learning that they'll likely be moved by the government for their own protection, Ben's mother tells his father, "'Don't take this the wrong way, but our lives could use a little shaking up.'" What does this remark help you understand about her? Are there ways in which you see similar qualities in Ben? Explain your answer.

7. As he searches for Erica to help prove her innocence, Ben states, "Why does she always have to be so cryptic? If she really wanted me to find her, you'd think she would just write it down in a simple, easy-to-understand way." Consider Ben's comment and what you've learned about Erica. Do you believe this is a fair assessment? If so, in what ways?

8. When Ben and Zoe eventually locate Erica at the Library of Congress, she tells Ben, "'I thought you'd be coming alone. I left the message for *you*. In your room. If I had wanted this to be a party, I would have sent out invitations.'" Consider Erica's reaction to Ben including Zoe in the search. Do you think Erica's response is appropriate? Explain your answer.

9. Erica tells Ben, "'I've told you before, friendships can be a liability in this business.'" Do you agree or disagree with her assessment? Review the events of *Spy School Revolution*. What are some specific ways that Erica is proven wrong? From your perspective, who are the most loyal friends you've encountered while reading the novel?

10. What have you learned about the Croatoan in *Spy School Revolution*? How does this mysterious evil organization compare to SPYDER? What do you predict will be most challenging about running a campaign against them?

11. Ben tells Erica, "'I can't believe Zoe's ratting us out. She's our friend.'" Consider Zoe's choice to double-cross Ben as a means of getting to Erica. Are her actions simply professional given Erica's wanted status, or do you believe the issue is more complicated than Zoe will admit? Explain your answer.

In what ways do Mike's questions about Zoe's involvement complicate the issue for Ben?

12. What are your earliest impressions of Agent Nora Taco? Given what is learned about her throughout the course of the novel, do you believe she's an effective agent for the CIA? Explain your answer.

13. While arguing about Erica, Zoe tells Ben, "'I thought she might be trying to kill you . . . and you were too blind to see it! You've always been blind where Erica is concerned. Ever since you met her, she has consistently put your life in danger to further her own career.'" Do you think Zoe's assessment of Erica is fair? What other factors might be in play? Explain your position.

14. In sharing background about the mysterious Croatoan organization, Erica tells Ben, "'Over the past four centuries, the Croatoan has become more and more fanatical, with one singular mission: to destroy the United States of America once and for all.'" In what ways does learning about Spain's early influence and unsuccessful intentions to colonize America lead to the Croatoan's frustration and desire for revenge? How does this ultimately drive the events that happen in *Spy School Revolution*? Given what you learn about the Croatoan and Agent Durkee, do you feel their anger is justified? Explain your answers.

15. After Erica tells Ben that the Croatoan found her weakness, Ben retorts, "'Weakness? . . . You don't have any weaknesses.'" How does learning about Erica's vulnerabilities make Ben feel? What's your reaction to this revelation?

16. In trying to determine why the Croatoan has suddenly targeted both Erica and Ben, Erica says, "'Because it's good business. In theory, they're plotting something big and don't want us causing any trouble. But now they also have the CIA looking for *us* and not them.'" If this is true, why is finding evidence of the Croatoan's existence so essential?

17. As Erica, Ben, and Catherine drift down the Potomac River in a rowboat, Catherine says, "'My goodness. It's a lovely night for a covert operation.'" What does this innocent statement indicate about Catherine's general disposition? What are some of the ways Erica is like her mother? Do you see any notable differences? What makes their general family dynamics so complicated?

18. After explaining to Ben why she's never told him about her sister, Trixie, Erica replies, "'As you know, my family isn't normal.'" Do you agree or disagree with her assessment? What does "normal" mean to you? What might "normal" mean to others? Does learning that Erica wants to protect her sister at all costs surprise you? Explain your answers.

19. In what ways does Ben and Mike's arrival at their former school cause disruptions? In what ways is returning to the campus complicated for them? Are there ways in which they are ultimately pleased with the outcome?

20. Catherine tells Ben and Mike, "'Especially in this business . . . More so than any other, perhaps. This won't be the last time you find yourselves with your job and your heart at odds.'" What are some of the ways that relationships might be challenging for secret agents? How does this apply to each of these characters?

21. Thinking back on events in this book and other novels in the Spy School series, what has been your favorite mission for Ben and his team? Explain your answer.

22. As the novel closes, Trixie tells Ben and Mike, "'I didn't only come looking for you because of Erica. For years, I've suspected something strange was going on with my family, but no one would ever tell me the truth. And now it appears you might know what that is. . . . There's a hard way to do this and an easy way. Which would you prefer? . . . I'm all ears, boys. So start talking.'" What do you predict Ben and Mike will ultimately tell Trixie? In what ways might Trixie's involvement with their team shift moving forward?

This guide was created by Dr. Rose Brock, an assistant professor in Library Science Department in the College of Education at Sam Houston State University. Dr. Brock holds a Ph.D. in Library Science, specializing in children's and young adult literature.

This guide has been provided by Simon & Schuster for classroom, library, and reading group use. It may be reproduced in its entirety or excerpted for these purposes. For more Simon & Schuster guides and classroom materials, please visit simonandschuster.net or simonandschuster.net/thebookpantry.

Turn the page for a
sneak peek of
spy school
at sea!

DEBRIEFING

Office of the Principal

Nathan Hale Building

The Academy of Espionage

Washington, DC

May 15

1500 hours

The principal was acting stranger than usual.

In my sixteen months at the CIA's Academy of Espionage, I had seen the principal display many aspects of his personality, none of which were good. He had been angry, bitter, paranoid, churlish, jealous, contemptuous, ornery, disdainful, mercurial, obnoxious, flummoxed, confused, passive-aggressive, and just plain mean. But the day I was assigned to Operation Deadly Manatee, his behavior was the most unsettling of all.

He was trying to be nice.

With most people, of course, this would have been a good thing. But with the principal it felt wrong, as though he was fighting every natural instinct he had. Watching him try to be nice was like watching a tiger try to eat a salad.

"Benjamin!" he exclaimed upon opening the door to his office, with what was obviously forced enthusiasm. "Such a pleasure to see you!"

"Er . . . thanks," I said warily.

"Please come in. Make yourself comfortable. Everyone else will be here soon." The principal waved me into his office and attempted to smile. It was evident that the man hadn't smiled very much and wasn't quite sure how to do it. Instead of appearing friendly and welcoming, he looked like someone suffering from a bad case of indigestion.

I cautiously stepped into his office—or rather, what remained of it. Nine months earlier, I had accidentally blown up the principal's office with a mortar round. (Which explained some of the principal's general ill temper toward me, but not all of it.) Budget issues and red tape had kept the repairs from proceeding quickly, forcing the principal to temporarily relocate his office to a broom closet, which he had been extremely peeved about. When I had been notified to report to his original office, I expected to find that it had been restored to its previous condition.

This was not the case. In fact, almost no work had been done on the office at all. The entire exterior wall was still missing. A haphazard attempt had been made to reinforce that side of the room with a spindly framework of two-by-fours, but there was still a gaping hole—and since we were on the fifth floor of the Nathan Hale Administration Building, this meant that a misstep could result in a quick plummet down to the campus quadrangle. The furniture hadn't been replaced and was all slightly charred, while what remained of the carpet smelled like a doused campfire. The principal's beloved desk, which had been incinerated in the blast, had been replaced by a wobbly piece of plywood laid across two sawhorses—although the principal had managed to procure a new rolling chair.

"I recognize that it's still a work in progress," the principal said weakly. "They won't be able to start the repairs until December. But I just couldn't take working in that broom closet anymore. And now that it's spring, it's not so bad. I kind of like the open design. All the fresh air is invigorating."

"I can see that," I said as supportively as I could. The hole in the wall certainly let in plenty of fresh air. And pigeons. A dozen of them were roosting in what remained of the ceiling, which meant that a good amount of the floor was speckled with pigeon droppings.

The principal ignored them and made a show of taking a deep breath. "Ah. It's far better than all the stale, recirculated air you'd get in a normal office. I suppose, in a way, I ought to thank you for destroying this place." He attempted another smile for me, although I had the sense that he didn't feel like smiling at all, and that he was only playing at being nice to mask his natural enraged state.

I wondered what was going on.

There was a knock at the door. The principal started back for it, intending to open it, but this proved unnecessary when the hinges simply tore free from the damaged frame, and the door toppled into the office.

This revealed four more people standing in the doorway, all of whom had apparently also been summoned to the meeting.

Two were fellow students from spy school: Mike Brezinski and Erica Hale. Mike had been my best friend in my normal life, back before I had been recruited to the academy. I was supposed to keep the academy's existence a secret from Mike (as well as everyone else on earth), but he had eventually figured out where I was really going and been rewarded for his cleverness by getting recruited.

Meanwhile, Erica had known about the academy for her entire life, as she was a legacy. She came from a long line of spies and had been training since a very young age to follow in her family's footsteps. Thus, she was significantly more talented than any of her fellow trainees at school—and most actual spies as well.

The other two invitees were Erica's parents. Catherine Hale was an exceptionally talented agent for Britain's MI6—and a doting mother. Somehow she found a way to balance both lives and was as adept at thwarting criminals as she was at baking cookies.

Meanwhile, Alexander Hale was a fraud. Until very recently, his greatest skill as a spy had been convincing people that he was skilled as a spy. This had worked for him for quite a long time, and he had been respected and admired by his peers, until he was finally found out and disgraced. Since then, he had managed to redeem himself slightly, after ending up on a few missions with me—along with Catherine, Erica, and Mike.

"Greetings!" the principal exclaimed as pleasantly as he could. "Welcome, everyone! I'm glad you could make it!"

The other four responded to this in varying ways. Catherine and Erica both regarded the principal suspiciously, probably wondering what could explain his friendliness, while Mike was more cautious, as though he suspected that perhaps the real principal had been kidnapped and replaced with an impostor. Alexander didn't appear to notice any difference at all.

"It's good to see you, too," he said, shaking the principal's hand. "I like the new layout of the office. Very spacious. So, what's the reason for this get-together?"

"I'd be happy to explain that." A woman I had never met brusquely swept into the room. She appeared to be in her forties, wore a tailored business suit, and had a briefcase handcuffed to her right wrist. She didn't seem at all surprised by the state of the principal's office, which indicated to me that she had been there before. "I'm Indira Kapoor, deputy director of operations at the CIA. I've been paying close attention to your careers, and I must say, most of you have done some very impressive work." She turned slightly away from Alexander as she said this, as if to make it clear that the phrase "most of you" didn't apply to him.

Alexander appeared not to notice this, either. "Why thank you," he said, flashing Indira a suave smile.

Alexander was a very handsome man, and I had seen his smile make other women go weak in the knees, but Indira was impervious to it. Instead, she kept her gaze locked on Erica, Mike, and me. "I recognize that, due to many mistakes on the part of the Agency, the three of you have ended up on missions far earlier than would normally be recommended for young agents. But you have all handled yourselves capably and acted with ingenuity and skill, which is obviously a testament to the education you have received at this institution." She shifted her attention to the principal.

"So I suppose I owe you congratulations as well."

The principal now flashed what appeared to be an actual smile. "Thank you, Deputy Kapoor. I've done my best to whip these junior agents into shape." He plopped down into his desk chair and waved the rest of us to a char-broiled sofa.

I suddenly understood the reason for the principal's shift in personality. *We were making him look good.*

To my side, Erica bristled with anger. There were plenty of good things about the Academy of Espionage, but the principal wasn't one of them. If anything, he'd been a deterrent to our education. The idea that he was getting credit for anything we had accomplished was upsetting enough to me; for Erica, who had achieved her excellence in espionage with zero help from the principal, it was infuriating.

Her mother was aware of this as well. I saw her catch Erica's eye and mouth, *Let it go.*

Erica petulantly sat on the blackened sofa, sending a small puff of soot into the air. Mike and I took spots beside her. The sofa still reeked of burnt leather from the mortar blast.

Catherine sat primly in a gently seared armchair close by.

Alexander stayed by the makeshift desk, reaching into a bowl of jelly beans that the principal kept there. Then he made a face of disgust. "Er . . . do you have any other snacks? A pigeon appears to have pooped in these."

Deputy Kapoor ignored this, setting her briefcase on the desk and unlocking it from her wrist. "The reason I'm here with all of you now is directly related to the lead you discovered on your most recent mission, indicating the latest whereabouts of Murray Hill."

I sat up at the mention of the name. Murray had been a fellow student at spy school when I had arrived, but I had discovered he was working as a mole for a covert organization known as SPYDER. Over the next sixteen months, Murray had double-crossed both the CIA and SPYDER multiple times, doing everything he could to stay alive and get rich. I had last encountered him making a shady deal for an organization known as the Croatoan, which we had subsequently defeated, although Murray had escaped. However, I had recovered a piece of evidence that indicated where he might have been spending his time. . . .

"Is he in Nicaragua?" Erica asked, intrigued.

"We believe so." Deputy Kapoor entered a combination to unlock her briefcase, then lifted out five dossiers. "We've had a team working down there, following up on your lead, and while they haven't seen Hill, they *have* heard rumors about his whereabouts." She began to hand out the dossiers, first to Catherine, then to Mike, then me.

My dossier was a thickly stuffed manila envelope stamped with TOP SECRET. HIGHLY CLASSIFIED INFORMATION.

HAND-DELIVER ONLY TO BENJAMIN RIPLEY. OPERATION DEADLY MANATEE.

"Deadly Manatee?" Mike asked, sounding disappointed. "Manatees aren't even remotely deadly."

"Of course they are," Deputy Kapoor replied. "They have razor-sharp teeth, and schools of them have been known to skeletonize a human being within a minute. You don't get much deadlier than that."

"I'm afraid you're thinking of piranhas," Catherine said diplomatically. "Manatees are rotund, herbivorous mammals also known as sea cows. They're quite docile."

"Oh," Deputy Kapoor said, looking slightly embarrassed. "Really?"

"The only way one of them could ever kill a human is if you dropped it off a tall building onto someone's head," Mike informed her. "Don't you have any biologists at the CIA?"

"We're not a zoo," Deputy Kapoor said testily. "We're an espionage organization. And besides, I'm not in charge of naming operations. That's the Department of Mission Nomenclature. If you have a problem, you can take it up with them." She quickly handed off the remaining dossiers to Erica and Alexander.

"Um . . . ," the principal said meekly. "I think you forgot me. I didn't get a dossier."

"Why would you get a dossier?" Deputy Kapoor asked. "You're not going on assignment. *They* are."

"I just figured, since they're my students, and I'm responsible for their education . . ."

"That's not the way it's done," Deputy Kapoor interrupted. "The nature of this mission is highly classified. In fact, I'll need you to leave this office while we discuss it."

"What?" The principal snapped to his feet so quickly that his brand-new desk chair rolled across the room behind him and tumbled through the gap in his wall. The principal was so upset, he didn't even notice. "But this is *my* office!"

From outside, there was a distant yelp of surprise, followed by the distinct sound of an office chair thudding into the quadrangle lawn.

Deputy Kapoor said, "We need a secure place to discuss this mission. When you volunteered your office, I thought you understood how these things worked."

The principal was definitely upset to be cut out of the meeting; I could see the rage in his eyes. He simmered for a moment, then managed to tamp down his emotions in front of Deputy Kapoor and forced a smile. "I *do* understand," he said through gritted teeth. "I just thought that I might be included this time, seeing as I have molded these students into the fine agents that they are today."

"No," Deputy Kapoor said firmly. "Now, if you'll please leave us, I'd like to proceed with this debriefing."

"Fine," the principal said peevishly. He stormed out of the room, shooting me an angry glare on the way. If his office door had still been attached to the doorframe, he probably would have slammed it.

While all this had been going on, everyone else had opened their dossiers and begun examining the contents. Even though we were all going on the exact same mission, Erica and Catherine were pointedly holding their official orders so that no one else could see them, indicating that we might not all be getting the same information. I noticed Erica look up from hers and give me a glance of concern.

"Oh," Catherine said suddenly. "This is intriguing."

She was holding a big, glossy brochure. I found one in my dossier as well and pulled it out.

It was for a cruise ship. The *Emperor of the Seas*. There was a photograph of it on the front cover, docked at a tropical island. The ship was absolutely enormous, eighteen stories tall and nearly a quarter mile in length. It looked like a floating office building.

"I've heard about this ship!" Mike exclaimed. "It's the biggest cruise ship ever constructed!"

"That's correct," Deputy Kapoor agreed, looking pleased

by Mike's knowledge. "It's the first of a line of mega-cruisers being built by a Chinese conglomerate in Beijing. The *Emperor* launched last winter and has been cruising in the South Pacific, but it is currently en route to the Caribbean. It's last port of call, ten days ago was in Hawaii, and it will be making some stops in Central America before passing through the Panama Canal."

"I assume one of those stops is Nicaragua," Erica deduced.

"Yes. Our agents on the ground have learned that Murray Hill plans to board that ship in the port of Corinto tomorrow morning."

"Why?" Alexander asked.

"We have no idea," Deputy Kapoor admitted. "Which is why we are sending all of you to Nicaragua. It's a joint operation between us and MI6. You'll be boarding that ship in Corinto tomorrow as well."

"We get to go on the *Emperor of the Seas*?" Mike exclaimed. "Awesome! It's supposed to be the most amazing ship ever built! There's a bunch of swimming pools and miniature golf and a ropes course and a rock wall and a water park!" He excitedly pointed to a photograph from the top deck of the ship: a spaghetti tangle of waterslides that dumped into a large pool.

It looked like a whole lot of fun.

Deputy Kapoor gave Mike a sharp look. "The purpose is

for you to be investigating Murray Hill, not going on water-slides."

"Do you want us to blend in and look like normal tourists?" Mike asked.

"Of course."

"Well, normal tourists go on waterslides."

Deputy Kapoor frowned. "I suppose you have a point."

"Are you sure this is prudent?" Catherine asked her, then looked to Mike, Erica, and me. "I know that you children have served your country well and faced considerable danger on several other missions. But you're still . . . well, *children*. Michael, you're only in your first year of training here. And Benjamin, your instructors still won't let you carry a firearm for fear that you'll accidentally shoot yourself with it."

I didn't take offense at this. I was in no hurry to carry a firearm for the exact same reason. And while I had been proud to serve my country on those missions, I hadn't been a big fan of the "considerable danger" portions of them.

It was only four weeks since I had thwarted the last enemy plot, in which I had nearly been blown to pieces—along with a considerable portion of Washington, DC. That had landed me in the hospital for a few days with some cracked ribs. They had healed, but I was still supposed to be taking it easy.

Deputy Kapoor said, "The Agency is not taking this

decision lightly. However, we have our reasons for activating the children. First, they have faced Murray Hill many times and are familiar with his behavior." She turned to me. "In fact, Agent Ripley, you probably understand Murray Hill better than anyone else at this agency."

"That's right," Mike said supportively. "You probably know what Murray's thinking before *he* knows what he's thinking."

I started to deny this, as Murray Hill had hoodwinked me plenty of times, but Deputy Kapoor continued talking before I could. "Secondly, this cruise ship has been designed for *families*. It turns out, there are many places on the ship where adults aren't even allowed to go, such as the teen clubs. And Murray is a teenager—albeit an extremely unscrupulous one. If he ventures into any of these adult-free areas, we need agents who can follow him without causing alarm."

"Good thinking," Alexander Hale said. "Only . . . don't you think it will look suspicious for the children to be traveling alone?"

Deputy Kapoor gave him a stern look, indicating she was disappointed that he hadn't grasped the nature of the mission yet. "They won't be alone. They'll be posing as part of a family. With *you*. You and Catherine will pose as the parents, while Erica, Mike, and Ben will pretend to be your children. Er, well, Erica won't be pretending, as she actually *is* your child. But the boys will be posing as your sons."

"We get to be brothers?" Mike asked, thrilled. "Best mission ever!"

"But we don't look alike," I pointed out. "And we don't look like the Hales, either."

"You're adopted," Deputy Kapoor replied. "Which also explains how you can be so close in age."

"This is so cool!" Mike exclaimed. "I always wanted a brother!"

"You *have* a brother," I reminded him.

"A *good* brother," he corrected. "One who doesn't pin me down and fart on my head."

Inside all of our dossiers were elaborately detailed biographies of the characters we would be portraying. I quickly perused them. We would all be posing as the Rotko family, since the Hales already had aliases under that name. Erica would resume being Sasha Rotko, who she had impersonated on previous missions, while her parents would be Bill and Carol. Mike's alias was Jack Rotko, a gifted middle school athlete, while mine was Quincy Rotko. I was thirteen—which made sense, as it was my own age—and I was captain of the math team at St. Smithen's Science Academy for Boys and Girls—which also made sense, as St. Smithen's was the cover for spy school, and I was quite gifted in mathematics. (Among other things, my math skills gave me an unusually accurate sense of time, and so I knew that we had been in our meeting for thirteen minutes and twenty-seven seconds without even looking at my watch.)

"I'm an accountant?" Alexander said disappointedly, perusing his own file. "That doesn't sound very exciting."

"It's not supposed to be exciting," Catherine told him. "You're supposed to blend in and not draw attention to yourself."

"So what are you?" Alexander asked.

"An ophthalmologist."

"You're a doctor?" Alexander cried jealously. "Awww. Can't I be an ophthalmologist too?"

"Do you know what part of the body an ophthalmologist studies?" Deputy Kapoor asked.

"The spleen?" Alexander guessed.

"Not even close," Deputy Kapoor said. "Which is why we made you an accountant."

"This is going to be great!" Mike was so thrilled, he was practically vibrating. "We get to go on another mission—on the coolest cruise ship in the world. And I get a fake brother." He turned to Erica excitedly. "And a fake sister, too!"

Erica gave us a faint smile in return, as though she wasn't nearly as enthusiastic about this as Mike.

Which was understandable. Erica and I had an unusual relationship. I'd had a crush on her since the very first moment

I saw her at the academy. Meanwhile, she had thought I was a pathetic loser who'd wash out within a week—if I didn't get killed first. Over the ensuing months we had ended up on several missions together, during which she had slowly come to respect me—and even consider me a friend. However, this made her extremely uncomfortable, as she believed relationships were a liability in the spy business. (Her parents were a prime example of this; being spies had been hard on their relationship, leading to a divorce, although they had recently been trying to work things out.) So Erica often dealt with her feelings by pretending they didn't exist. On our last mission, she had actually hugged me, but since then, she had been avoiding me completely.

So, in theory, going on a cruise with her should have been a good thing. As my fake sister, she would be forced to spend plenty of time with me—and I had heard that cruises could be very romantic. The glossy brochure for the *Emperor* was filled with photos of loving couples walking hand in hand on tropical beaches and standing at the railing of the ship, staring out at the sunset.

But going on a cruise with Erica *wasn't* a good thing. Not at this point. In fact, it promised to be a disaster.

Because, for the first time since I had met her, I wanted to avoid Erica Hale.

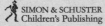

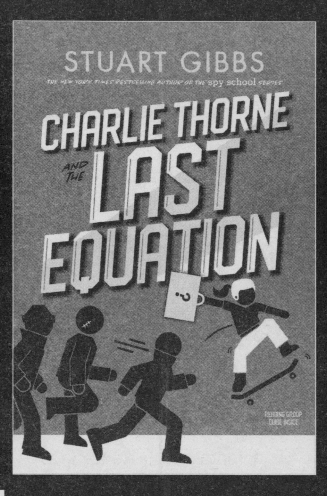

STUART GIBBS

THE NEW YORK TIMES BESTSELLING AUTHOR OF THE spy school SERIES

CHARLIE THORNE
AND THE
LAST EQUATION

READING GROUP
GUIDE INSIDE

From *New York Times* bestselling author Stuart Gibbs comes the first novel in a thrilling new series about the world's youngest genius, who must use her unbelievable code-breaking skills to outsmart Einstein.